YOU NEVER KNOW

YOU
NEVER KNOW

NIOBIA BRYANT
MELANIE SCHUSTER
KIMBERLEY WHITE

ARABESQUE®

YOU NEVER KNOW

ISBN 1-58314-688-1

© 2006 by Kimani Books

The publisher acknowledges the copyright holders
of the individual works as follows:

COULD IT BE?
© 2006 by Niobia Bryant

CHAIN OF FOOLS
© 2006 by Melanie Schuster

TO HAVE IT ALL
© 2006 by Kimberley White

www.kimanipress.com

Printed in U.S.A.

CONTENTS

COULD IT BE?

Niobia Bryant

For my Sistahs in the Word,
Melanie Schuster and Kim Louise

What would I do without our
three-hour-long conference calls?

1

"Rise and shine, girl."

One cat-shaped eye of onyx popped open. Then the other.

Ameena Jones's eyes focused as she lay sprawled in the middle of her king-size bed. One by one she looked up into the faces of her girls, her best friends, her sist*ahs*. First Eva. Then Demi. And lastly, Winifred—who refused to be called Winnie.

"I have got to change my locks," Meena drawled, her voice heavy with interrupted sleep as she pulled a satin emerald pillow over her face.

"Yeah, right," Demi countered, reaching down to remove the pillow with one hand and balance the crystal flute she was holding with the other.

Meena groaned, kicking the bed in pure childlike frustration. "I just got in at three this morning from a video shoot and my behind is—"

"We got mimosas," Eva said smoothly in that raspy

voice that drove all the brothas from Wall Street to the street thugs wild.

Meena sat up in bed. She *loved* a good mimosa. "If you three were really on point you'd have—"

"Breakfast burritos from the Burrito Bar," the three ladies finished in unison.

Demi passed Meena the flute. "This will taste so much better if you handle that morning breath."

Meena frowned. "Is it that bad?" she asked, breathing into the hand she cupped over her rosebud-shaped mouth.

The three ladies held a hand over their noses and nodded with mock solemn expressions.

Meena flung a fuchsia silk neck roll accent pillow at them as they left the spacious master suite of her loft located in the trendy Tribeca section of Manhattan. They left behind the scent of their various perfumes and the echo of their laughter.

She climbed off the platform bed, her petite frame dressed in nothing but white low-cut boy shorts and a shrunken wife-beater tee that she refused to let go.

Meena *loved* the city. The energy. The fast, electric pace. The endless nights. The constant movement.

She was all about New York, and New York was all about her.

Meena studied her reflection in the large oval mirror over her pedestal sink as she brushed her teeth. She used her free hand to pull off her silk scarf and rake her fingers through her stylish and spiky pixie haircut of deep shiny ebony. It was so Fantasia and she loved it!

I need a trim, she thought, making a mental note to make an appointment at Luxe Studios.

As a fashion stylist for some of the biggest names in entertainment, Meena knew that appearances were everything. She was proud that she was able to shape the careers of stars—both new and seasoned—because she had a flare for knowing what looked good on whom. A degree from the Fashion Institute of Technology in New York and a solid five years in the industry didn't hurt her natural abilities either.

"Hold up. Wait a minute," she said suddenly, quickly bending over the sink to rinse her mouth.

Mimosa, breakfast burritos, and all of her friends here at once could only mean one thing: trouble that was spelled M-A-N.

Meena opened the frosted glass door of her ultra-modern spa bathroom, eventually striding out of her bedroom.

"I think I heard her playing with Troy in the bathroom," she heard Winifred whisper.

Troy was the sizable vibrator the girls had given her as a gag gift one Christmas.

"That was my motorized toothbrush, thank you very much," Meena said, walking up to where they sat around her steel-topped dining room table that could easily seat twelve.

Eva and Winifred shared a knowing—and totally unbelieving—look.

"*Anyway,*" Meena stressed.

Eva used tongs to place an assortment of fresh fruit and an oversize breakfast burrito onto a paper plate to hand to Meena.

Meena frowned. "Why the paper plates?" she asked.

"You know we're all scared of your kitchen," Demi answered, using a plastic fork to push around the scrambled eggs and sausage falling from the inside of her own burrito.

"Last time I tried to use your corkscrew I damn near lost an eye," Eva said with a deadpan expression that was too phony to be believed.

The ladies all shared a laugh at *that* memory.

True, her kitchen—like the rest of her house—was a picture in the marriage of modern-day technology and a sophisticated and comfortable decor. Just about everything was controlled by a remote or was activated by sensors. She took modern convenience to a whole other level.

Meena took a healthy bite of her burrito and a deep swig of her mimosa before she asked, "Okay, who has the man drama?"

When Eva's and Winifred's eyes shifted to Demi, Meena's feline eyes fell on her as well.

"Damien thinks they need a break," Eva offered into the silence.

Meena immediately felt for her friend. "Dem—"

"I'm not sweating it," Demi said, cutting her off.

Meena thought of the pain she had dealt with after her own breakup with Roderick last year. Two years of what she had thought was a good relationship down the toilet. She'd cried like a baby for weeks after—even though he hadn't been worth one drop. With a pang, she thought of the woman who had to have borne his child by now, a child conceived during her association with him.

Yes, it *still* hurt, so she could only imagine how Demi felt to lose Damien when he had seemed so perfect.

Demi released a breath as she leveled each of them with a stare. "Trust me, I don't care," she insisted. "He was lousy in bed anyway."

Eva used a spoon to scoop out the last of the sweet flesh of her slice of cantaloupe. "No need to lie to us. Girl, that brother had you sprung."

Demi let out a little soft moan that was all too telling as she got lost in her thoughts.

Meena raised her flute. "Here's to good sex," she mused. "Or in my case, memories of good sex."

"No...*great* sex," Demi added with a wink.

"Now *I'll* drink to that," Eva countered, before sipping down the last of her drink.

"Surprise, surprise," Meena muttered good naturedly into her drink with a smile.

"Don't hate my appreciation of a well-formed and skillfully used penis," Eva said with an Eartha Kitt–like drawl.

"Just too bad such a wonderful *thing* is usually attached

to an idiot," Winifred threw into the mix as she refilled Eva's flute with more mimosa.

The ladies all toasted to *that* one.

Meena was just about to agree with Demi when she noticed the empty bottle of champagne sitting amongst the clutter of their brunch. "Is that my bottle of Dom Perignon?" she squealed, rising a little from her seat to snatch up the gold bottle. "Jay-Z gave that to me last year. I was saving it for a special occasion."

Winifred took the bottle back. "What's the special occasion? A wedding. You need a man first."

"Here, here," Eva chimed in.

"I go on lots of dates," Meena defended.

"Nothing serious, though," Demi added.

"When's the last time you had sex—sans Troy, of course?" Eva asked.

Meena had not been intimate with anyone since her ex over a year ago. "What does sex have to do with it?" she asked, avoiding the question.

Eva arched a finely threaded brow. "Because you don't have casual sex—no matter how much I sing the praises of it. So if you were remotely serious about one of your boy toys, you would have given up those sweet lacy La Perla panties by now, darling."

Meena hated to admit it, but her ever observant friend had a point. In the space of a week, when her hectic schedule allowed it, Meena had fun enjoying dinner at La Bernadine with a Travis on Thursday night, watching a movie with a Jamal on Friday, and dancing with a Rasheed on Saturday at her favorite club, The G Spot. Still, for the last year, fun had not included sweat-your-straight-roots-nappy sex.

"What are y'all up to today?" Meena asked, purposefully changing the subject.

Eva just laughed lightly in victory.

"We're going to Bliss Soho. You game?" Winifred asked, flipping her soft straight hair behind her ear.

Meena thought of the upscale spa and longed for the time to be pampered and calmed by one of their signature treatments like the rose petal wrap, but her schedule wouldn't allow it. "I wish," she sighed, using slender fingers to massage her own neck. "I have a shoot I'm styling for *Essence*, and I have to start working on the wardrobe for a new artist over at Platinum Records."

Now Meena loved her girls. These three women were like sisters to her. Twelve years of friendship and a million tears, secrets, and laughs formed a bond that Meena relished. These women were real. They kept her grounded and didn't let her rising celebrity swell her head. She loved knowing them and being around them. And in the face of both her parents being deceased and having no real siblings, Meena thought of them as her family. Still, she was busier than a lone hooker working the docks and had to get her day rolling, so she was glad to walk them to the door.

"Seven...eight...nine...two thousand."

Marcus Daniels flopped back onto the mat, a fine sheet of perspiration coating his bared muscular chest as he wrapped up his daily exercise routine of a 45-minute run on his treadmill and 2,000 ab crunches to keep his rock-hard six-pack from spreading to twelve.

Allowing himself a few precious moments of peace and quiet, Marcus closed his hazel eyes and inhaled and exhaled, deeply and slowly. He blocked out the forty-five-minute commute to his Manhattan office and the twelve- to fourteen-hour day ahead of him at the sports and entertainment law firm, MDDL Law Inc., which he owned with his best friend, Derek Lyles.

And so in the words of one his favorite rappers Fabolous, he just had to *breathe*.

Allowing himself just a few precious moments, he rose from the floor with surprising ease for his 6'9", 225-lb, all-muscular frame. Stepping out of his fitted boxers, Marcus strode nude into his adjoining bathroom for a shower. As he stood beneath the pulsating spray in the center of his old-fashioned claw-foot tub, he ran over his appointments for the day and shook his head at the nonstop pace ahead of him. Their firm was growing by leaps and bounds every day, with Derek and his junior associates focusing on legal matters, and Marcus branching off and building their work as sports agents. In fact, they were planning to expand MDDL into Los Angeles next month.

After a weekend of just relaxing in his brick colonial home in the Thomaston suburbs of Great Neck, New York, Marcus was actually ready for the crazy work week ahead in the city that never sleeps. Not that he abhorred the Big Apple, he just preferred the quiet, laid-back style of suburbia, and Great Neck offered a small-town feel that he enjoyed.

He flung his blazer over his arm and grabbed his briefcase and keys before leaving the house to climb into his Mercedes Benz G55. Just as he started his forty-five-minute commute into Manhattan, Marcus reached into his briefcase and removed his cell phone to turn it on. It was the same one he had since 1995. It looked like an ice cream sandwich in shape and had no special bells and whistles— no text messaging, no pictures, no color screen, no special ring tones. To Marcus, technology and most of its trappings were overrated.

Marcus preferred writing letters on his custom stationery to sending e-mails to friends and family. Unlike many of the brothas in his age bracket, he preferred a challenging and methodical game of chess to playing the latest sports video game. In fact, he usually avoided computers at all cost if not directly work related.

He understood the usefulness of modern technology but disdained it when it replaced person-to-person communication. In his home, he had the standard electronics out of sheer necessity, but he didn't mind at all walking across the room to turn on the lights—or the TV station. Once when they were in college, Derek watched six straight hours of Lifetime movies because he couldn't find the remote and refused to rise from his sofa. Absolutely ridiculous.

Marcus laughed at the very thought of his masochistic friend trapped watching the usual fare of women-oriented movies on the cable station.

Thankfully, he was able to enjoy his commute into Manhattan without any major traffic backups. The ringing of his cell phone didn't even interrupt him. It was just him and *Miss Jones in the Morning* on HOT97 FM.

The Manhattan office of MDDL was located on Madison Avenue. Marcus steered his vehicle to the reserved parking spot in the underground parking garage. Minutes later he was riding the elevator up to their offices on the twentieth floor, then striding through the rotating glass door emblazoned with their graphic MDDL Law symbol.

"Good morning, Mr. Daniels," the receptionist, Alexandria, greeted him with a polite smile behind the counter of their front office.

"Morning," Marcus returned with a nod as he continued toward his suite of offices made up of his paralegal's Aaron's office, a mini conference room, and then his larger corner office. Derek had an identical set of rooms to the left of the front office. The rest of the space was smaller offices for the other attorneys and staff, an exercise room, and a kitchen.

Marcus's office was so different than the majority of their office space. He had insisted on a decor that suited his style more than the modern chrome and hard angles Derek preferred. Basically, he was open about the decor of everything but his personal space. The warm, rich tones, mahogany wainscoting, and shelves of books had the feel of a study—and he loved it.

Marcus was just settling in when Derek came strolling into the office.

"Whaddup, dawg,"

Marcus dropped his Cross pen and leaned back in his chair. "Nothing much. Whaddup with you?"

Derek propped his tall, slender frame on the edge of Marcus's desk. "You probably noticed I didn't call you all weekend," he began, a toothy grin in place on his boyishly handsome face.

Marcus crossed his fingers behind his head, his arms bent. "What's her name?" he asked, cutting to the chase.

"This little freak named Yvette. Whoo-eee!!" Derek did an exaggerated shiver. "Her tongue should be bronzed."

Marcus just laughed at his easy-going, fun-loving friend. "Club Speed or Xbar?" he asked, naming their two favorite spots.

Derek picked up the football Marcus had sitting on the edge of the desk. "Neither," he said, tossing it up into the air several times. "Met her at church last Sunday."

"Man, you ain't nothing but the devil."

"A *well*-laid devil."

They both laughed.

"She has a friend named Deshan," Derek offered with a roguish wiggle of his thick eyebrows.

"Naw, I'm straight," Marcus said, scooting forward in his chair to begin checking his e-mails—which were all work related.

Derek shrugged, rising to set the football back on the base. "Deshan might be the one."

Marcus frowned as he sat up straight in his chair. "Lady in the street and only a freak in *my* bed?"

Derek's grin widened until he was all teeth and cheek-bones. "Deshan's definitely not the one then."

Marcus shook his head as Derek left the office. As he focused on clearing out his in-box, Marcus silently wondered if there was really such a thing as "the one."

2

One Week Later

Meena moved easily through the hustle and bustle of the relentless pace of New York's body traffic as she made her way to her favorite spot for a quick, easy, and totally inexpensive lunch at Gray's Papaya on 8th Avenue.

"One special to go, please," she told the man behind the counter with a beguiling smile.

A special was two hot dogs and a fruit punch drink for under three dollars from the legendary corner eatery open 24 hours a day.

She was just brushing past someone while leaving the restaurant when her cell phone began to chime her "Disco Inferno" ring tone.

Balancing the cup and the small paper bag holding her lunch with one hand, Meena flipped open her cell phone with the other. "Meena Jones," she said, moving close to the building to shield her call from some of the sounds of New York living.

"Meena, this is Lala." Lala was Meena's personal assistant.

"Yes, Lala. What's up?"

"Where are you?"

"I'm at Gray's, but I'm 'bout to head uptown to finish shopping for a video shoot next week." Meena frowned at the angry squeal of tires behind her. She swung around to see a cabbie leaning out of his window to argue with a bike messenger.

"That rapper Money you just signed on wanted your private cell phone number, but after you told me he actually tried to holla at you, I wanted to run it by you first."

"Definitely not," Meena said, doing an eye roll as she knocked her oversize shades down over her eyes with her wrist. "I don't know if he was serious or just flirting to pass the time, but I want to keep this as professional as possible, especially with all this drama going down with Savor."

Savor was a multiplatinum hip-hop star who Meena was now suing for breach of contract. He had made one sexual advance toward her too many, and Meena had proceeded to check and wreck him right in the middle of a photo shoot. Embarrassed, the rapper and his management team fired her on the spot. Well, for the last three months Meena had unsuccessfully tried to collect her fees for all work that had been completed. She made the decision two weeks ago to sue him. Her deposition was this coming Monday, and Meena couldn't wait for the whole matter to be over.

"Thought so, just wanted to run it by you first."

"That's why I love you, La," Meena said honestly. Her assistant was top rate, and having Lala watching her back and covering her rear gave her the ability to focus on her work.

Meena stepped to the corner and held out her hand, still clutching her lunch, to flag down a taxi. "I'm off to Sean John," she said as a taxi slowed to a stop in front of her.

"Cool, do you want me to send a car?"

"Nope, I'm cabbing it. I'll be fine."

"Talk to you later."

Meena opened the door and settled onto the backseat, dropping her phone into her Louis Vuitton jean purse. "Fifth Avenue and Forty-first Street, please."

As the cab sped through the metropolis, Meena took a well-deserved moment to do nothing but sit back, chill, and relax as she finished her lunch. As a celebrity stylist, her days were filled with varying appointments and engagements throughout the city—sometimes the country, depending on where her clients were when they needed her. Dashing to a meeting to work with a label's creative team for image consulting on an artist or going to the showrooms and upscale stores of the trendiest designers for personal shopping of up to five to seven clients at one time was just a piece of the Jones's Style pie. She also had to be on set or location for various video and photo shoots, make TV appearances, and even write editorials for several fashion and lifestyle magazines about the latest trends.

Truth, though? Meena loved her career, but she wanted, no needed, to find the time to start her own fashion line, MeenaMeena. With her degree from F.I.T. and over five years working in the fashion industry under her belt—first as an assistant fashion display stylist for an upscale department store to now owning her own business—Meena knew she was creatively and maybe even financially ready. Now all she needed was the time.

Her ring tone sounded from her purse; she clamped the dog with her teeth, freeing her hands to dig into the purse for her phone. She flipped it open and took the time to view the caller ID. She smiled as a playful picture of Eva sticking out her tongue filled the screen before a text message was displayed:

LOOKING FOR MR. OR MS. RIGHT—
OR EVEN MR. OR MS. RIGHT NOW?

ONE NIGHT OF 10 ELIGIBLE SINGLES
WITH 10 GETTING TO KNOW YOU DATES.
COME OUT AND GET YOUR FLIRT ON . . .
YOU NEVER KNOW.
PAYABLE TO: Meena Jones

You game or what?

—Eva THE Diva

Speed dating? Was Eva crazy?

Then again: Was *she* crazy? Ten black brothas to flirt with in one night. None of the drama of a man wanting a commitment for more because he brought you a cosmopolitan. None of the agony of wanting to end a date early without hurting someone's feelings or striking a cord in an unknowing psychopath.

He could be a cock-eyed, buck-toothed, second coming of Buckwheat with breath kicking like a kung fu marathon, and in ten short minutes he would be out of her face and her space—no questions asked, no explanations given.

Her girls, a cosmo or apple martini, and ten dates in one night? It didn't add up to a love match in Meena's book, but it was beginning to sound like fun, and that was what Meena was all about.

Hell, why not?

"Whassup, dawg?" Derek asked as he and Aaron, Marcus's paralegal, strolled into his office.

He looked at them over the top of his reading glasses. "What's the plan for tonight, fellows?" Marcus asked.

"How does a room filled with beautiful women sound?" Derek asked, slipping his hands into the pockets of his charcoal linen slacks.

Marcus nodded, removing his glasses to place them in their case. "Sounds good."

"A room filled with beautiful sistahs *with* jobs," Aaron added with comedic emphasis, taking a seat in the club chair in front of Marcus's desk.

Marcus's charming smile broadened. "Sounds even better."

"Ten dates in one night," Derek added, after which he turned his head to exchange a long look with Aaron.

Marcus's million-watt smile dimmed quite a bit.

"There's this speed dating thing for black professionals tonight," Derek explained.

"Nah, kid, I'll pass."

Derek and Aaron both released an exaggerated moan.

"What?" Marcus asked, holding up his hands. "Can you imagine the kind of women that'll be there? Nah, go 'head, roll out without me."

"You don't know what you're missing," Aaron said, rising. "I met my last girlfriend there."

Marcus pierced Aaron with his eyes. "And this is the one who stole your credit cards while you were sleeping and took her other man to Atlantic City."

"That's cold, man," Aaron said, nudging Derek when he saw the man's shoulders shaking with laughter.

"Listen, man, bump *his* drama," Derek said, leaning forward on Marcus's desk. "Ten chances, if not more, to tap some new ass with only half the work. Some desperate new ass. Oh, I'm all over speed dating."

"You give new meaning to dogs, man." Marcus laughed as his friend pulled a six-pack of Magnum condoms from his wallet.

"Woof, woof," Derek barked loudly, pounding his chest with his fist.

"Let's go speed dating."

Derek was obviously confused. "I thought you didn't want to—"

"Can't a brotha change his mind?" Marcus asked.

* * *

"All right, ladies, are we ready to run this show," Meena asked as the four friends stood in the doorway of the jazz club/restaurant where the speed dating soiree was being held.

"That's a given," Eva stated, looking gorgeous in a short turquoise blazer and camisole paired with low-rise khaki capris.

Winifred flipped her long, straight hair behind her shoulder as she reached in her clutch for the tube to touch up her lip gloss. "Can you two try to be a little humble for once?" she asked.

They both just shrugged.

"Let's order some drinks," Demi offered, still dressed in the chocolate silk suit she'd worn to work.

"Yes, I need an apple spritzer," Meena stated, leading the ladies to the circular-shaped bar where they all grabbed a stool.

After ordering their drinks, the ladies were trying to agree where to go for a late-night dinner when the event was over. Suddenly, Meena felt a chill shimmy over her delicate skin. She didn't know why she felt the need to look over her shoulder toward the entrance, but she did.

There were three men standing there, but her eyes immediately settled on the brotha in the middle. *Jesus, he's fine,* she thought, taking a moment to enjoy the view before turning back to her friends and her drink.

"If desperate women are looking this good, then thank God for the supposed male shortage," Derek whispered to Marcus, standing to his left.

"And they all have jobs," Aaron chirped from his right.

Marcus just shook his head and stepped down into the lounge area. They found a table near the back to sit. Several women turned their heads to openly stare at them, and Marcus felt like a piece of meat going through inspection. He glanced down at his Jacob & Co. watch. It was *still* early.

He looked around and his eyes fell on the four attractive sistahs sitting at the far end of the bar. His eyes focused on the profile of the one with the short, spiky hair. Unable to look away, he watched as one of her friends leaned forward to whisper something to her. Seconds later she flung her head back in laughter.

He watched as a pretty face was completely transformed into beauty. *She's gorgeous,* he thought, silently wishing she would turn so that he could see if the full view of her face was as delectable as her profile.

Aaron nudged him, and Marcus's eyes reluctantly and slowly shifted to him. "Huh?"

"Not so bad in here, right?" Aaron asked as his eyes continued to skim the women in attendance.

Marcus shifted his eyes back to the beauty at the bar just to discover neither she nor her friends were there. "What the hell?" he muttered, wondering where they could have vanished to so quickly. He raised up from his seat a little to look around the dimly lit area. His head swung to the left, and then the right. He turned and looked behind him.

Both Derek and Aaron leaned back in their chairs to look up at him like he had lost his mind.

"What's up with you, dawg?" Derek asked.

Marcus didn't know the answer to that himself. The only thing he did know for sure was that he wanted to see his mystery lady again.

"Whew, I feel a thousand times better," Meena sighed as she left the bathroom stall and washed her hands at the sink.

Eva, Winifred, and Demi were all touching up their makeup in the mirror over the sinks.

"Right now I'm ready to flirt," Meena said, quickly checking her own makeup before they all moved to the door.

"You need to be ready to fu—"

"Eva!" Winifred scolded sharply.

They all burst into laughter.

A tall, robust sistah with locks as thick as fingers stepped onto the stage and adjusted the mic. "Welcome everyone. Welcome. I'm Pauntice Vanderbilt, the owner of Modern Dating Solutions and the organizer of this event, this evening. I just wanted to go over a few of the guidelines of the event, and then we can get started."

She looked down at the clipboard she held in hand. "There will be ten dates of ten minutes in length. The men, our gentlemen, will move from table to table about the room, following the order you were given on your card at the door. Please, no exchange of private or personal information. We collected everyone's info at the door, and if you are interested in getting to know someone a little better, let us know and we will contact that person to see if they agree to the exchange of information. Also, there is a two-drink maximum."

There was few groans at that.

"When the bell chimes the date is over and it is time to move on to the next person."

She looked around the room. "Looks like we have another full house tonight. So if there are no other questions, let the dates begin."

A tall brotha with neat, slender dreads stepped up to Meena's table. *Well, all right now. He's cute.* She gave him her best smile.

"Hello, I'm Majig."

"Hi, I'm Mee . . ." The rest of her words trailed off as the fine, buff brother in the suit walked past her table.

His head turned, and their eyes locked.

Her heart raced.

He smiled just a little.

It was enough to make Meena tilt her head to the side and smile in return. She was in full-flirt mode.

The brotha with the dreads, Majig, stepped into her line of vision, and her eyes shifted up to him.

"Nice to meet you, Mee," he stated, holding out his hand.

Meena laughed a little as she accepted his hand. "My name's Meena and nice to meet you."

Majig took the seat across from her.

Her first "date" of the night.

"Okay, Majig, tell me all about you," she said, placing her chin in her hands as she leaned in close to him.

Marcus tried his best not to frown as his third date of the night continued to rattle on about her love for her dog, Gucci.

"So...do you have any pets?" she asked.

Mind you, this was the first question she bothered to ask him during her entire five-minute lovefest of her poodle.

Marcus couldn't have been more pleased when the bell rang.

"I saw you on MTV last week. You're even more beautiful in person."

During this particular date Meena had mastered the art of smiling and holding her breath, because although the man before her was sexy in a Shemar Moore kind of way, his breath was kicking like kung fu.

"You have this sexy as hell Clark Kent thing going on."

Marcus's thick, slashing brow rose as the woman, a fair-skinned beauty whose heritage was a toss-up, reached across the table to trace the back of his hand with her finger.

"Thanks," he told her, a little put off by her directness. He leaned back in his chair to cross one ankle over his knee. "So, what do you for fun? What are your hobbies?"

She laughed, low and husky, as she easily uncurled her tongue and touched it to the tip of her nose. She then made the tip quiver as she boldly locked her eyes with his.

Marcus shifted in his seat and swallowed over a sudden lump in his throat.

"I love a petite woman."

Meena took a sip of her drink—her second, and thus final one during the event. She looked at the buff brother who was three times her size sitting across from her. "Oh, really?" she asked.

"Yeah, shoot, little things like you are usually flexible as hell, and I can flip—"

"Sshh." Meena held up a hand, shaking her head.

"But we could—"

"*Please* hush. Not another word," Meena told him, refusing to listen to him talk of some great sexual experience that wasn't going down anyway.

"I—"

"Eh-eh."

Meena pulled out her Smartphone and began checking her e-mail.

The buff brother crossed his massive arms over his chest. They both waited for the ten minutes to tick by...*slowly*.

"After graduating from law school, I—"

Bzzzzzzzz...bzzzzzzzz.

Marcus swallowed the rest of his words as his latest date proceeded to answer her vibrating cell phone without a second glance in his direction. With her acrylic nails, fuchsia hair, and gold trunk jewelry, Marcus knew she was looking for a roughneck, and he couldn't guess what profession she worked in that allowed her to dress that way.

"Hey, Reesie, girl, what *you* doing?"

* * *

Meena was willing to give most things a try, but this speed dating was beginning to get on her last nerve. She was more than ready to go.

Seven down and three more to endure.

She turned to dig in her bag for a piece of gum or mint when the fine hairs on her nape suddenly stood on end in unspoken awareness. She felt a slight hum of electricity shimmy over her entire body.

Meena looked over her shoulder and her eyes traveled up the chocolate pinstripe suit to the face of the cutie from the door.

That hum intensified.

"Hi, I'm Meena," she said, her voice as breathless as she felt.

"I'm Marcus."

"Nice to meet you," they said in unison.

3

Marcus thought Meena was beautiful.

Her skin was the deep, rich complexion of hot chocolate, and it was perfectly complemented by short, spiky hair the color of midnight. The hairstyle brought emphasis to her slanted eyes—her best feature to him—and full, pouty lips that were tinted with a sheer gloss that made them beg to be worshipped with kisses. He was intrigued by her fierce, almost exotic beauty that was very Nia Long–like.

Even her pointy, elflike ears suited her and made her even more adorable.

He smiled at her—a genuine smile—and held out his hand to her.

She returned his smile with a brilliant one of her own.

Marcus's heart swelled.

There was *something* about Marcus that made Meena's knees weak. It wasn't just his killa body that even his tailored—and stylish—suit could not hide. Nor was it his rugged, handsome features. Pecan tan complexion. Strong jaw. Prominent cheekbones and almond-shaped eyes. The small scar on his left cheek didn't deter from his attractiveness; in fact, it made him even more sexy and daring to her. Nor was it the faint scent of his cologne—she had already identified it as Gucci. No, it wasn't only those things that intrigued her. But it was *something*.

He stretched his hand out to her and Meena felt excited at the thought of touching him. She reached for it and their hands clasped like two lovers in a sexual embrace.

A shiver of pure, unadulterated awareness filled her entire body, and the hum was nearly deafening.

"This is a little awkward," Marcus began, actually nervous in this woman's presence—something he hadn't felt since his teens.

Meena smiled at him. "Tell me about it. Coming to this was one of my friend's idea."

"Mine, too."

"It's been...fun," Meena said, twirling the stirrer in her drink as she fought the desire to trace his scar with her finger.

The corner of Marcus's mouth lifted. "Yes, very enlightening," he quipped.

"What's really sad is some of these poor souls are hoping to find love."

Marcus snorted. "Picture that."

"Yeah, right."

Their eyes met, and they both laughed away the sudden feeling of nervousness.

Meena cleared her throat and took another sip of her drink as she studied his profile over the rim. "What would you be doing right now if you weren't here?" she asked from true interest, and not just a need to fill the air with words.

Marcus leaned forward on the table. "Straight up?" he asked.

The scent of his cologne intensified and Meena enjoyed the air. "That's right."

Marcus studied her with his eyes. "Can I tell you what I think you would be doing instead?"

Meena's brow lifted a bit in surprise. "Okay, I'll bite."

Marcus smiled, thinking of a lovely region he would like to bite. "You are obviously a woman who takes care of herself. Well maintained, but not high maintenance."

Meena inclined her head as she relaxed back into her seat and watched him. "Thank you."

"I see you at home listening to some Anita—"

"Mary J," she corrected with a shake of her head.

"You're lounging in silk pajamas—"

Meena shook her head again as she smiled at him. "Tank top and boxers."

"Sipping on white wine—"

Meena just laughed.

"Don't tell me. Wrong again?" Marcus asked, his white teeth flashing brilliantly against his bronzed complexion. "I'm not very good at this, am I?"

"No, not at all," Meena teased, leaning forward to pat his hand reassuringly. "But that's okay."

Marcus followed his impulse and covered her hand with his own.

Heat rose like they were in an inferno. Such a simple gesture a testament to the chemistry between them. A chemistry both were well aware of.

"Now's my turn," Meena said, arching her brow devilishly.

Marcus was curious how she perceived him. "Okay," he said, gently caressing her hand with his thumb.

"Okay, let's see," she said, wiggling her bottom in her seat. "You would be somewhere with your friends with one hand down your pants and the other on the remote—"

Marcus flung his head back and laughed—full, rich, vibrant, sexy as all get out.

"You and your boys are eating hoagies and drinking Heinekens—"

Marcus held up his hand. "No, no, no," he admonished. "You were doing pretty good, but I don't drink, and I don't eat meat."

Meena's face showed her surprise. "You're a vegetarian?"

"A vegan, actually."

Meena's eyes darted down to his leather shoes.

"Yes, they're leather," he assured her with a smile, pleased that he didn't have to explain exactly what it was to be a vegan. "I've cut milk and dairy from my diet to stay healthy, not because I'm spiritual like Russell Simmons."

"Oh, that's right, I forgot Russell was a vegan," Meena said, her thumb now tracing circles on Marcus's wrist.

"Do you know him?" Marcus asked.

Not wanting to name-drop, Meena told a little lie, "No."

"Well, I'm not that deep—trust me."

"Still, I admire a man with convictions."

"Well, I was chubby growing up, and I decided to get in shape once I hit college."

"Job well done," Meena complimented, taking in his broad shoulders.

Marcus smiled bashfully—something else he hadn't done since puberty. And his honesty about his weight struggles growing up amazed him as well.

"Well, my drama growing up was acne," Meena admitted, squeezing his hand.

He eyed her smooth, bronzed complexion.

"Trust me, Proactiv don't play," she assured him.

Marcus loved Meena's sense of humor, and he laughed at the oddball expression she made as if to accentuate her point. "We're a couple of before and after pictures, huh?" he asked, getting lost in her spirit.

Meena raised her glass with her free hand. "Here's to getting better with age."

Marcus picked up his glass of cranberry juice and touched it to hers. "Here...here."

"Do you really want to know what I would be doing right now?" she asked as she sat her glass down.

"Tell me, Meena, what would you be doing?"

"Sleeping like a hibernating bear," she told him frankly. "I have the most comfortable king-size bed that I would like to spend more time enjoying."

An image of her petite and shapely frame in the center of a king-size bed in only a tank top and tight boxers made him take a deep sip of his drink.

"I firmly believe in making time to relax. I schedule time for it just like most people schedule appointments," he told her, so lost in her company that he almost forgot they were not alone.

"Sometimes there's just not enough hours in my day," she said, letting her head fall into her hand.

"Make the time," Marcus stated simply, now tracing the lines in her palm with his finger.

"In the city that never sleeps?" she asked in disbelief.

"True, but that's why I commute to work in Manhattan, and then carry my black behind home every night to the 'burbs."

The bell jingled and Meena felt like Cinderella at the ball when the clock struck twelve. She didn't want her time with Marcus to end.

The looked at each other in regret.

Marcus released her hand as he rose with obvious reluctance. "It was a pleasure meeting you, Meena," he said with warmth and honesty.

"You, too, Marcus," she admitted softly as she looked up at him.

Even as the other men shifted to other tables for their next date, Marcus remained standing there, looking at her. Marcus reached down and lightly stroked Meena's cheek. She leaned her face into his grasp.

"Excuse me, bro'," came a masculine voice from behind him.

Marcus looked over his shoulder at the man behind him. Meena's next date. His next date waited as well.

"Is it okay if I let them know we want to exchange information?" he asked, sticking to the rules of the event—no matter how silly he thought they were.

Meena thought that this tall, obviously confident man looking slightly bashful about asking her that was adorable.

"Definitely," she told him in a husky voice.

He turned and walked away. Meena's eyes devoured the sight of his well over six foot, muscular form in a suit that was clearly tailored to fit him so well. That same suit, so refined and distinguished, was a contrast to the raw and almost wild maleness that his body movements hinted at. He was in total control of his body. The kind of control that would have the woman in his bed clawing the sheets, climbing the walls, and screaming his name until she was hoarse.

And she watched him like a hawk until he took a seat at another table across the room. She leaned forward in her seat to check out his next date.

She frowned.

It was Eva!

"Hel-lo," her next date said in a singsong fashion that was only slightly annoying.

Meena forced her eyes away from the sight of her sultry friend giving Marcus her "come-and-get-me" look. "Huh?" she asked, focusing her eyes on the man as he stretched his hand to her. "Oh, I'm sorry. I'm Meena. Nice to meet you."

"I'm Shawn," he said as Meena shook his hand.

He was nice looking in a Gerald Levert, big and sexy way, but Meena had her mind and her heart set on Marcus.

She reached for her cell. "So, Shawn, tell me about yourself," Meena said, even as she began to type in a text message to Eva's cell.

"I live in Newark, New Jersey, actually, and I own a res-idential construction company . . ."

Meena knew she was being rude, but she had to pump Eva's brakes before she really got revved up and made a move on Marcus.

"Give Marcus your cell phone", she typed.

Meena hit SEND, and then leaned forward to watch as Eva reached down to pull her cell phone from her purse that was on the floor.

"Is everything okay?" Shawn asked, following her line of vision in confusion.

Meena watched him out of the corner of her eyes with-out even turning her head. "Uhm, yes. Yes, everything is co-pacetic," she said, turning to face him. "Now, how long have you been in plumbing?"

"Actually, it's construction . . ."

Meena's cell phone vibrated in her hand and she flipped it open. It read, "OK."

Meena's head whipped to watch as Eva handed Marcus the phone. She started to hit the number to call Eva's phone via her programmed speed dial. She paused.

"I'm not usually this rude, Shane—"

"It's Shawn."

"Right. Uhm, but I believe I just met the man for me and—"

He actually smiled, full and bright. "Do you?" he en-couraged.

Meena laughed bashfully. "I'm sorry," she said.

He shrugged. "It's cool, because I got my eye on some-one else, too," he assured her.

Meena hit the button to dial Eva's cell phone as Shawn rose, raised his glass in toast to her, and walked to the bar.

As the phone began to ring in her ear, Meena looked over to see Marcus looking at her with Eva's phone to his ear.

"Hey, Meena," he said, his voice filled with obvious pleasure.

"I didn't want our date to end," she admitted without an ounce of shame as they stared at each other from across the room.

"I didn't either."

Meena watched as he closed the phone and handed it back to Eva before he rose and slowly made his way back to her table. She closed her phone and it instantly vibrated. Meena looked down at the screen: "YOU OWE ME HEIFER." Meena laughed, closing the phone just as Marcus came to a stop beside her and held out his hand.

Meena took it and rose.

4

The next morning Meena was laying in the middle of her bed with a soft smile on her face. It was a Saturday morning—an early Saturday morning—and she was wide awake. She had no appointments to go rushing off to, no train, planes, or automobiles to hop into. She was just too excited to sleep because she had Marcus on her mind.

She went to sleep with him there, and there he remained when she woke up this morning.

The man was...incredible.

Intelligent. Handsome. Charming. Romantic. Driven. Focused. Considerate. Gentlemanly. And sexy as all get out.

And these are the qualities in him that she had discovered in just one night, which to her meant that the best was yet to come.

Last night when they left the speed dating event they had thrown the event coordinators' rules to the wind and decided why not take matters into their own hands. They walked across the street to enjoy the good food and even better company in an intimate Portuguese restaurant. After dinner they strolled through the Soho district, had drinks at one of her favorite martini bars, and then caught a cab to Central Park for a carriage ride.

It was a long, enjoyable, and romantic night. It was exactly what she needed.

Neither had wanted the evening to end, but it had. And so at 1:00 A.M., with one final hug they both climbed into two separate taxis and went their separate ways. Like a true gentleman, Marcus had called her to ensure she got home safely, and that led to a two-hour phone conversation where they discussed everything and nothing.

Meena glanced at her clock. It was 8 A.M. She'd already planned to give him a call around 10 A.M. Okay maybe 9.

Forcing herself to do *something*, Meena reached for her Smartphone and began checking her e-mails.

Her house phone began to ring just as she was reviewing an article the editor of a fashion magazine had sent to her for revisions.

Thinking it could be Marcus, Meena reached across the bed to snatch her cordless from the base. "Hello."

"When did you change your locks?" Winifred asked.

Meena reached for the remote and turned on the small TV hooked to her security system. She smiled in satisfaction at her friends' scowling faces on the screen.

Without answering, Meena hung up the phone and rolled out of bed. Her doorbell squealed—long and grating.

She pushed the button on the intercom system by the light switch to open the door of her private side entrance downstairs. She was just walking out to the front door to unlock it when she heard the service elevator halt. "Good morning, ladies," she called over her shoulder as they stepped off the elevator.

"Do you have company?" Demi asked, peeking down the hall into Meena's bedroom.

Meena paused on the way to her kitchen to look over

her shoulder at her friend. "Now's a good time to ask," she said dryly. "That's *exactly* why I changed my locks."

She reached into the fridge for a small personal can of apple juice. She turned and was startled to see all three of her girls standing together. "What?" she asked, defensively.

"Why didn't you answer your cell phone last night?"

"Where were you?"

"Is he still here?"

"Are you crazy?"

"We were worried."

"Meena, girl, you tripping."

"Details...details."

The questions and comments flew so fast and furious that they began to blend. Meena didn't know which of her friends said or asked what.

Still dressed in her usual night attire, Meena climbed onto a stool, the can of juice still in her hand.

"Girls, I think I fell in love last night," she began honestly.

They each grabbed a stool from around the bar that separated the kitchen from the living room area of the loft.

"When we left, Marcus and I went right across the street to have dinner."

"Does this end in Marcus getting rid of your coochie cobwebs?" Eva asked.

Meena looked at each of them long and hard. "Ladies, what happened last night was about more than sex—"

"That good?" Demi asked, swinging the leg she had crossed.

"*Or* that bad," Eva added.

"Focus, ladies," Meena admonished. "Last night was an amazing evening with an even more amazing man. We're so different, and that's what I like about him most . . ."

The dinner

"You really don't use your cell or e-mails unless it's for work?" Meena asked Marcus in amazement as they sat across from each other in the restaurant.

Marcus nodded his head in earnest as he took a large sip of his water. "That's right."

"But...why?" she asked, setting her fork down to settle her cat-shaped eyes on his handsome face.

"I think personal e-mails are actually impersonal, and cell phones are a nuisance to me on a early Sunday morning when I just want to read my newspaper. Everything in today's society is so in an instant, so quick. Slow and steady wins the race."

"I guess you have a point, but I love all my gadgets," Meena admitted.

"Tech junkie, huh?"

"Definitely. I have a cell phone, a Smartphone, a two-way pager, my laptop, my portable DVD and Mp3 players. And Lord, don't get me started on all the things rigged up in my loft. Just about anything can be done with one touch of the button."

"Twelve steps to recovery," Marcus joked.

"You know I just thought of something," she said softly, a hint of a smile in her eyes spread to her luscious lips.

He stopped eating, crossed his arms on the tabletop, and gave her his full attention.

"I think I would prefer to get love letters written by the hand of my man. Maybe they'll be a hint of his cologne on the paper or the distinct slashing of his handwriting and the joy of knowing the effort was made."

Marcus reached across the table and took her hand into his warmly. "If I was your man, I'd write you love letters and little notes every day," he told her in his deep, masculine tone. "Would you keep them all?"

Meena caressed his fingers, blown away by the intensity in his eyes. "Each...and...every...one, for as long as I live."

"Good morning, son."

Marcus looked up from the newspaper he was reading

to see his father walking up the back walkway to enter his screened porch.

His parents lived just a few miles away, and they visited each other frequently.

"Morning," Marcus said, sliding his glasses up onto his head.

"I been standing here watching you. Look like you got a lot on your mind." Thelonius chuckled as he took the wicker seat across from his son. "What's her name?"

Marcus looked over at his father—an aged reflection of himself—and smiled. "Her name is Meena."

He thought of her. Her scent. Her touch. Her smile. Her infectious laughter. Her sense of humor. Her body. Her beauty.

He'd known this woman for less than twenty-four hours and already he missed her petite presence by his side.

"Is it that deep?" Thelonius asked as he peered at his son looking off into the distance with a hint of a smile.

Marcus licked his lips and couldn't beat the grin off his face with a stick.

"In a good way or a bad way?" Thelonius asked with concern.

"In a good way...a damn good way, Pops . . ."

The stroll

"Favorite movie?" Marcus asked as they strolled arm and arm.

"Comedy, drama, or sci-fi?" Meena asked as she let her head rest against his arm.

"How 'bout of all time periods?" Marcus countered, smiling broadly as she playfully pinched him.

"Uhm, that's hard one, but I think I'll say *Love Jones*. A nice movie about black love," she told him. "Definitely *Love Jones*."

Marcus nodded. "Good movie."

"*Great* movie," she said with emphasis, looking up at him and thinking how much she would like to taste his lips. "Now, what's yours?"

"Any of the *Star Wars* movies," he admitted.

Meena's mouth fell open. "Oooohh, you're a Trekkie?" she asked, tossing her head back to fill the air with her bubbly laughter.

"No, I'm not. I said *Star Wars,* not *Star Trek.*"

Meena shrugged. "Same difference," she said as she stopped to peer into the window of a fabric store. "A sci-fi fan who doesn't like technology. You're an odd duck, Marcus Daniels."

"I like all kinds of movies," he told her.

"Yeah, me, too. I cry every time I watch *Terms of Endearment.*" Meena reclaimed Marcus's arm as they continued forward. "When I have time to watch a movie, that is."

"We'll make time," he said, following an impulse to swing her easily up into his arms.

"Sounds like a date to me," Meena said, burying her face into his neck to inhale deeply of his scent as her heart pounded wildly like African drums.

"Sure does," he answered, touching his chin to the top of her head.

Meena raised her head suddenly to look at him with a raised brow. "You *do* have a DVD player, don't you?"

"He twirled you right there in the middle of the street?" Demi asked, almost absentmindedly filling her mouth with plump grapes as they all listened to Meena's tale.

"Yup, and it was fun and spontaneous," Meena told them, wishing that she was in Marcus's arms at that very moment. "Umpf...umpf...umpf."

Demi, Winifred, and Eva exchanged a look as Meena visibly shivered.

"The brotha that good?" Eva asked, her interest even more piqued.

Meena gave her a long, hard stare. "Did I not say this was not about sex, Miss Eva the Diva?"

"So what is it about?" Winifred asked, reaching forward to lightly touch Meena's hand.

"I know this is so corny and so cliché, so *not* me, but—"

"Barf bag alert," Eva teased.

"I think I found my soul mate. . . ."

The drinks

"Do you believe in love at first sight?" Marcus asked Meena as they sat in an intimate corner of one of her favorite spots—The Martini Bar.

"Not really, not until—"

"Tonight, right?" he asked, his thigh pressed intimately against hers.

Meena couldn't tear her eyes away from his. "Right," she answered softly.

Marcus rose his glass of seltzer water and lime. "Here's to finding your soul mate."

Meena touched her apple martini to his glass. "Here, here," she said softly.

"Your soul mate, huh?" Thelonius asked his son with a chuckle. "This little lady had your nose wide open. Wish we weren't leaving for Florida today so we could meet her."

"Me, too," Mercus said. "I've just never met anyone like her."

"Take your time, son," his father warned. "It's all the good things, the great times...in the beginning. No one's perfect."

Marcus nodded, but he couldn't help but think Meena may not be perfect, but she just might be perfect for him.

The carriage ride

"I love New York," Meena sighed, as she cuddled close to Marcus's side. "I need to do a tourist day and try to see it from a visitor's viewpoint."

"We'll see it together," Marcus told her, his arm comfortably settled around her shoulders.

"Is that a promise?" Meena asked, enjoying the feel, the scent, all of him.

"My word is my honor."

She believed him.

"My girls are not going to believe this," Meena sighed.

Marcus leaned forward to look down at her, suddenly filled with the need to plant dozens of kisses over her face. This woman brought out the mushiness in him—and he didn't mind one bit.

"That was your posse with you tonight?" he asked.

"No diggety, no doubt." Meena said.

They settled closer to one another.

"Were you looking for a love match at all?" Meena asked, curious.

Marcus shook his head.

"Well, I wasn't looking to find anyone either when Eva gave me the invite, but let's just say I owe her the Christian Louboutin leopard pumps she wants."

Marcus squeezed her close to his side as the carriage lurched forward, and they both tilted their heads back to look up at the star-filled night sky.

5

Meena hung up the phone after calling Marcus's home number for the third time that morning. "Okay, Meena Nishon Jones, that was absolutely the last call," she chided herself as she sat her cordless phone back onto its base.

She let the towel she had wrapped around her naked, damp body fall the floor as she made her way to the dresser.

Okay, maybe she'd jumped the gun last night in thinking she had lucked up and found "the one." Maybe he woke up and thought she wasn't quite as cute and appealing as he did last night—okay, maybe not—but what was his deal?

Meena yanked a matching pair of bra and panties from the drawer.

She was disappointed. She had really liked Marcus. "Suspender-wearing, big-head fool," she muttered.

Brrrnnnggg.

Meena paused in pulling up her panties at the shrill cry of the phone. She tugged the delicate lace up around her hips as she moved over to pick up the phone. She was disappointed that it was not Marcus, and then was annoyed at herself for caring.

"Hello," she said, just a hint of a snap in her voice.

"You must be one hell of a woman."

Meena's breath caught in her throat. It was Marcus. She would know that voice anywhere.

She sank down onto her bed. "Oh, really?"

"Oh, definitely."

"Why's that?" she asked, fishing for compliments.

"I have never used my cell phone for non–work-related or non-emergency reasons," he mused.

"So why start now?" she asked, laying back among the pillows on her bed.

"I just had to hear that sexy voice of yours."

A fine layer of goosebumps raced across her body. "I try to please," she said in a voice she deepened to a husky, playful whisper.

She was rewarded by the sound of his infectious laughter filling the phone.

"I called you this morning," she admitted, lifting one slender leg up to flex her foot.

"I'm not home."

Meena raised a brow. "Kinda figured that."

"Don't you want to know where I am?" he asked.

Meena rolled over onto her stomach. "Well, I didn't want to be too forward and ask."

"Ask," he prompted.

She shrugged. "Okay, where are you?"

"Downstairs."

Meena froze. She rolled off the bed and was about to shoot over to her open window when she realized her size 32Bs were exposed.

She covered her breasts with her forearm and moved to the window to see Marcus standing next to a black SUV down below. He was dressed in lightweight linen pants and a white T-shirt.

He tilted his head up and waved at her.

Meena couldn't explain how excited she was to see him. "I would wave, but both my hands are in use and I don't want to flash you the twins," she quipped.

"I wouldn't mind at all," he said.

"I'm sure you wouldn't," she drawled.

"I have a surprise for you."

Meena smiled. "I'll buzz you up."

"You have to come down to get it," he insisted.

"Why?"

"If I told you that it would spoil the surprise, right," he told her, now leaning against the passenger door of the SUV.

"Where are we going?" she asked, completely guessing.

Marcus just laughed.

"I have to know how to dress, Marcus," Meena protested.

When he still wouldn't answer, Meena childishly stuck out her tongue to him and turned away from the window. "Be down in five," she told him, walking back to her closet.

"I'll be waiting."

Meena hung up the phone, and then tossed it over her shoulder onto the bed.

Based on his outfit, Meena chose a flirty ivory cotton skirt that showed off her legs and paired it with a chocolate lace tank with a deep V-neck. She kept her makeup to a minimum and wore no jewelry except her diamond studs and a cross pendant.

Within five minutes she was walking out the building and going around the corner to walk up behind Marcus as he bent over the hood reading his newspaper.

Meena lightly tapped his shoulder, stepping back as he whirled around abruptly. "It's just me, handsome," she told him, looking at him with his glasses on. "Damn, you even look good in glasses."

Marcus slid his hands into his pockets as he looked down at her and rocked on his heels. "If you make your clients look half as good as you do right now, I can see why you do what you do."

"Thank you."

Marcus moved to open the passenger door. "Ready to roll?"

"Yes, but where are we rolling to?" she asked. "And where's my surprise?"

"We're headed to it right now."

Meena settled back against the plush leather as Marcus folded up his paper on the hood, and then climbed into the driver's seat.

"I only ask you to promise me one thing," he stated as he started the luxury vehicle and pulled away from the curb. "Promise me today you will relax. No checking your e-mails on those fifty different cell phones and PDAs you have—"

Meena laughed.

"No answering your cell phone every time it rings."

Meena just looked at him.

"Articles, photo shoots, shopping for people, talking to your girls, making sure other people look good are all important. I respect what you do," he assured her. "But *your* life, *your* peace, and *your* well-being are just as important."

Meena smiled and reached over to lightly caress his face. "Marcus Daniels, you are just what I needed when I needed it," she said with a fierceness that showed just how much she meant those words.

He smiled, showing two deep dimples in his cheeks.

"Now, I will make that promise if you promise me something," she said softly, innocently, deceptively.

"Name it."

"You have to toss this brick you call a cell phone and let me pick out a new phone for you," she said, trying not to laugh.

"What's wrong with my phone?"

"Mess around and drop it on your foot and you'll be

wearing a cast, that's what. Now, do we have a deal?"
Meena asked, loving that she had the upper hand.

"I thought I was the lawyer," Marcus muttered as the
light turned green and he accelerated the vehicle.

"Huh?" Meena asked, exaggerated as she leaned close
to him, cupping her hand to her ear. "I didn't hear you."

"Deal."

Meena took the archaic phone and tossed it onto the
next row of seats.

"Marcus, this has been wonderful," Meena sighed as
she leaned back into his embrace.

Her surprise was a ride on his sailboat, *Destiny*. They
spent the day with Marcus at the helm, eventually dropping
anchor so that they could prepare lunch together in the gal-
ley downstairs.

Now the sun was setting and the sky was a blend of
beautiful hues of blues, oranges, and brilliant reds as they
sipped sparkling cider and enjoyed the crisp scent of the
ocean and the cool feel of its breeze where they sat.

"It seems like so much has happened in just twenty-
four hours," Marcus said as he rose to pull Meena into his
embrace, setting his chin atop her head. "I feel like I've
known you forever. I feel like I don't want to ever not have
you in my life. Am I crazy?"

She balanced her flute of cider behind his back as she
tilted her head back to gaze up at him. "If so, we're two
crazy nuts together," she whispered into that sweet, intimate space between them. "I never believed that I could
feel so strongly about someone so quickly . . . until now.
Until you."

Marcus used the strength of just one solid arm to pick
Meena up by the waist so that they were directly face to
face. Together, they slowly moved in close to bless one another with one firm kiss. But that led to a dozen more until
finally Marcus flung his flute over the boat to free his hand

so that he could grasp the back of Meena's head and deepen the kiss. He released a moan of abandon and pleasure.

Meena tossed her own flute into the darkening waters as she freely caressed the strong lines of Marcus's back with her eager hands.

Framed by the fierce beauty of the sky, Marcus and Meena gave in to their passion and kissed each other like they were starved for one another.

Marcus backed up until he felt the bench press into the back of his thighs. He sat down, gasping hotly as Meena immediately climbed into his lap and grinded against the full, heavy length of his erection.

He shifted his hands down to place them under her skirt and feel the warmth of her soft buttocks in his hands. To discover she wore nothing but a delicate lace thong caused a hungry growl to escape from him.

Meena raised her hands to grasp the sides of Marcus's handsome and strong face. She licked the outline of his full lips before suckling them into her mouth. "Uhhmm, tastes good," she sighed.

"It does, does it?" Marcus asked, looking into her hazy eyes and seeing the reflection of the sun setting behind him.

Meena reached behind herself to clasp Marcus's hands, pulling them up to her aching breasts. The warmth of able palms radiated through the lace of her top, and Meena wondered if anything in the world felt better.

Using his skillful fingers, Marcus rolled the taut nipples, causing Meena to squirm against him with her hips as she leaned back in wild abandon.

He raised the top over her head, trying to control the desire to tear it from her body. He dropped it onto the deck as the sight of her breasts, bared to his eager eyes, made his heart rate erratic. Small and plump with dark nipples that were so full and round, they were the most divine breasts he'd ever seen.

While his hands moved to cross her bottom beneath her

skirt, Meena steered his head until his mouth surrounded a taut nipple. "Yes," she moaned, leaning to the right a little to look down as Marcus released his full tongue and licked from the base of her breast and up to the upturned nipple. As he drew the taut flesh into his mouth, Meena felt the bud between her legs throb and become soaked with her arousal. The ache radiated to her thighs and abdomen, and Meena wondered if she could truly go another minute without having Marcus inside of her.

Marcus leaned back to quickly snatch his T-shirt over his head. As Meena trailed her quivering hands over the smooth, contoured lines of his body, he unzipped her skirt, and then rose with his arm securely around her. The skirt dropped onto the deck with ease, and Meena wrapped her legs around Marcus's waist as they kissed each other with passion and ardor.

"Are we moving too fast?" Marcus whispered against her lips.

Meena released a breath heavy with desire and frustration. "I don't know," she answered honestly, touching her forehead down upon his. "But I do know that right now at this moment it feels...right."

"I feel like I've known your sexy ass forever," he told her, his voice husky and barely above a whisper.

"And I feel like I have loved you forever," Meena admitted, speaking from her heart as she stared into Marcus's eyes with tears brimming in her own.

Marcus's chest exploded with her words. "When we're gray and old with a million picky-headed grands, just remember you said I love you first," he said with a boyish grin.

Meena lightly caressed his nape as she smiled softly. "It'll be your word against mine."

Marcus pulled out his wallet and removed a condom before putting the wallet back into his pocket. He reached beneath Meena's bared bottom to undo his belt, zipper, and button. His linen pants slid down his legs to the deck and his boxers soon followed. Quickly, he sheathed himself for their protection.

There on the deck of his boat named *Destiny*, Marcus and Meena claimed their own bit of fate beneath the wide expanse of stars now glittering against the velvet backdrop of the night sky. Unashamed and wanton, they kissed, stroked, enjoyed, and pleasured, lost in a world all their own.

As Marcus placed his hands on her buttocks to guide this woman—his woman—down onto his thick, throbbing rod, Meena gasped hotly. She was filled not just physically, but emotionally.

Marcus buried his face into her neck, biting his bottom lip as Meena's core fit him like a vice.

She arched her back and began to circle her hips, pulling Marcus deeper within her.

"Damn, girl," he moaned in pleasure and some amazement at her skill. "Oh, so you showing out, huh?"

Meena lifted her head to look down at him as they were framed by the moon's light, thankfully surrounded by nothing but the water. "Everything I do, I do well."

Marcus put his feet wider apart, bracing himself with every muscle in his form as he held himself stiff as Meena worked her hips to her own rhythm.

Gasping for breath. Heated kisses. Deep massaging with trembling hands. Racing hearts. Fast and furious strokes. Slow and sensuous ones. The line between passion and lust blurred.

Marcus felt a tightness in his chest and his loins as his member stiffened before each spasmodic jerk released his seed.

Meena clutched him as her own wave after wave of release shook her body as she came with him, coating him with her juices.

They both gasped deeply as if trying to draw air as their hearts pummeled in their chests in perfect sync with one another.

6

Meena glanced down at her watch as she paced the length of the conference room in her attorney's Manhattan offices. After the glorious weekend she had just shared with Marcus, the last thing Meena wanted to do on a Monday morning was handle legal issues so that she could receive the money she was owed and the respect she deserved.

At least it was the beginning of the end, and Meena just prayed that both Savor and his management company knew she was serious now that she was suing them for breach of contract for a sum that was ten times the fees they had refused to pay in the first place.

For them to countersue for breach of contract was absolutely ridiculous.

Releasing a breath heavy with aggravation, Meena looked down at the busy street below through the large window, trying hard not to feel like a caged animal. She leaned forward suddenly at the sight of a tall, muscular brother in a tailored suit crossing the street.

Her heart raced, and then double pumped.

Suddenly the brother looked up. He was a stranger, not her Marcus like she thought.

She had started to fill him in on her legal woes but didn't want to put a damper on their fun weekend. Meena was far too independent for that anyway. Besides, when she was with Marcus she wanted to forget anything troublesome or worrisome in her life and just enjoy being happy for the first time in a long time. Too long.

So she would get through this bit of drama today, go to work, and then prepare for her dinner date with Marcus tonight. She mischievously smiled at the thought of dessert.

"Glad to see you're in a better mood," Danice Richardson said as she strolled into the conference room.

Meena turned and looked at the dark-skinned, Ethiopian beauty with her waist-length dreadlocks and the regal features of a queen. "Just reminiscing on a really good weekend."

Danice waved a hand toward one of the leather chairs at the conference table as she took a seat herself. "All ready for today, then?" she asked, the hint of her accent at the very edges of her voice.

"Ready as I'll ever be," Meena said, taking a seat and crossing her slender legs.

"We've had a change of representation for Savor and Hitmaker Management," Danice said as she opened the file in front of her.

"That's no big deal...right?"

"Shouldn't be. I'm familiar with the attorney. His style's a little cutthroat and in your face, but it's nothing we can not handle."

Meena nodded, her face reflective. "And he is?"

"Derek Lyles of MDDL Law."

Marcus was tired. He let his body relax against the elevator as he rode up to the office. He reached on to his hip for the new digital data phone Meena had picked out for him yesterday.

Funny that she was able to accomplish in one weekend what his best friend of the past twenty years couldn't get him to do. Scrolling to his gallery of pictures, all taken during their day of fun in the sun at Battery Park, Marcus enlarged a snapshot of Meena sitting cross-legged on the blanket as she sketched designs.

"Damn, girl, you know you got me jacked up," he admitted softly, shaking his head as he smiled boyishly.

The elevator slid to a stop, and the door opened with ease. Marcus closed his phone and placed it back in the clip as he stepped forward.

He almost collided with Derek, who was obviously leaving. "Whaddup, dawg?" Marcus greeted as he pressed his back against one of the doors to keep them from closing.

The men gave each other a pound—the black man's handshake.

"How did the meeting go with Roderick Steele?" Derek asked.

Marcus wiped his hand over his mouth. "I think he might go with a larger sports agency. In fact, I'd like your help on this one. Busy?"

Derek looked down at his watch. "We just got a new client over the weekend. I called you at home but I couldn't reach you, and I know not to try that thing you call a cell phone. Had a little freak of the week over, huh?"

Marcus couldn't stop the cheesy grin that spread across his face but refrained from telling his friend and business partner about Meena—she was too special for their usual locker room type discussions on women and sex.

"Who's the new client?" he asked, deliberately changing the subject as the elevator began to emit a high-pitched wailing noise like an alarm.

Derek stepped into the elevator and pulled Marcus in so that the door could close and the noise would cease. "Savor.

You know that kid that sings that song all the ladies love, 'Gimme an O!' Well, he fired his attorney last week and we were recommended to step in and get the job done."

"Standard deal?" Marcus asked as Derek pushed the button for the lobby.

"Actually, he's in the midst of a lawsuit and I'm headed to the deposition right now," Derek said as the elevator slid to a stop. "Tell you what. Ride to the deposition with me, and on the way we'll brainstorm about Roderick?"

"Cool," Marcus said, following Derek to his vehicle.

Meena watched Derek Lyles as he sauntered into the conference room like he owned the building and everything and everyone in it. He was all confidence and cockiness in his black Gucci suit. He smiled at her like he knew what color her panties were as he extended his hand.

She allowed him to briefly take her hand before she turned her attention to Savor. She had to force the look of astonishment from filling her face when she clearly recognized one of the suits she'd selected for his new wardrobe. She pierced him with her eyes and could have literally spit when he winked at her.

"My partner's going to be joining us after he finishes a call," Derek began as he undid the single button of his suit jacket and took a seat across the table from Meena and Danice. "May I begin?"

Danice inclined her head, her pen poised over her legal pad as she boldly met his stare.

Meena heard her cell phone vibrating against the keys in her purse, but she ignored it as Derek's questioning started.

It became evident rather quickly that his intention was to paint her as the one who became sexually aggressive toward his client. *Ain't that a bunch of b-s.*

"Are you kidding me?" Meena snapped, leaning forward in her chair as Derek just asked her if she'd been sexually active with one of her celebrity clients.

Danice put a restraining hand on Meena's arm. "Irrelevant, counselor. My client will not answer that."

Derek looked as pleased as the wolf in a den of sheep. "It's amazing how what you won't answer is just as telling as the answers to the questions that you will."

Meena absolutely hated his guts.

"I believe the question is very relevant—"

The conference room door opened and all eyes shifted to it.

Meena's face shifted from pleasure to surprise to confusion, and then suspicion.

"This is Marcus Daniels, my business partner," Derek stated.

Meena pierced Marcus with her eyes.

Marcus slipped his cell phone back into the clip, having been unable to reach Meena on hers. He closed the conference room door and moved over to take the seat to Derek's left directly across from...Meena?

His body froze at the first sight of her, and the seconds it took for his bottom to press against the seat seemed to take forever. *What the hell?*

"So, Ms. Jones, please answer the question: Have you ever been sexually involved with one of you clients?"

Marcus felt his stomach drop and tried to keep his face neutral even though his insides screamed "Nooooooooooo-oooo!"

Meena's eyes shifted to Marcus for one brief moment before she answered. "I'm not answering that."

Marcus frowned.

As Derek's questioning continued, Marcus saw Meena's anger and discomfort. He felt like someone had dropped him into the middle of a tank filled with ice-cold water. He wished like hell he wasn't sitting in the room.

He was lost to all the minute details, but the picture was becoming clearer as the deposition winded to an end. Several times he had to force himself not to flinch at Derek's line of questioning. It was true Lyle style: undermining, cold, calculated...ruthless. His partner was showing his cards to Meena: Continue with the lawsuit and be demolished in court.

Marcus released a heavy breath.

Meena looked to him with obvious expectations of his help, but Marcus felt this was a battle between his business and a woman he cared about, felt connected to on a level he had never known...only known since Friday.

There was no way he could openly defend Meena and go against his client. And there was no way he could reveal that he was involved with her—and if Meena was smart, she'd continue to keep that detail to herself as well. It wouldn't be the best move to reveal that she had sex with him just one night after they had met.

Meena left her attorney's office and was proud of herself for not breaking down as she walked to the curb and hailed a cab.

The hairs on the nape of her neck and arms stood on end.

"Meena."

She knew before she heard his voice that Marcus was behind her.

She ignored his tired behind.

"Meena, we need to talk," he said, stepping around her body to stand in front of her.

Meena laughed bitterly at that. "Your ass ain't had diddly to say in that sham of a meeting, so go to hell with whatever you have to say now."

Marcus reached out to touch her, but the look Meena gave him made him withdraw his hand.

"Why aren't you off with your jackass of a partner, Mr. MDDL Law, celebrating trying to make me look like a whore and a slut," she asked as a yellow cab finally pulled to a stop beside her.

"Meena, I didn't know anything—"

Meena opened the back door of the cab. "You damn right you don't *know* anything. *Your* client invited me to give him a freaking blow job when I was bending down to hem his pants."

"He's not my client—"

"*Your* firm, *your* partner, *your* damn client."

"Hey, lady, are you getting in or out?" the burly cab driver called to her through the passenger window.

Meena climbed into the back of the cab. "Go to hell, Mr. MDDL Law," she spat, fighting the tears and waves of hopelessness flooding her.

The cab door slammed behind her.

Marcus watched the cab fade into the hundreds of other vehicles moving up the street. "Damn," he swore, wanting to emit a scream that would bounce against a concrete skyscraper that nearly blocked the sun.

7

One month later

Meena had a busy weekend ahead of her. Dating was like riding a bike, and she was hopping back onto it and riding away full speed.

Dinner with Antoine tomorrow night. Church and then brunch with Elliott Sunday afternoon. A concert with Marc Sunday night.

And tonight was dinner with Brandon, a handsome Blair Underwood-looking brother who owned a chain of urban retail apparel stores.

In preparation for her first date in weeks, Meena had taken the day off and was pampered at Bliss Soho all day, had her hair and makeup done at Luxe, and had relished in a one-hour bath scented with her favorite coconut-scented bath gel from Carol's Daughter. A new short and flirty cocktail dress in vibrant shades of aqua and strappy sandals that added three inches to her height emphasized her shapely legs.

She was determined to start living her life to the fullest again. No more moping about the coulda, woulda, and shouldas with Marcus.

So when she left her loft, her plan was to flirt until she couldn't flirt no more and get back to the old Meena.

Easier said than done.

"Food bad?"

Meena stopped pushing her shrimp étouffée around on her plate to look up at Brandon. The food was delicious. Brandon was more than easy on the eye, and his attempts at conversation were on point.

So why wasn't she having a good time?

Memories of Marcus that's why.

Not Brandon nor any of the other brothas she had lined up for dates could compete. She wanted more than a line of dates with brothas she wouldn't even consinder dating seriously. She wanted more than diversions with the ultimate goal of fun and not longevity.

She wanted Marcus.

"The food's good," she admitted, trying her best to give him her best smile—but it didn't quite reach her exotic eyes.

So as Brandon began to tell her an amusing story of catching shoplifters in his Bronx store, Meena leaned in close and tilted her head to stare at him with feigned interest. She knew even as she put on a good show of the old Meena that her life had been forever changed by Marcus, and she wondered how in the hell she was to cope without him.

Meena was in his blood, and Marcus could not get her out of his mind. He honestly wondered if he ever would.

"Damn," he swore as he leaned back in his chair and brought his hands up to wipe his mouth. The woman had made his toes curl with her sex and his life happier with her laughter.

"Here late again, man?" Derek asked as he strolled into Marcus's office.

Marcus removed his glasses as he looked up at his friend. "Working on the Roderick Steele contract," he eased out as if it wasn't good news.

"That's *my* dawg," Derek said in an animated fashion as he extended his fist to his friend.

Marcus leaned forward to lightly tap his fist atop his partner's. "Thank you...thank you."

Derek loosened his tie as he settled down into one of the leather club chairs facing the desk. "Word is Savor settled out of court with Meena today."

Marcus put way too much attention into unnecessarily shuffling papers on his desk. "Oh yeah," he said, trying to sound nonchalant.

Derek could only shake his head in amusement at his friend.

"Thanks again for supporting my decision not to represent Savor."

Derek nodded. "I just wish I could turn back the hands of time. Maybe my boy wouldn't be walking around acting and looking like his damn dog died."

"Derek, man—"

Derek held up both his hands. "Naw, man, let me finish," he said, wanting to speak his piece. "Meena's pissed at you and you're pissed at yourself because you didn't stand in and stop me from getting the job done at the deposition. At that moment you chose your business over pleasure. Fine. Big...damn...deal. You don't throw away something special over some straight b-s."

Marcus settled back into his chair, forcing it to recline as he studied his friend.

"I've known you since before you had hairs on your chest, and I have never seen you like this over a woman.

'Round here singing Lionel Richie, either moping around or working like a madman all time of the night and weekends. You're working yourself ragged."

"The firm is growing. We're expanding into the West Coast. More work. More hours to put in to make it successful," Marcus said, sweeping his hand above the various stacks of files and paperwork on his desk. "In fact, I think we should start considering Zion as a full partner—"

"You love her."

Marcus placed his arms on his desk as he leaned forward to lock eyes with Derek. "You asking me or telling me?"

"Telling you," Derek quickly responded without a doubt.

Marcus released a heavy breath. "What you want from me?" he asked.

"I want you to pull your head out of your ass and go get your woman," Derek spouted. "She's fine as hell. Mess around and I'll—"

Marcus shot daggers at his friend. "Don't play—"

"Yup, thought so," Derek said with satisfaction at Marcus's obvious show of jealousy. "I never knew you to give up so easily."

"Maybe it wasn't worth fighting for," Marcus lied.

"So get your act together then."

"This trip to L.A. is just what I need," Marcus stated.

"Go 'head and get you a lovely L.A. dip to relieve some of the pressure," Derek said, rising from the chair. "Mess 'round and have zits big as skittles all over your dang on face."

Marcus just laughed. He hadn't had sex since Meena— the longest he'd gone since he was a chubby virgin who couldn't buy a piece of tail.

Derek's phone played Marques Houston's "Naked" from his hip. His face lit in a huge devilish grin as he flipped his phone open. "Whassup, baby. I'm still at my office."

Marcus began packing items into his briefcase, being

sure he had his airline tickets for his 10 A.M. flight out of La Guardia the following day.

"I'm on my way, baby. Put it on ice for Big Daddy," Derek cooed. "No, don't you start without me. I'm leaving right now."

Derek snapped his phone shut decisively as he moved to the door. "Marcus, man, safe trip. You know I'm flying down next weekend to start interviewing the personnel in L.A. May your night be as...*fulfilling* as mine. Gotta go."

Marcus just laughed at Derek's speedy departure.

His friend's words remained with him, though. He reached onto his hip for his phone and pulled up a picture of Meena playfully winking at him. *I got to get over her.*

Thinking quickly, and probably rashly, Marcus picked up his office phone and dialed a number with his forefinger. He leaned back in his chair as the phone rang.

"Hello."

"Hey, Wendi. What's up?" he asked, forcing a casualness into his tone.

"Marcus? Oooh. Long time no hear from," she purred in obvious surprise and pleasure.

Marcus pictured the voluptuous mocha-skinned beauty whose sex was as soothing as hot chocolate on a cold winter's day. Just the hot toddy for a little "Meena-don't-love-me-blues."

"Been real busy with work lately, that's all," he said, playing with his Cross pen.

"Now it's time for pleasure, right?"

"Definitely."

"Your place or mine?"

"Yours."

"Give me an hour."

The line went dead.

Marcus looked down at Meena's photo one last time before he deleted that and every other picture of her from his phone once and for all.

* * *

Meena sipped her apple martini but didn't really notice the flavor of the liquid. It was an automated motion.

Everything in her life seemed that way lately.

After her date with Brandon drew to a tragic end, Meena had called her girls and they all met up at the G-Spot.

"Brandon the beautiful wasn't enough to get you out your slump, huh?" Winifred asked.

"I'm not in a slump," Meena protested without much enthusiasm.

"Come on, Meena," Eva urged. "You haven't been yourself since—"

Meena shot her a look to keep her friend from saying his name. "I'm cool," she lied, looking around the club as she bounced a little in her chair to the music pressing and beating against the walls.

Admitting to them about the weekend she had shared with Marcus had been easy—even the part about her foolishly believing she had experienced true love at first sight. The hard part was admitting that even though she had told him to go to hell that day at the cab, she wanted Marcus to fight for her and to fight for what they had shared that weekend and could share for their rest of their lives.

But he never called her, and she never called him.

So obviously what they thought they shared had been more hype than reality.

"Well, at least all that drama with Savor is over," Demi said, pushing her shoulder into Meena's at their favorite table.

"Here's to punks jumping up to get beat down," Eva joked, raising her classic martini into the middle of the table.

"Damn right," Meena agreed, glad that she had these three women as her friends.

Savor and Hitmaker Management were dropping the counter suit and were willing to settle out of court. Yes, that was a victory. Discovering that she had so foolishly and so easily given her heart and her body to a man she didn't know, no matter how right it had felt at the time, that was one of the biggest disappointments of her life, and it had weighed heavily on her since the day of the deposition.

"To hell with Marcus," Meena said aloud, voicing her thoughts.

The women all toasted to that with a sistah-like "Humph."

Her girls had hardly left her side even though she told them she was cool. They had even stayed over three times and brought over enough burritos and mimosa to keep them all on the Stairmaster for a solid day to work off the sinfully delicious calories.

Demi leaned in close and said, "Better said than done, my friend."

Meena said nothing but allowed herself to get lost in the memories of the moonlit madness she and Marcus had created on the yacht that night.

"You ain't got to go home, Marcus Daniels, but you got to get the hell out of here!"

His clothing smacked him dead in his face where he sat naked in the middle of the bed. Through the leg of the underwear on his head he looked at Wendi, gloriously naked and obviously mad as hell, standing at the foot of the bed with her arms crossed over her chest and her toe tapping like crazy.

Marcus rose from the bed and began pulling on his boxers first.

Wendi gave him a long once over that was meant to be mocking. "Damn shame. You know they got pills for that shit."

Marcus paused in pulling up his pants to look at her like she was out of her mind. She mumbled under her breath as she strutted around the room snatching up her discarded clothing.

Marcus shoved his tie into the pocket of his suit jacket. "Wendi, I'll—"

She shot him daggers as she sucked air between her teeth. "Negro, *please.*"

Marcus said nothing else as he walked out of her apartment. He couldn't really blame her. It wasn't easy for a woman like Wendi to swallow not being able to arouse a man. Not that she hadn't tried like hell.

Still, he had been right there with her, ready to seal the deal, when he looked down into her face and *really* saw her.

The body was more voluptuous and full. The face not as slender and exotic. The hair far too long.

She wasn't Meena, and he felt like a heel for almost using her body as a receptacle for his release and pretending she was another woman.

No, Marcus wouldn't be calling Wendi anymore because he doubted she would ever let him forget this night.

Meena climbed into bed definitely feeling the effects of her night out. She rolled over onto her back and closed her eyes. Finding no comfort, she flopped over again and bunched the many pillows on her bed. Unfortunately, the feel of the pillows pressed intimately against her body made her think of the night she had spent in Marcus's bed wrapped securely against his length by his strong arms and muscled legs.

Meena gave in to the memories of him, and a moan of arousal came forth from the back of her throat.

Marcus had laid between her open thighs, planted deep within her core. Each stroke had embedded him deeper inside of her until the soft hairs of his groin tickled the bare skin of her shaven mound.

"Lord...have...mercy," she groaned, shoving a neck roll between her thighs to ease the throbbing ache of her core.

Marcus had been so strong and able to lift her and flip her with ease while he stroked long and deep...in and out...in and out...in and out...and then a slow, sensual circle of his hips that caused his penis to press against every bit of her.

Meena felt a fine sheen of sweat coat her body as she kicked away her sheets and flung away the useless neck roll in pure sexual frustration and heat. A heat that had begun in her core was now setting her entire body on fire.

A fire only Marcus could quench.

"Woo-oo-ee!" she sighed, fanning herself as she prayed for the desire she felt to wan.

As sleep began to make her eyelids heavy and her breathing slowed, Meena prayed that she would be released from her distraction of Marcus in her slumber.

Meena woke up with a jolt, sitting up straight in bed. Disoriented and a little confused, she looked around her bedroom with wide eyes as her heart pounded rapidly in her chest. "What the hell?" she whispered.

She looked at the digital clock on the bedside table. It read 1:23 A.M.

Still half asleep, Meena kicked off her bed covers and dragged herself out of bed to the bathroom to relieve herself. She was headed back to bed when lightning suddenly filled the sky, briefly illuminating the entire loft as the thunder soon followed with a loud rumble.

Meena was glad for the rain; she always slept better in this type of weather.

Stopping at the foot of the bed to stretch her petite frame, Meena gave a cursory glance at her monitors for her security system before climbing in bed.

Meena froze with one foot on the floor and one knee pressed into the bed. She turned and looked over her shoulder at the monitor to see a large, masculine figure walking away from her front door.

"Marcus," she whispered, her heart swelling to twice its size.

Meena dashed to the window, nearly slipping. She looked down at Marcus making his way back to his SUV. He hadn't rung the bell. He hadn't made his presence known. But how odd that she woke up at that exact moment to see him.

Lightning and thunder echoed again, but she was deaf to its roar as the furious pounding of her heart filled her ears. She snatched up her phone and dialed his cell phone number, but it went straight to voice mail.

Clad only in her boy shorts and tank top, Meena dashed through the house and raced through the front door to take the stairs like they were nothing. She pushed the industrial-strength metal door so hard that it slammed back against the wall with a loud BANG.

"Marcus!" she yelled as he climbed into his SUV, rain coating her and plastering her hair and clothes to her body. But she didn't care. She had to get to him. The desire to do so was too great to be ignored.

His SUV pulled away from the curb, and Meena ran to the curb to watch his crimson lights fade behind the curtain of pouring rain.

"Damn," she said huskily.

Meena turned and made her way back to the private entrance of her loft apartment as the rain splattering against the streets and the buildings nearly deafened her.

The blare of a horn caused her to stop and whirl around. She nearly fainted at the sight of Marcus's SUV parked at the curb. He jumped out of the SUV and ran to her.

"I thought I imagined you," Marcus said, fighting the urge to touch her and hold her as he stared down into a face he could look at for a lifetime.

"I just woke up and there you were, Marcus," she admitted as she fought the tears welling up in her throat.

"God, I have missed you," he admitted fiercely as lightning flashed in the skies. "I had to see you, Meena. I *had* to."

Touched by the conviction and emotion she saw even

through the rain, Meena reached up and stroked his face. "This thing between us is scary, you know."

He saw that she craved his kisses and used one strong arm to pull Meena close to him and pick her up to mold her body to his. And for the first time in weeks, Marcus felt whole again as he placed his hand on Meena's nape and steered her head down to him for a long kiss that could've made steam rise from their bodies from the heat they created.

"I'm sorry," Marcus whispered against her lips.

Meena just nodded and captured his tongue for a long, leisurely suckle as she wrapped her legs around his waist.

Marcus carried her into the building and up the stairs. When he reached the top, he pressed Meena's back to the wall and grinded his lengthy erection into her with a growl. "I haven't been with anyone since the last time we were together," he admitted against her ear as he trailed kisses down her throat.

Meena grabbed his head and forced him to look at her as she searched his eyes for honesty. "Me, either."

Marcus kissed Meena with all of the passion and emotion he had for her.

"Make love to me, Marcus," Meena commanded, her hands massaging deep circles into his muscled back.

Marcus walked them into the loft as the onslaught of the rainstorm thundered outside. He set Meena on her feet as he peeled the wet clothing from her body, and then rushed off his own clothing until they both stood naked and slightly shivering from the wetness and the desire they had for one another.

And there in the middle of her living room as the flashes of lightning illuminated their sculptured bodies, Marcus and Meena laid on the floor together. He opened her legs with his knees and poised his lengthy erection to enter her, but Meena placed a restraining hand on his rigid abdomen.

"The condom, Marcus," she whispered, even as she used shaking hands to stroke the length of him.

He laid down atop Meena and reached out in the darkness for his pants to pull out his wallet and retrieve a condom. Quickly, he tore the package and sheathed himself, eager to be inside her.

Again he positioned himself for entry, and Meena gaped her legs as wide as she could for him to fill her.

Inch by delicious inch, Marcus stroked until he was planted deep within her, her body accepting all of him. "Damn," he swore at her snug fit, raising up on his hands to look down at her as he grimaced from the smooth, tight feel of her walls against him. "I understand why we need the condom, but I can not wait until I feel you against me," he admitted, before lowering his head to capture her lips.

"In due time. In due time," she answered. She began to work her hips as her hands stroked the contours of his back and shifted down smoothly to playfully swat his firm buttocks.

Marcus's lips pursed as she drove him wild with her movements. "Work it, Meena," he urged, now gyrating his own hips so that they moved in unison.

For the next hour their coupling varied from making sweet, intimate love to a fast and furious stroking that made their hearts race and their bodies become coated with sweat as Meena begged him for a reprieve. The rumble and flashes of lightning intensified their actions as nature claimed the skies. The two enjoyed a physical connection that was as natural as the weather outside. It was as if they were made for one another. Meant to be joined. Meant to *be*.

They both cried out hoarsely as the first waves of their release coursed over their bodies. Their cries mingled with the thunder and lightning until they were both spent. Their hearts beat in a furious pattern together.

"God, I love you, Meena," Marcus whispered against her forehead as he reached beneath her body to hold her against him as he rolled over onto his back.

"This thing between us is so scary. I'm not the fall in love at first sight type, Marcus, but I know that since I first saw you at the speed dating thing I felt a pull toward you. I felt like I needed you even then."

"I felt the same way when I saw you."

"I know that you had nothing to do with the way your partner treated me in the deposition," she said, going back to why they had been apart all these weeks. "But I felt you could have stepped up for me. For a minute, I thought you set me up."

Marcus held her closer if that was at all possible. "Derek didn't know who you were and what you meant to me. This was all just a crazy coincidence that I wish I could have stopped sooner. I guess you know we're no longer representing Savor."

Meena nodded against his chest as her fingers massaged his arms.

"Congratulations on your settlement. I know you deserved it, and it was one of the reasons that I asked Derek not to represent him any longer."

Meena raised her head and looked down at him. "That's behind us. We've got a lifetime to make it up to each other."

Marcus thought of the plane he had to catch in just eight hours. He just got her back in his life, and now he was headed across the country for three months. Damn. "Uhm, baby?"

"Yes," Meena said, placing tiny kisses against his nipples.

"You like L.A.?"

EPILOGUE

Five years later

"Remember, ladies, work like you have never worked before. I need those beautiful faces and those beautiful bodies to bring MeenaMeena clothes to life."

Meena clasped her hands together, a bundle of nerves as she finished up her speech backstage to her first runway show at New York's Fashion Week.

Everyone applauded her, and Meena couldn't hardly believe that finally her dreams were a reality.

"Meena, your cell phone," Lala said, walking up to her with it in her hand.

"Who is it?" she asked.

"That sexy husband of yours."

Meena's heart double pumped. Four years of marriage and the man still had that effect on her.

"Hey, you," she said into the phone with a smile, moving to the rear of the tent for some semblance of quiet. "Where are you?"

"Front row, baby," he assured her.

Meena turned and went back to the front, anxious to just look at him even if she couldn't hold him until this circus was over. Through the tent her eyes went straight to him where he sat with their three-year-old daughter, Destiny, in his lap. To his left were his parents. And to his right was her sistah-girls: Eva, Winifred, and Demi. Her family.

The lights dimmed in the tent.

"We're 'bout to start," she told him, blowing him a kiss. "Wish me luck."

"Nothing but luck, baby."

Meena stepped back from the break in the curtain as the music began, and her eyes lit up with joy as the first model took her stance on the runway.

Dear Readers,

Love at first sight, huh? If only everyone could be as lucky as Meena and Marcus to feel the explosion of pure love at first sight of each other. Their relationship was rushed, but that was because neither could deny their feelings. I wish for a love like theirs for all of you hopeless romantics out there. Hey, you never know—smile.

Love 2 Live & Live 2 Love,

Niobia

ABOUT THE AUTHOR

Niobia Simone Bryant has taken the romance world by storm since her 2000 release of *Admission of Love*. With national best-selling status, award wins, and five critically acclaimed releases under her belt, she truly believes the best is yet to come.

When she's not tied to her computer, she loves cooking, reading all genres of literature, and spending time with her boyfriend, family, and friends.

For more on this author who cannot be stopped, go to her Web site: www.geocities.com/niobia_bryant. There you can also join her free online book club Niobia_Bryant_News. Or you can e-mail her at: Niobia_Bryant@yahoo.com.

CHAIN OF FOOLS

Melanie Schuster

Dedicated to my online
family, who keep me
laughing, happy, and sane every day.
Stay blessed, all of you!

And to Regina Hightower,
a Renaissance woman,
a true friend, and an amazing prayer warrior.
Thank you just isn't enough.

Acknowledgments

Thanks so much to Niobia Bryant and Kim Louise for all the caring support and friendship. You'll never know how much it has meant to me.

A special thanks to Derrick Meyer for the understanding and the long talks. You really helped me hang in there.

To Clint Stanford, who has gotten even better with age like a fine vintage wine, thanks for finding me! Big hug!

And my eternal gratitude to Jamil, who knows me better than anyone and who always knows what to say.

1

A fierce rumble of thunder sounded in the distance, followed by the faint, static crackle of lightning. The insistent pounding of rain on the big, tempered, plate glass windows drowned the rattle and brought with it the fresh smell of rain, permeating the room through the patio doors left open for just that purpose. Soft music played in the background, and a fragrant fire provided an amber glow, the only light necessary. The two people entwined in each other's arms didn't need any other illumination, nor did they require the music; they were too consumed with each other.

Liz was completely naked on the soft plush blanket, laying on her back with her knees bent and her legs parted. Her eyes were closed and her hands were on the broad shoulders of the man who was bringing her the ultimate bliss, who was awakening her to pleasures she'd only imagined until now. His smooth, dark skin glistened in the flickering flames as he kissed his way down her body. His lips were hot and tender as he sucked her nipples, teasing her with his teeth and lavishing his tongue around the hard, tingling tips. When he finally ended the sweet torture, he continued to ravage her body. Liz tried to be still and enjoy the sensations, but they were coming too fast and he was too powerful; every stroke of his tongue was bringing her closer to the explosion only he could create.

She could feel a faint sheen of perspiration coating her limbs as her legs began to tremble and open wider. Her hips began to move in anticipation of what she was about to share with her man. She could feel his huge erection on her leg as he eased down her body, and the weight of it made her start to lose control. His tongue toyed with her navel, stroking it in ever-widening circles that led him down to the sweet muskiness of her private treasure. She moaned aloud as he slipped his hands under her hips to bring her closer to his yearning mouth, burying his face in her softness to begin the long, unending kiss that would render her helpless with the fire of his loving. She opened her eyes and gasped as she saw how huge her nipples had become; only he could do that to her. "Oh, baby," she groaned, as he began to sing "Crazy in Love."

The song continued and Liz's soft cries turned to vicious cursing as she snatched up her cell phone. "I hate you," she growled into the little instrument of torture. The sweet release of her dream had been just that, another fragment of the erotic fantasies that plagued her with increasing regularity. The voice on the phone, however, was her reality.

"Liz, one day it's not going to be me on the phone. One of these days you're gonna snarl into the phone like that and it's going to be your mama or your dream man on the other end, then what're you gonna do?" The lighthearted, sexy male voice on the other end did nothing to cheer her and only served to aggravate her more.

"Fletch, it's always you. No one else calls me at this ungodly hour, and no one else manages to call right when I'm...oh, never mind," she snapped. "Hold on a minute."

She tossed the phone aside and managed to sit up in the bed, dislodging several of the books that were scattered, as usual, over its surface. She opened and closed her eyes several times, feeling around in the corners of her eyelids for the crumbs that always accumulated when she was deeply asleep. Shoving her thick black hair out of her face, she frowned at the phone before putting it back to her ear. "What do you want, you slave driver? Can't it wait until I get to the office?"

Fletcher Raymond, incredible as it sometimes seemed to both of them, was her boss. After his retirement as one of the highest paid players in the NBA, Fletch had parlayed his good looks and engaging personality into a multimillion dollar development package at one of the networks, and he was doing very, very well with it, thanks in large part to Liz. He was profoundly grateful to her for all she did as his executive producer, but he wasn't above trying to manipulate her into doing what he wanted. Like now.

"Actually, no, it can't wait until you get to the office. I have a great idea I'd like to run past you, and I was going to take you out to breakfast to discuss it," he said in the warm, appealing voice Liz had come to know and dread. Normally she would've told him to go jump in the lake, but it so happened she had a little proposition of her own. She crossed her arms over her breasts and smiled, a sly and feline grimace Fletch would have recognized at once if he'd seen it. If he could interrupt her dream life with one of his schemes, the least she could do was stir up his waking life with one of hers. *Nothing like a little* quid pro quo *in the morning*, she thought with satisfaction.

"Okay, Fletch. That sounds like a great idea. Where are you taking me?"

She ended up meeting Fletch at his private athletic club, a lavish establishment frequented by all the movers and shakers in Beverly Hills. The membership roster consisted of actors, models, agents, producers, athletes, and social-ites—the Hollywood A-list Liz tried with all her heart to avoid as often as possible. She hated all the trappings of Hollywood and tolerated her environment only because it gave her an opportunity to do what she loved. Liz Walker excelled at making things happen; she liked being in con-trol of creative projects. She loved making quality television shows and movies, and thanks to her plum job with Fletch-er's production company, she had an opportunity to do just that. If she could have figured out a way to do it without setting foot in California, she'd have done it. To her mind, California was a polarizing environment. People either loved it or hated it, and she pretty much despised it. Fletcher said it was because she was a corn-fed, midwestern milkmaid at heart.

Fletcher always said whatever popped into his head; the little governor in most mature adults' brains that told them the difference between polite commentary and insult was completely missing from Fletcher. He was already at the table in the lushly furnished dining room when Liz arrived. He looked her over appreciatively as she walked to the table with a slight frown on her face. She was wearing a slim-fitting silk jersey dress in a brilliant peacock blue. It had a high turtleneck and deeply cut armholes that showed off her firm, nicely muscled shoulders and her long neck. It also gave the impression of modesty since her rather small but perfect breasts weren't being showcased. Yet the snug fit of the dress made it impossible to ignore how enticingly round and sexy they were, how they looked made for a man's touch.

Fletcher raised an eyebrow as he watched heads turn while Liz made her approach. *She wants something*, he mused while admiring her long, shapely legs. She was wear-ing four-inch heels, which caused her to walk with a seduc-tive sway completely unlike her normal businesslike stride. And the simple, elegant dress had slits on both sides to allow tantalizing glimpses of those fabulous legs. Liz frowned slightly when he failed to stand up when she reached the table. He knew how lapses in manners annoyed her, but he wanted to see how badly she wanted a favor from him. Plus, he didn't trust himself to stand right then. Despite the fact they were good friends, as well as colleagues, Liz still tempted him mightily from time to time, and this was one of them.

She swiveled her hips into her chair in a manner that caused an older gentleman at a nearby table to groan aloud, something Liz luckily didn't hear. Fletcher heard it and grinned, which served to further annoy her, although she was doing her best to hide it. She sat up ramrod straight and took a deep breath, then turned to Fletcher with a surprisingly natural smile. "Good morning, Fletcher. You're looking well," she murmured.

Fletcher had to take a deep swallow of ice water before speaking. Liz, although definitely not a Hollywood glamour girl, was beautiful. She was tall, elegant, and forceful with rich, dark brown skin, big, juicy lips with a perfect cupid's bow, and thick black wavy hair. She wore her hair in a stacked, layered bob that framed her features and drew attention to her big black eyes with their long lashes. Her eyes were her best feature; they reflected the unmistakable intelligence that demanded respect from everyone she encountered. And she was built like a real woman, too, with hips and a booty that said "touch me if you dare" on the few occasions she dressed to show it off. The only time Liz dressed like this was when she wanted something really bad and she wanted to soften up Fletcher. They might be totally platonic friends, but she knew how to work him. And today he was going to let her.

"You're looking pretty good yourself. I already ordered for you, if that's okay."

She raised an eyebrow, but her face relaxed into a smile as the server appeared with her order of *huevos rancheros* and a petite filet mignon, grilled medium well, the way she liked it. There was also an icy glass of pineapple juice and a plate of fresh strawberries with *crème fraîche*. Her mood improved as soon as she saw the delicious meal. "Fletcher, you know me too well," she said happily. Saying a quick grace, she began to partake of her steak with real enjoyment.

That was another of Liz's non-Hollywood ways; she ate anything and everything and refused to succumb to fad diets. Fletcher could feel his nature rising again as he watched her devour her food with real appetite and decided to get down to business while he still could. He couldn't resist teasing her a little, though.

"Are you sure we made the right decision? It's not too late, you know, we could forget about working together and explore the possibilities of passion. Travel the road of romance and find out what awaits us at every turn," he said in what he hoped was a seductive voice.

"Fletch, that's incredibly weak. How do you manage to pull with lines that lame?" She took a sip of pineapple juice and shook her head. Pointing at the hash browns on his plate, she asked if she could have some and smiled when he put a helping on her plate. Then she went right back to the subject at hand. "The day I interviewed with you we made a decision to ignore whatever attraction we felt and concentrate on business because we both had goals. That hasn't changed, and you know it. Besides, we know each other too well. What fun would a relationship be? What about the mystery that makes things exciting and stimulating? With us it would be like dating a cousin or something. There wouldn't be any challenge," she reminded him patiently.

Fletch frowned the same way he had when she came to interview with him. He'd taken one look at her and had gotten flustered and angry because she was so well qualified and so darned sexy. He'd practically snarled at her that they had to make a vow never to touch each other because the work relationship would be doomed. Staring at her balefully, he had announced, "I'm too stupid to keep a woman as talented as you as a girlfriend, so I guess you'll have to come work with me. But you keep your hands to yourself, or I won't be responsible, hear me?" Liz had burst out laughing and agreed to come work with him, the salary he was offering was too tempting, even though it meant moving from New York to L.A. And despite any misgivings he may have had about hiring a beautiful and sexy woman as producer, bringing her on board was a brilliant move.

He looked at Liz again, watching her enjoy her meal and half listening to her chatter. Suddenly he smiled, a big, sneaky grin that would have put her on red alert if she'd been looking at him. *So you like challenges, do you? Well, kid, I've got the challenge of a lifetime for you.*

Liz savored her coffee as she watched Fletcher perusing her proposal. He'd gently plied her with questions during their meal, and as though she had no control over the situation whatsoever, she'd put all her cards on the table. Her passion was documentary filmmaking, and she wanted Fletcher to greenlight her in making movies close to her heart. The first project was on Oscar Micheaux, the legendary black film pioneer. Liz wanted to start a series of biographies on historical figures, and she had prepared an impressively well-documented pitch, which Fletch was looking at now. She could tell from his body language and the rapt expression on his face that he was really taking in every word, that he could see the obvious merit in her project. It was at these times she could look at Fletcher objectively and see him as an intelligent, attractive, powerful man. Too bad he was her boss. There were some lines she wasn't about to cross for anyone. Still . . .

She sighed and rested her chin in her hand as she continued to watch him. Fletcher had smooth skin the exact color and texture of a Hershey bar. He had big eyes with long, curly lashes and a deep dimple in one cheek. His smile was almost the best thing about him. It was so genuine and infectious, it made the recipient smile automatically. He had big, dazzlingly white teeth with just a hint of a gap in the front, a slight imperfection that was sexy for some reason. He laughed often, and despite a truly goofy sense of humor, he had a mind like a steel trap and could grasp even the most obscure concepts quickly. His long-limbed body was both graceful and athletic. All in all, he was pretty irresistible, but Liz held her ground. Fletch was way too satisfactory as an employer to even contemplate a relationship. Besides, they were like brother and sister, familiar and trusting. Why muck up the water with lust?

"Liz, this is brilliant. You did your usual professional job in bringing this to the table, and I have no reason not to think it will be successful. In fact, once we get another project out of the way I don't see any reason why you can't get started on this."

She was so thrilled by his positive response she completely missed the carefully benign expression Fletch adopted. "You like it? Oh, Fletch, I'm thrilled. I really put my heart into this one because it means so much to me. This is going to be the most brilliant series anyone ever . . ." Her voice trailed away as she finally noticed the look she referred to as the "Fletcher fish-eye," a totally insincere effort on his part to look like he gave a rat's behind. Liz's brow furrowed deeply as she recalled his last words. "After *what* project? Don't try to play me, Fletch," she said, her eyes narrowing in suspicion.

Fletcher tried looking innocent, switching quickly to his concerned face. When he saw that wasn't going to wash either, he leaned forward and answered her questions directly.

"Look, Liz, there's a program I want to buy. I haven't mentioned it because it's not the kind of thing you'd ever want to be involved with, but I need your help on it. If you help me get it up and running, you'll have carte blanche to do whatever you want with the documentaries. In fact, I'll let you develop a full twenty-six-show package with an option for two full-length films, one of which can be a theatrical release," he told her.

Liz's mouth dropped open and she snapped it shut, only to have it fall open again. She caught herself and leaned forward to stare at Fletcher. "Okay, who are you and what have you done with my boss?"

Fletcher had to laugh at the look on her face. "It's me, I swear. I haven't had my brain sucked out by zombies from the planet Doobie, and I'm not under mind control from some enemy nation. I think your idea is a good one, and I want you to run with it. All I ask in return is that you do me this tiny little favor. I just need you to participate in this new program as a sort of acid test," he told her, using the persuasive voice she'd have recognized if she'd been giving him her full attention.

Right then her head was so full of possibilities she didn't have room for anything else. She was already picturing the results of all her hard work airing as a finished product, exciting a new generation to the genius of Oscar Micheaux. Her eyes were soft and dreamy as she envisioned the fruits of her long labor brought to life on the screen. She was completely caught up in the images, so much so that she had to ask Fletcher to repeat what he'd said.

"Sorry, Fletch, I didn't hear you. You want me to do what?" she asked distractedly.

Fletcher looked into her eyes with not a hint of shame. He even smiled a little as he told her what he wanted. "I need you to be a contestant on the show I want to buy. It's called *Meet Your Mate,* and it's a new kind of reality dating show. The concept is different from most of those shows and I think it has real potential. That's why I want someone who can be objective to participate in the pilot and give me feedback I can trust without all the hype."

While he was talking Liz's face went from totally blank

to confused to dismayed, and by the time he was finished her expression was blank again. Her words, however, were quite distinct, leaving no chance of a misunderstanding.

"You must be out of your mind," she said in a flat, ominous voice.

Fletcher tried to look innocent with little success and asked what was wrong. "What's the matter, Liz, doesn't it sound like fun?"

Liz didn't bother to answer, as she was too busy picking up her proposal and her Prada tote bag. She opened her mouth twice to try to respond to him and finally ended by holding her hand up to him like a crossing guard warning off oncoming traffic.

"See you at the office. Thanks for breakfast," she spat out, before leaving the table and walking out of the dining room so quickly all that remained was the faint promise of her fragrance.

Fletcher grinned as he looked at the seat she'd just vacated. When he got back to the office, that was when the fun would begin. It wouldn't be easy, but he would get what he wanted and, in turn, she would get what she wanted. It was a win-win situation all the way around. It might take her a few days to realize it, but he knew he'd get his way.

2

By the time Fletcher reached Liz's office he hoped she'd had time to cool down. It had been two hours since she left the club, and past experience had taught him she didn't stay mad long. He left his glass-walled office and strolled down the corridor to Liz's domain. Her secretary was off on an errand, so he went to the door of her private office and knocked politely.

"Come in," she said, then looked up from her work with a smile that faded when she saw who it was.

Fletcher also lost his smile when he realized she'd changed clothes. She was now wearing a shantung shirt in a romantic pink color with a pair of nicely tailored, wide-legged, cuffed trousers in chocolate brown. "You changed," he said glumly.

Liz didn't pretend to misunderstand him. "You're a mean, manipulative man. You don't deserve to look at my legs," she sniffed. "I'm updating my résumé right now because I'm going to be seeking other employment."

Fletcher sat on the long leather couch and stretched his legs out to their full length, almost knocking over the coffee table as he did so. "Liz, now you know you don't mean that. I'm just asking for a little favor. Can't you just do me this one tiny favor after all this time?"

Liz crossed her arms on her desk and leaned on them. "Fletch, it's not a *little* favor, and you know it. First, you know how I feel about so-called reality television. I think it's abysmal and a real indication of the intellectual death of our society. And second, you also know how I feel about dating shows in particular. They're awful, just dreadful. People making fools out of themselves on national television to get what, a free meal and a night of miniature golf or something? They're all orchestrated so the contestants will have horrible things to say about each other and make the other person look as ridiculous as possible, that's what gets the ratings," she said emphatically. "How could you even think of being involved with something like that?"

Fletcher watched her pretty face get redder and redder with righteous indignation before he replied. "You said the magic word, Liz: *ratings*. No one ever went broke underestimating the bad taste of America, and I don't intend to be the first. Reality shows are huge right now, they make tons of money for a relatively small investment, and they're hot, red-hot *smoking* hot. This development deal I have with the studio is contingent on me making money, and I don't intend to lose this deal by being too refined to make the big bucks." He leaned back and stared at Liz for a moment before continuing. In his most reasonable voice, the one he used when he was about to zero in for the kill, he asked for her cooperation.

"You know, Liz, a lot of people use nontraditional means to meet dates these days. People are too busy to try and meet people the old-fashioned way. It's more expedient to use dating services and online dating and personal ads than trying to get out and do the boy-meets-girl kind of thing. Look at you, Liz. Look how busy you are. When was the last time you had a date?" he probed gently.

Liz bared her teeth in a feral grimace and pointed her finger at him. "Don't even go there, Fletch. Don't try that concerned brotherly crap with me. I date enough, as if it's any of your concern. It just so happens that I don't find the dating scene in L.A. all that compelling. When I'm not out in it, I don't feel like I'm missing anything, thank you very much. Quiet as it's kept, the men out here aren't exactly the answer to my prayers," she said with a sniff.

Fletcher tried to hide his grin of triumph, this was going just the way he wanted it to. He tried to sound both disarming and caring as he kept digging at her. "You're not turning into one of those East Coast snobs, are you? One of those women who're impossible to please, looking for Mr. Perfect?"

Liz fell back in her chair and looked up at the ceiling while she moaned out loud. "I'm not looking for Prince Charming, I just need someone with the intellectual wherewithal to sustain a decent conversation. Someone with more brains than brawn, with more ambition than abs, and more imagination than ego; I don't think that's asking too much. Someone who can follow a conversation that contains words with more than one syllable," she said heatedly. "I've met more moronic pretty boys out here than you can shake a stick at. And every one of them was an aspiring singer or actor or model or worst of all, a professional athlete, not a one of them with a real job."

"I resent that remark about athletes; playing ball is hard work," Fletcher protested. "But I'm going to let that go for the time being. See, you're actually proving my point. You need to use a nontraditional means to meet a man. It would actually give you a better chance of meeting the right person," he said. "You meet people that share the same interests and attitudes you do, and your chances of success are greatly increased . . ." His voice faded as Liz stared him down with a look of utter disgust on her face.

"Okay, you can save that," she said dryly. "It may seem as though I'm just an uptight woman who can't get a man, but trust me when I tell you I've explored many avenues of modern dating, and they're all dead-end streets. Come around here, let me show you something," she said as she beckoned him with her forefinger.

Fletcher obeyed at once, pulling a chair around to her side of the desk and watching in fascination as Liz tapped on her computer keyboard, bringing up a file titled "Chain of Fools." When she opened it, the unmistakable voice of Aretha Franklin poured out as the contents of the file revealed themselves.

"Here you go, Fletch. Here's my experience in so-called nontraditional dating, chronicled so future generations won't make the same mistakes I did," she said with grim satisfaction. "Let's take this guy here," she said, clicking on the face of a moderately attractive bespectacled man.

"This is a guy I met online. He's an insurance broker, very successful. He also owns a lot of real estate. We chatted back and forth for a couple of weeks before we started talking on the phone and he's a great conversationalist. Intelligent, very funny, witty, really seemed to have his head on straight," she said, staring at the screen.

"So what went wrong? He looks okay to me," Fletch said. The guy wasn't gorgeous, but he looked prosperous and friendly.

Liz curled her lip in a delicate show of distaste. "Well, things were going along fine and we were about to meet in real life when one day he sent me a long letter he obviously thought was erotic. It was actually quite pornographic considering the fact that I'd never met the bozo, but that's beside the point. The thing is, he attached another picture of himself to the letter. He was booty-butt naked," she said disgustedly.

Fletch burst out laughing. "Aw, girl, quit playing, he wasn't either."

Liz pursed her lips and clicked on a link, which brought up a picture of the man standing in front of a full-length mirror taking a picture of his completely bare body. "He looks pretty naked to me," she said with no emotion.

Fletcher was speechless for once, but Liz wasn't. "That's the most perfect combination of arrogance and stupidity I've ever seen. Because you *know* I'm not the only recipient of this little jewel. He's sent this gem to many other women, count on it. He doesn't know me from a can of paint, and he has no idea what I might do with this picture. He better be glad I didn't forward it to my friend Jimmy in Detroit. It would have been in eighty million in-boxes within ten minutes with a caption: DO NOT BUY INSURANCE FROM THIS MAN. Jimmy would have put his name, address, and phone number on it, too. He doesn't play when it comes to freaks like that. And if I was supposed to be wowed by his endowment, ol' boy was dead wrong. I was all like Glinda the Good Witch in *The Wizard of Oz*," Liz sniffed. She leaned toward the computer screen and tilted her head to the left. In a spot-on, perfect imitation of Glinda, she piped, "Is it a good penis or a bad penis?" before tilting her head to the right, and then turning to look at Fletcher, who was howling with laughter.

"He could have at least sent an *alert* picture. I can't even tell what I'm looking at here with his little friend just hanging there like a limp noodle. Although frankly it would have been much grosser if the thing was ready for action 'cause then I'd have been wondering why it was ready for action, and I don't need that imagery in my mental Rolodex," she said with a delicate shudder while Fletch shouted with laughter. Waiting for him to stop guffawing, she grinned wickedly. "Now, here's a fellow who had enough nerve to show me the real deal."

Pointing the mouse at another face, she brought up a

link and cautioned Fletcher. "This was a guy who seemed like he had a lot of potential, but he was getting impatient. He kept wanting to come meet me, to visit me in person, and I kept trying to explain to him that I had a very busy schedule, and furthermore I needed to get to know him a lot better before meeting him up close and personal. He got miffed, I guess, and sent me a picture of what I'd be missing out on."

With a double-click, she revealed a chiseled body displaying a massive erection the sight of which made Fletcher cringe and cover his eyes. "Okay, I get it! Dang, that brother wasn't playing, was he?"

"Now do you understand? There are some sick puppies out there. It's not just me, Fletch; these people have some real issues. And you want me to go on some crackpot TV show to meet some stranger? I don't think so, boss."

"Yeah, okay, I can see why you wouldn't want to meet someone online," he conceded. "But there are other ways to meet people," he began, only to be silenced by a wave of her hand.

"Here's a joker my cousin introduced me to," she said, clicking on a very handsome man with a charming smile. "We had dinner at her house with her husband and kids; then the two of us went for a long drive and he brought me home. We talked about everything from art to music to religion, and I was really looking forward to seeing him again. We got comfortable in the living room and I went into the kitchen to make coffee. When I came back, he was sitting on my sofa wearing nothing but a smile," Liz reported. "Now, on a scale of one to ten, how happy was I to see that?"

"He took his clothes off?" Fletcher was dumbfounded.

"Yep, he was sitting there in his birthday suit looking just as happy as a pig in mud. A very *eager* pig, I might add."

"What did you do?"

"I gave him a big, fake grin and picked up all his clothes

and his shoes. I walked over to the front door, opened it, and threw the clothes out onto the lawn. I told him to go get them while I called 911. He took me at my word because he flew out the door. Oddly enough, he hasn't called me anymore," she said thoughtfully. "Do you think I was a little hard on him?"

Fletcher was trying not to laugh, but his amusement got the better of him and he let go with huge roars of laughter. "Liz, you have the worst luck I ever heard of. What is it about you that makes men want to take their clothes off?"

"I have no idea, but I have about five more penis portraits and at least four more naked stories. Would you like to hear about the guy I met at the singles group at church? Now he had a fetish for . . ."

"Stop! No more, please. Okay, so you've had some hard luck with meeting decent men by traditional and nontraditional methods, that just makes you more of a challenge. In a way, that's what *Meet Your Mate* is all about. The whole premise of the show is to find suitable mates for eligible, discerning, and sophisticated people. It's going to be different from the other junk that's out there, which is why you're the perfect candidate for the show. Trust me on this one, Liz. I promise you won't be disappointed. And you'll also have my blessing and my backing on the documentary series," he added.

Liz locked her eyes on his and hated what she saw. He looked so warm and sincere she wanted to believe him, wanted with all her heart to trust that he'd honor his commitment. And for the merest split of a second, she almost believed she'd meet her soul mate on that stupid show Fletcher was so determined to buy. But her common sense kicked in, and she had to challenge him.

"Okay, Fletch, so you'll get on board with my series if I go along with this madness. But tell me this: What makes you think I'm going to meet a decent man on a sleazy dating show? I'm doing it because I'm being blackmailed into it. Now what kind of loser goes on TV to meet a woman?" she asked pointedly.

Fletcher leaned back with a huge cheese-eating grin on his handsome face. "Just let me worry about that," he said smugly.

The four men sitting around the card table were all good looking and all were very good moods, to judge by their laughter. All except one. Romare Alexander looked at each of his brothers in turn with very little emotion. He was used to being the recipient of their ridicule, especially when the conversation turned to women. He was the oldest, the most serious minded, and the most accomplished of the four brothers, and they took an inordinate amount of pleasure in giving him a hard time. It wasn't often that Romare was at less than his best, but when they had the advantage, his younger siblings Dante, Adrian, and Dorian loved to get on his case. Dorian had the floor and he was relishing every second of the unusual opportunity to get all up in his brother's business.

"So, Rom, I hear you lost another one. I hear you and Kinesha are no longer an item," he said with an unholy grin.

Romare didn't even change his expression. He looked into a face that was almost his mirror image and raised an eyebrow. All the Alexander men looked alike, with smooth dark chocolate skin; close-cut, curly black hair; sculptured features with sexy, chiseled lips; and the unmistakable family trait of a deep cleft in the chin. Right now, though, there was a distinct difference between Romare and the other men. He looked cool and disinterested while his younger siblings looked wildly amused. In a voice devoid of emotion, he finally spoke. "I don't know why my love life is so interesting to you, but if you must know, Kinesha and I are no longer seeing each other." His dry delivery would've discouraged a wise man, but his brothers felt free to keep dipping.

"Man, you've got to be kidding," Adrian said incredulously. "As fine as Kinesha is, you mean to tell me you dropped her?"

Romare pretended great interest in the cards he held in his hand. "What makes you think she didn't drop me?" he asked in a too-casual manner.

"Because we know you, and we know how picky you are. You meet these incredibly fine women, they throw themselves at you, and you can't wait to find something wrong with them. Like their table manners aren't up to par, or they only have an associate's degree, or they don't have the proper appreciation of Mississippi Delta Blues, or something equally inane," Dante said scornfully. "You're just too picky, Rom. You're gonna end up old and alone, the quintessential eccentric bachelor uncle if you don't watch yourself."

Romare ignored that last remark long enough to pick up the cards on the table. After a quick and lethal trip to Boston at the expense of two of his unprepared brothers, he neatly gathered up the cards and stacked them back into a deck. Rom could always kick their butts in bid whist, and they knew it. "That's fifty bucks you owe me. And you're exaggerating as usual. I've never broken off a relationship for a petty reason, only when there was no hope of making it work," he said mildly.

"And why couldn't you make it work with Kinesha?" Adrian demanded. "She is built like a brick house, she has a good job, and I know she has a master's degree, so you can't say she's ignorant. And she had that bangin' body besides," he groaned.

"The bangin' body was the problem," Romare said dryly. "Apparently you have no idea the amount of maintenance involved in getting a body to bang like that. All she talked about was her percentage of body fat, her nutrition plan, and her exercise. When she wasn't talking about exercising, she was working out; and when she wasn't working

out, she was taking supplements; and when she wasn't taking supplements, she was buying workout gear. That body
of hers was her main occupation. And when we were in the
bed, forget about it. If I didn't tell her at least nineteen
times how beautiful she was, she'd pout for a week."

He shook his head as he stood up and stretched.
Adrian was unconvinced, however. "But what about that
other woman, what was her name? The one with the long
black hair?"

Romare rolled his eyes. "Her name was Karen and she
did have really beautiful hair. Hair that she had to get done
at least twice a week, sometimes more. Hair that couldn't
go swimming, that couldn't go horseback riding, that
couldn't stand to have the top down on my convertible,
that couldn't be touched while we were having sex because
something might happen to it." He shuddered theatrically.
"It was like the hair was her twin or something, it had that
much significance in her life. I never had one conversation
with her that didn't involve her freakin' hair. That damned
hair had to go, man, which meant she went with it."

Dante wasn't buying it. "Aw, man, fine as she was, I'd a
paid to get that hair done. You're just too picky, man."

"I'm not that particular, I'm really not. I just like what I
like, that's all. I want to meet a bright, educated woman
who can have a decent conversation and not obsess over
her looks. I don't think that's too much to ask," he said
firmly. As he crossed to the bar that separated the dining
area from the kitchen Dante and Dorian both burst out
laughing.

Dorian wiped the tears from his eyes and asked the
question that had gotten the evening started. "So why the
hell are you moving to California? What chance do you
have of meeting your kind of woman out there? It's like the
headquarters of the shallow and self-absorbed."

Romare grimaced as he acknowledged the truth of the
statement. He was going to California for a course in culi-

nary arts that would round out his education. After spending years in corporate America and making a pile of money in shrewd Wall Street trading and investing, Romare was pursuing his passion: gourmet cooking. He'd taken a very early retirement and attended the Cooking and Hospitality Institute of Chicago. Now he was enlarging his repertoire by taking an internship to learn Pacific Rim fusion cooking. The thought of being in California for three months was daunting, but he had the steely determination to make it work.

"I can handle it. I'm going out there for a purpose, and I can worry about my lack of a social life when I get done. I'm not ruled by my genitals unlike some in this room who shall go nameless." He was getting a bottle of wine out of the special cooling unit built into the kitchen and totally missed the look that passed around the card table.

"So, Romare," Adrian began, stroking his cleft with his index finger. "If there was a way for you to find a woman who meets your ridiculously stringent standards, would you be interested?"

"No, not really." Romare uncorked the wine and sniffed the cork, then held the bottle under his nose to fully appreciate the bouquet. "There's no point to it. I'm only going to be in Cali for a few months, and I don't have a lot of time to waste chasing after someone who doesn't exist." He poured a little of the wine into a stemmed glass and tasted it, making an admiring face as he savored its essence.

The card game came to a halt as Adrian pressed his point. "What if there was a way to guarantee you'd meet your perfect match, would you be interested?"

Romare raised an eyebrow as he looked at his brother, who was trying his best to look casual. Romare spoke loudly and slowly, moving his fingers in sign language. "I-said-no-thank-you."

Dorian leaned back in his chair and stared up at the

ceiling. "Not even if there was a large sum of money riding on it?"

Romare picked up the bottle with one hand and picked up four glasses by their stems with the other. He went back to the table with a grin he tried to hide. "Okay, let's have some details," he said as he sat down and began pouring the wine.

3

One month later

"Liz, I ought to shave your head. How many times do I have to tell you to stop doing that? Do you want to be bald or what?"

Liz tried to look repentant, but she was far too used to hearing this particular lecture from her hairstylist. She took a deep breath and pasted on her most winning smile, hoping to distract Tasha from her standard sermon on follicular abuse. "Tasha, I promise I won't ride with the top down anymore. I swear I won't," she said solemnly.

Tasha sucked her teeth and thumped Liz on the head with a rattail comb. "Girl, quit lying. You love that little goofy car too much to ride with the top up. If I know you, as soon as you're a block away from here you'll have the top down and the music blasting with your hair flying all over your head. All I ask is that you put a scarf on it, or a hat. Split ends are no joke, and when your hair is relaxed you have to be gentle with it. You swim in chlorinated water with no cap, you let the wind whip it to death, and you don't even have the decency to sleep on a satin pillow-case. All this beautiful hair and you treat it like straw. Well, that's what it's gonna look like in a few weeks, a pile of straw."

As she wound up her sermon, Tasha sucked her teeth again and shook her head in disgust. She could afford to be outspoken, her salon was one of the most popular in L.A. She'd been caring for Liz's mane since Liz moved to California, and she took her job seriously, constantly fuss-ing at Liz over her cavalier attitude toward her tresses. Liz just hoped that Tasha wasn't so ticked off that she wouldn't help her. Liz looked around the stylish salon decorated in black, pale green, rose, and silver and tried to look as con-trite as possible, which wasn't hard.

"Tash, I really will invest in a couple of caps and some scarves to keep my hair under control when I'm in the car. And I'll stop on the way home to get some satin pillow-cases, I really will. But I have a really big favor to ask of you; I hope you'll help me out," she said humbly.

Tasha was a good advertisement of her own work. Her shining black hair was always perfectly groomed and stylish, even on days when she had clients back to back to back. Tasha was almost six feet tall with a lush, curvy body and a beautiful smile. She was also down-to-earth and friendly, at least she was when her favorite clients weren't abusing their manes. And she couldn't resist a cry for help from anyone.

"Of course I'll help you, Liz. What can I do for you?" she asked with concern in her voice.

"I need you to make me into a chickenhead," Liz said firmly.

Tasha's large, almond-shaped eyes widened and she stared at Liz's reflection in the big mirror that faced the styl-ing chair where Liz sat. "Do *what*?" she asked incredulously.

Liz turned around so she was facing Tasha. "I need a makeover. I have to go on a TV show and I don't want to look like myself. I want to look as far from me as possible, as a matter of fact. I want to look like a true Rodeo Drive hoochie. Can you hook me up?"

Tasha tilted her head to one side and stared at Liz. "I can make you look like RuPaul if you want me to, but I'm not lifting a finger until you tell me why. Are you running from the law or something?"

"No, but I might be running from Fletcher after this escapade," Liz admitted with a big smile.

Once Liz realized that Fletcher was completely serious about this project and that he was determined not to make a single move on her project until she cooperated, she decided to do just that. She would go on his sleazy little show and give him just what he wanted, but it would be on her terms. She was going to prove to her stubborn employer once and for all that when it came to men, she knew what she was taking about. The first step in that direction was a total transformation of her looks, albeit a temporary one. She rapidly explained the situation to Tasha and outlined her plan.

"It's like this, Tash. Any man will make a fool of himself over a woman if she has the right look. If she dresses a little on the slutty side and has big, bouncy boobs and lots and lots of hair she can have the IQ of a loofah sponge and it won't make a smidge of difference to your average shallow, salivating man. Intellect, character, personality, and talent mean nothing, all they want is someplace hot and hollow to stick their . . ."

"Liz!" Tasha sounded shocked, and Liz felt terrible about being so vulgar. Tasha was such a lady; she didn't need to hear that kind of stuff.

"I'm so sorry, Tash, I got caught up. I just want to prove a point by going on this show, and I also don't want anyone to know who I am. I want to be taken seriously as a producer in this town and being on this dopey show could make that really difficult. I want to look like someone else entirely. I want to look like a California bling-bling diva, if there is such a thing. I want to look like, like . . ."

"Like the Beverly Center meets the Crenshaw Swap Meet," Tasha murmured, staring at Liz.

"That's it! You got it, Tasha. Can you do it?"

"Honey, when I get through with you, your own mama won't recognize you. Just sit back and let me do what I do."

The afternoon of the taping arrived with as little fanfare as Liz could manage. She finally convinced Fletcher that she'd be too nervous if he accompanied her to the studio as he had planned. "Why don't you stay here? They're going to send over a video by messenger right after the taping, so you'll see it soon enough," she said casually.

They were seated in his spacious office and Fletcher was being more cooperative than Liz could ever remember. He didn't make a single protest; all he said was, "Okay, fine, that sounds like a good idea." He leaned across his desk to look intently at Liz, who was sitting in one of the two Eames chairs that occupied the space in front of the huge desk. "Look, Lizzie, I really hope you enjoy yourself tonight. It could be the start of something really great. You never know," he said with a warmth and sincerity that was most unlike him. Liz found herself at a loss for words.

"Well, thanks, Fletch, that's really nice of you," she said distractedly. "Listen, I need to get going if I'm going to make it to the studio on time. I'll let you know how it goes." With a breezy wave, she rose to leave the office and Fletcher spoke again.

"Just keep an open mind, Lizzie; that's all I ask."

Liz started backing out of the office with a strained expression on her face. Fletcher only called her Lizzie when he was in friend mode, not boss mode. He seemed genuinely concerned about her, which was touching, as well as surprising. She had to get out of there right now, before the guilt over her deception started eating at her. "Okay, I'll call you later," she said breathlessly, then turned and fled. She really did have to hurry; Tasha was waiting for her to begin the transformation.

A few hours later, Liz was standing backstage, waiting for the cue for her entrance. She willed herself to be calm, to remember why she was doing this. In three short weeks it would all be over and she'd be free to pursue her dream, to create artistic and insightful documentaries. She was about to drift into a daydream when she caught a glimpse of herself in a dusty mirror mounted on the wall. She jumped, thinking someone was staring at her, and immediately felt silly. It was just that Tasha was a little bit too talented. Thanks to her skill, Liz doubted that even her parents would recognize her. She was totally transformed.

Her thick, wavy, chin-length bob was slicked back with a cascade of streaked hair attached. She now had thick bangs with thin strands of auburn and copper hair blended in so the crown of her head looked as streaked as the high ponytail. It was layered, lacquered, chic, and sexy, but it didn't resemble her real hair at all. Her eyes also looked foreign, with meticulously placed individual false lashes at the outer corners and expertly applied eyeshadow in a smoldering deep charcoal shade. Plus she was wearing nonprescription contact lenses in a smoky gray, which made her look alluring, albeit like a life-sized doll. Tasha had put her makeup on so well she looked almost like she wasn't wearing any, or she would have if it weren't for the chocolate brown lipstick with a gloss so shiny it was blinding. Her thoughts went back to the moment she'd seen herself in all her artificial glory in Tasha's salon earlier in the day.

Liz had taken one look in the full-length mirror and gasped. "Heavenly Father, I look like Bling-Bling Barbie the Rodeo Drive Harlot," she murmured.

Tasha laughed at her chagrin. "See? You need to be careful what you wish for. You know, you can take some of that off, you don't have to do this."

Liz had looked so torn at her appearance that Tasha had felt sorry for her. She was wearing a cream leather bustier and a matching leather jacket that stopped just below her waist and was cut close to the body to accentuate her figure. The jacket zipped down the front, and she had it down far enough so that her curves were exposed. She had curves aplenty, too, thanks to an amazing push-up bra with water-filled inserts that made her look two cup sizes bigger. Her legs looked even longer than usual, as well they should, she was wearing stiletto heels with the most expensive pair of jeans she'd ever had in her life. She hated to admit it, but they fit better than any other jeans she'd ever worn, and they made her booty look like a sculpture. With her new hair caressing her shoulders and the giant gold hoop earrings she borrowed from Tasha, she really looked like someone else—a very unhappy person, to judge by the strained look on her face.

"You don't have to go through with this, Liz. You can go on dressed in your regular clothes, we can take out those lenses, and you can be yourself. Did it ever occur to you that you might just meet a nice man on this show? You might meet someone you can really get to know; he might even be your soul mate. Did you ever think of that?"

Tasha's comforting words had the opposite effect on Liz. She'd suddenly squared her shoulder and looked resolute, saying, "No, not at all. Anyone stupid enough to come on this show to meet their dream woman is too lame for me. Okay, Tash, thanks for everything, I'll let you know what happens."

And picking up the Louis Vuitton bag she'd borrowed from Tasha's sister, she had hurriedly left the salon. Now she looked as determined as she had felt earlier. She knew exactly what she was doing, and the end result was going to be worth every minute of the charade. The stage manager signaled her that it was time to come onstage, as the show's host had just announced her.

Liz walked onstage confidently, and the sway of her hips made her look sexy and assertive, too. She smiled and waved at the small studio audience. The host, a medium height, mundanely good-looking man named Wes, resplendent with a bleached set of capped teeth, smirked and grinned at her as he air-kissed her cheek and led her over to a long, slippery leather sofa.

"So, Raquel, I understand you're a production assistant at a television station, correct?"

Liz blinked, and then remembered she'd used her middle name in filling out the show's questionnaire. "Yes, Wes, that's right," she said in the breathy voice she'd practiced. She gave him a wide smile and endured a few minutes of questions, then braced herself as he prepared to bring her date onstage. By now she was nervous, so nervous she really couldn't understand what he was saying, it sounded like "blah, blah, blah" to her frenzied ears.

"And now, Raquel, it's time to meet the man who could be your mate, Romare Alexander!"

Liz felt her stomach implode and a cascade of fireworks burst in her temples as she watched a very tall man walk out onto the stage. She wanted to die right on the spot. Romare Alexander was the best looking man she'd ever seen in her life, and there she sat looking like a beauty queen gone criminal. Life couldn't get any worse.

4

Romare stood on the balcony of his sublet apartment, staring blankly at the California scenery. The best word for him right now was confused. Sipping the aromatic coffee he'd just prepared, he enjoyed the morning breeze as he pondered his situation. Reliving the events of the night before should have helped him assimilate things, but it really didn't. He'd stupidly accepted one of his brothers' bets before coming out here, and now the chickens had come home to roost. At least one had come a-flappin' in the form of a very tempting woman who could mean nothing but trouble.

Point one: he'd been punked. He couldn't recall the exact words that had led him into saying he'd take the bet, but before he could figure a way out of it, he'd ended up on this stupid dating show with a very large sum of money riding on the outcome. Obviously he needed the services of a mental health professional, and soon.

Point two: more proof of his deteriorating mental state

was his inappropriate reaction to his date, Raquel. She was everything he despised in a woman. Her contrived hair, fake smile, fake eye color, and ridiculously expensive clothes were all indications that she was the kind of beautiful dimwit he strove to avoid at all costs. Unfortunately, there was something about her that attracted him. Damned if he knew what it was, but it was there simmering along the surface just waiting to boil over. He knew it from the moment their hands touched in a brief handshake. A tiny jolt of electric sensation had coursed through his body, as unexpected as it was unwelcome. He was supposed to be repelled by women like Raquel, not attracted to them.

Point three: regardless of how ill-advised the whole enterprise was, he was committed to it, and like all the Alexander men, he was stubborn enough to see it through to the end. He called it honor, but his mother thought it bordered on fanaticism with Romare. Once he committed to something, he was in it all the way. He was going to be the perfect gentleman and show Raquel a wonderful time on each of the dates they were forced to go out on.

He shuddered at the thought of looking into those artificially colored eyes all day; it would be like talking to a ventriloquist's dummy. *I could avoid those eyes by checking out her booty all day*, he thought with a grim smile. She did have a pretty one; although the rest of her had the gaunt look he associated with overly vain women. He called it the EAT SOMETHING look, as in "dang, baby, you need to have a decent meal or two." Nothing was more annoying to him than a woman who picked over her food.

Romare finished his coffee and tightened the towel around his waist. He certainly didn't want to lose it; it was all he had on at the moment. He stroked his rock-hard stomach and smiled. A sudden burst of assurance surrounded him; this was going to be the easiest money he ever won in his life. He would treat Raquel like a queen, starting with the date he'd planned. Of course, if she wasn't a good sport, this date could be a disaster, but it wouldn't be for lack of effort on his part. Singing "No Woman, No Cry," he went inside to get dressed.

While Romare was having coffee and doubts, Liz was getting royally chewed out by Fletcher. He was standing in the middle of her living room letting her known just how little he appreciated her new look. And he was doing it in a voice loud enough to raise the dead.

"Why did you do this, Liz? Why did you have to complicate everything? This could have been nice and easy; but no, you have to show up looking like you fixin' to audition at a booty club!"

Liz, dressed for her first date with Romare, was trying not to take his caustic remarks personally, but his last remark really stung. "Excuse *you,* I didn't look like I was about to go dance on a pole," she said indignantly. "And you need to back off me, I already feel like Boo-Boo the Fool," she mumbled.

Surprisingly, Fletcher calmed down at once. He stopped yelling and walked past Liz into the kitchen where he opened the refrigerator and started poking around. "So you feel foolish, huh? Why is that, Lizzie?"

Liz followed him into the kitchen and sat down heavily on one of the tall stools next to the breakfast bar. "Don't bother looking in there. There's nothing but cottage cheese, boiled eggs, and those vile chicken breasts with no skin and no flavor. And lots of water," she added glumly.

"Dang, woman, are you trying to starve me or something?"

"No, I was starving myself. I've been on a low-carb diet for the past few weeks. Thanks for noticing."

Fletcher raised his eyebrows as he emerged from his scavenging with a bottle of Aquafina water in one hand and a grilled chicken breast in the other. "Well, it worked. I thought it was my imagination, but you definitely look skinny. Underfed, really." After washing down a mouthful of chicken with a huge gulp of water, he joined Liz on the stool next to hers.

"Talk to me, Lizzie. What in the world made you dress up like a bachelor party blow-up doll? And why do you feel like such a fool?"

Liz blew out a huge breath full of despair and stared at her hands. "I decided that since you were blackmailing me into going on this stupid show I could make a point while I was doing it. I had the brilliant idea that I could prove that men are only interested in long hair and big boobs, and I got my girl Tasha to hook me up."

Fletcher stopped eating long enough to comment, "Well, she did a good job. Where'd you get those knockers from, anyway? Those aren't yours; I have yours committed to memory," he leered.

Liz straightened her slumping posture and cupped her breasts. "Fletch, this bra is amazing! It's like a little water-bed for your bosom. Wanna see?"

Fletcher's face contorted in horror and he spilled water down the front of his expensive blue Polo shirt. "Oh, hell, no. Please leave me my illusions and delusions. Quiet as it's kept, men don't want to know how you women manage to look like you do." He took the linen dishtowel Liz handed him and swabbed at his shirt awkwardly. When Liz took the towel from him and finished the job properly, he pressed for more details. "So you wanted to prove all men are dogs and you got all hoochied up. Now you feel stupid, why is that?"

Liz rose from the stool, tossed the towel in the sink, and sighed. "Because, Fletch, the guy is *fine*. Not only is he fine, he's *smart*. He was this big time attorney for a long time and he invested all his money and made a pile, and now he's decided to pursue his long-time passion for gourmet cooking. Can you believe it? He walked away from all that money to pursue a dream." Liz paced around the kitchen looking miserable.

In a voice devoid of guile, Fletcher asked what the problem was. "He sounds like a nice guy to me."

"That is the problem, genius. He *is* a nice guy, a fabulous guy, in fact. And here I am perpetrating big time. If I keep this charade up, I'm screwed, because a man like him isn't going to be interested in all of this," she said angrily, gesturing at her hair and her new outfit of a halter top and skin-tight capri pants in a brilliant shade of orange with matching stiletto-heeled mules with pointed toes.

"Well, you can always tell him the truth and go back to your real self," Fletcher suggested.

"Right, the truth. 'Romare, I don't really look like this, I just put on this little disguise because I'm such a neurotic man-hater I think that all men want a skanky broad to call their own.'" She gave Fletcher a baleful stare. "That'll work, right? He'll in no way think I'm totally deranged and run away from me if I tell him that, I'll betcha. Thanks, Fletch, great advice," she said bitterly.

"Hey, don't get mad at me. I didn't do this, it was all your own doing. I'm just surprised that you care so much; it's just a stupid TV show, after all. And besides, this guy might not be as nice as you think. Maybe he's a jerk in nice guy's clothing," he offered.

Liz's eyes lit up and a look of pure relief flooded her face. "That's true, isn't it? He might be a real idiot; maybe last night was just a front! Hurry up and get out of here. He's going to pick me up in about fifteen minutes, and I have to finish putting on my skanky, wet look lipstick. You'd be surprised how much time it takes to look this cheap," she said hurriedly.

Fletcher was more than happy to leave, although he demanded details as soon as the date was over. "Hit me on my cell phone; I want to hear all about it." Taking the bottle of water with him, he gestured at the refrigerator. "And don't cook no more of that chicken, it was nasty."

* * *

Romare arrived promptly and saw right away that his idea of casual attire was very different from Raquel's. He was wearing old jeans and a prized Hawaiian print shirt whose heyday was long past but had a lot of sentimental value attached to it. Raquel was festive but way too dressy for what he had planned. He greeted her and tried to suggest she might want to bring an extra pair of shoes for where they were going.

"Oh, really? Where exactly are we going?" she asked guardedly.

"Disneyland," he answered.

Liz/Raquel stared at him with her mouth open. "You have *got* to be joking," she said.

"No, I'm not," he said calmly. "I thought it would be fun."

"I'll be right back," she answered. "Have a seat," she added as an afterthought.

Romare did sit down, looking around her living room with interest. There was a small fireplace, lots of tropical plants, and a long teal blue sofa, which faced the patio. There were two comfortable looking chairs and a coffee table with interesting looking magazines stacked neatly on either end. There were some beautifully framed Paul Goodnight and Jack Vetrianno prints on the walls, giving the room a warm and artsy feel. Family pictures were scattered around the room, and there were big throw pillows of bright colors on the floor. The tables beside each chair also held books, as well as intriguing items that begged to be picked up and handled. Romare had just reached for a kaleidoscope when Raquel announced she was ready.

"Okay, let's go," she said happily.

Romare's eyes got big when he beheld the new Raquel. She was now wearing Nike Shox, a pair of jeans at least as old as his, and a tight-fitting white T-shirt with a deep scoop neck. She had a baseball cap in one hand and a digital camera in the other. All of a sudden she looked approachable, relaxed, and fun. Even her breasts looked better, like perky apples instead of weirdly pushed up melons. "I'm not going to take a purse, can you put my keys and my driver's license in your pocket?" she asked with a winsome smile.

"Uh, what about your cell phone?" he asked in a slightly dazed voice.

"Who needs it? If someone calls they can just leave a message," Liz responded. "Let's not worry about phone calls, let's just go have fun."

They really did have fun; it was one of the best dates Romare could remember. He had a hard time reconciling the laughing woman at his side with the brittle mannequin of the night before. This Raquel was easy to talk to, charming, and intelligent, with a great sense of humor. And a sense of adventure, too, as she was game to ride every ride and didn't seem to mind standing in the long lines either. He also discovered she had a wonderful appetite, and they seemed to be eating all day long. Almost every food vendor they passed got some of their business; they ate hot dogs, hamburgers, popcorn, cotton candy, nachos, French fries, funnel cakes, and anything else that caught their fancy. He offered several times to take her to one of the many sit-down restaurants in the park, but she refused.

"This is so much more fun, it's like being at the fair when I was little. The Michigan State Fair was one of the highlights of the summer for me and my brothers and sisters. All that's missing is the farm exhibits," she said with a smile.

Romare looked down at Liz and returned her smile. She looked extremely cute with mustard and ketchup stains on her pristine-white shirt and a small dribble of blue sno-cone on her chin. He licked his finger and wiped it off, then put his finger in his mouth as she stared at him. "Sno-cone," he said. "All gone. So you liked looking at the farm animals and stuff?"

Liz laughed. "We raised farm animals," she admitted. "I grew up on a dairy farm in Michigan and my siblings and I always had animals in the judging. We won a lot of ribbons and medals, too. My mom would win for her quilts and preserves. You're looking at a real farm girl, Romare," she said with a twinkle in her fascinating black eyes.

Romare tilted his head and stopped walking to get a better look. "Your eyes," her said softly. He leaned down even nearer, bringing his face nearer to hers.

She stared back at him, not breathing, not even blinking. "What about them," she said in a near whisper.

"Your eyes are a different color," Romare said thoughtlessly. "They were gray last night, now they're black."

Liz was jolted out of her growing reverie by his words, but she was always a fast thinker. Affecting a bland expression, she airily assured him he was wrong. "Oh no, they're the same color they always are," she said quickly.

"You sure? I could have sworn they were a different color last night."

"I'm positive. Studio lights do funny things to your eyes. How about going on the log ride?"

Romare allowed her to lead him in the direction of the ride, acknowledging the fact that he'd have followed her anywhere. She was just that enchanting, but for the life of him he couldn't figure out how she'd gotten to him so thoroughly in so short a time.

5

They walked to the door of Liz's small house holding hands. The evening air was punctuated with the sound of their laughter as they recalled the enjoyable day they'd spent together. When they reached the door, Romare gallantly took the keys from his pocket and held them out to her. She pointed out the door key and he opened it, entering before her. "I don't want you to think I have no manners," he explained, "I'd just like to make sure everything is okay before you come in."

What was left of her heart melted at the simple words. She put down the bags of Disney paraphernalia he'd purchased for her on the sofa and turned to watch him as he checked her kitchen, the back door, and the windows. He looked at her for permission to continue his inspection and she nodded mutely. As he opened the door to her bedroom, she followed with her heart beating madly. He checked the windows and she watched his broad shoulders move up and down, admiring the way his taut behind looked in his jeans. Her bedroom was impeccable, thanks to a mother who instilled in all her children the habit of making their beds daily and hanging up all their clothes. Even the discarded orange outfit of the morning was neatly put away.

Just then Romare turned around, his warm brown eyes traveling up and down her body. He smiled at the charming picture she made, all mussed and grimy from their Disneyland adventure. She smiled back. "We look like a couple of hoboes, don't we?"

He agreed. "But you're the cutest hobo I've ever seen. Do you think those stains will come out of your T-shirt?"

Liz glanced down indifferently. There were traces of mustard, ketchup, barbecue sauce, and a few dribbles of blue and purple sno-cone. "Maybe. I think the log ride helped," she laughed.

Romare swallowed hard at her last remark. The log ride might have helped her shirt, but it had caused him great pain. He would never forget how she looked after that ride, the wet T-shirt clinging to her and outlining her breasts so that her alert and provocative nipples showed clearly. She'd looked so incredibly sexy he'd wanted to drag her to one of the many nearby hotels and have his way with her for a few days or weeks or months.

"You should probably get it in the wash pretty soon," he mumbled, taking a step toward her.

"I will," she murmured, taking a step toward him.

It was hard to say who made the next move, but suddenly they were in each other's arms, taking their first taste of one another and loving it. Romare's lips were as smooth and soft as his skin, and they tasted as chocolaty as he looked. His tongue was hot and sweet, and the feel of it was driving Liz crazy. She moaned and opened her mouth wider to better accommodate the tender assault. She stretched up on her toes, her arms encircling his neck. A soft gasp escaped her as he suddenly picked her up, bringing her to his eye level and introducing her body to his hardened one.

Romare couldn't ever remember being so aroused by a mere kiss, not since he was about sixteen. But her lips were so soft and yielding and her tongue so enticing, he surrendered to the hypnotic rapture he found in her arms. He couldn't stop kissing her, he couldn't stop touching her, bringing her closer to him. When he picked her up his big hands cupped her bottom and her long legs wrapped around his waist so she was anchored on top of his massive erection. They began moving against each other, their bodies begging for more and more, for a release from the sensual pressure that was building inside. Bracing his legs, he held her even closer as she moved her hips in a way that could lead to only one conclusion. He tried to pull away from her but it was too late, she had captured him completely.

Romare still couldn't believe how soft her skin was. He had stroked her all over and his lips had followed his hands into an exploration of every inch of her incredible body, and it still wasn't enough. They were laying in her bed with him turned on his side so he could touch her to his heart's content. Right now she was on her back with her knees slightly bent and her legs open wide enough for him to play in her most feminine recess. His fingers were busy caressing her, relishing the hot moistness of her womanhood, while his thumb stroked the center of her pleasure. Her eyes were closed and she was making little sounds of enjoyment that made him want to please her even more. He couldn't stop looking at her; the sight of her comely form increased his hunger, and he took one of her hardened chocolate nipples in his mouth.

He sucked hard at first, then softer, pulling the tender flesh in and out of his mouth, very gently exposing it to his teeth, which made her soft moans get louder and faster.

"Oh, Rom, what are you doing to me?" she moaned.

"I'm making love to you, just like we did last night, baby. Like we're going to do all day. I'm hungry for you, baby, and I have to have my fill of you," he growled.

When he could feel the honeyed moisture spurt from her body he dove to capture it with his mouth, using his tongue and his lips to drive her into a frenzy of passion. He positioned himself so he could lick the sweet juices and suck her so they would continue to flow. He could feel the pulsing of her private pearl and hear the cries of passion torn from her throat; they sounded like...like...his cell phone.

"This better be good," he said roughly. "You'd better have a damned good reason for waking me up out of a sound—" He stopped, remembering the incredibly hot dream he'd been having. "For waking me up," he amended in the same rough tone.

"Sounds like somebody had a pretty bad day," said the familiar voice on the other end.

Recognizing the caller, Romare groaned. He knew why he was getting this call, and he wasn't in the mood for it. "Aww, man, what do you want? Do you want to gloat? To say you were right and I was wrong? Well, screw you. Why I let you jokers talk me into this I'll never know. I hate all of you, I want you to know that."

"So was it a bad date? Is she that scary, man?"

"No. Yes. No. I don't know," Romare groaned. He writhed his naked body around in the wrinkled sheets and sighed deeply. "At first I thought it was going to be a disaster because she looked like your typical chickenhead, you know the type. Show 'em something shiny and they'll do anything, right?"

Romare stared up at the ceiling for a moment before continuing. "Well, looks are deceiving, man. She's smart and funny, has a dynamite personality, in fact. We went to Disneyland on our first date and we had a ball, came home looking like two grubby kids. Get this, man, she grew up on a farm in Michigan. Can you believe it? I really think she's too smart for her job; she's some kind of a production assistant at a TV station. That's double talk for go-fer. She's way too intelligent for that," he said thoughtfully.

"So where are you going next? That's how it works, right, you have two dates with her or something?"

Romare sat up and groaned. "That's the problem. We're supposed to have three dates; each one is one week apart. And we can't have any contact between the dates. No phone calls, no nothing. It's part of the show; we agreed to it when we came on."

"Oh yeah? What's wrong with that? This way she's out of your hair and you don't have to deal with her. Sounds like a good plan to me."

"That's because you didn't kiss her good night," Romare retorted and immediately wished he hadn't. The hooting and catcalls that came through the receiver were deafening.

"It wasn't like that, it was just a nice kiss good night." The fact that his overactive imagination had turned an innocent kiss into something out of a book of urban erotica was his own business. "And I really want to see her again. I don't see how I'm going to wait a whole week.

The week went by faster than either of them could imagine, although it was a week Liz put to good use. For one thing, she had to get her hair redone. "Tasha, this time can we make it a little simpler? Not so high and not so long? And not so poufy in the top? I need something a little more casual," she explained.

Tasha was more than happy to do her bidding. "Anything you say. I'd sure like to know what you did with this hairdo, though. Girl, you looked a hot mess when you walked in here."

Liz explained her trip to the amusement park. "Tash, I haven't had that much fun in years. I love fairs and amusement parks of all kinds, and I hadn't been to one in ages. I've wanted to go to Disneyland and ride those teacups since I was a little girl. It was wonderful," she said with a tinge of sadness in her voice.

"Well, why are you so down in the mouth? Is he not nice?" Tasha demanded to know. She sounded like she'd go kick his butt if he was being less than a gentleman.

Liz sighed deeply. "First you have to promise not to say I told you so."

"I promise," Tasha said solemnly.

"Tash, this is the nicest guy I've ever met. He's warm and genuine and intelligent, and he's so danged fine he makes my teeth hurt."

"I told you so," Tasha said at once. "I told you this masquerade was a mistake, that you might meet your soul mate and you'd regret this whole farce. Didn't I tell you?"

"What happened to not saying I told you so," Liz pouted.

"I forgot. So how fine is he?"

"Picture a chocolate Boris Kodjoe with curly hair and a dimple in his chin. Is that fine enough for you?"

All Tasha could do was nod her head in silence.

Romare was singing as he approached Liz/Raquel's door. He carried a bouquet of flowers and a bottle of champagne. He raised his hand to push the bell, but the door opened before he had a chance to ring it.

"I was watching for you," Liz admitted without a trace of embarrassment.

"You look beautiful," Romare said with warm admiration.

"So do you," she said shyly.

She was looking really festive in one of her normal outfits; a coral-colored knit camisole with a matching sweater and a pair of perfectly tailored ivory boot-cut slacks that rode low on her hips. On her feet were low-heeled, open-toed, coral mules that matched the sweater set. She had on medium-sized gold hoop earrings and two gold bangle bracelets, gifts from her brothers when she got her master's degree. Even though the high ponytail was still in place, it was much more subdued, as was her makeup.

While Romare feasted his eyes on her beauty, she admired the way he looked in khaki slacks and a pink Oxford cloth Polo dress shirt open at the neck. The color looked wonderful against his smooth ebony skin. He was wearing Italian loafers and a really expensive-looking belt, and he smelled heavenly.

"Are those for me?" she asked teasingly as she looked pointedly at the flowers.

He smiled and handed her the bouquet and the wine. "It serves you right for being so pretty. I got so caught up looking at you I forgot to hand them over. So where are we going today?"

It was her turn to plan the date, and she'd put a lot of thought into it. "It's a surprise. I'll tell you when we're on the way. Do you mind if I drive?"

After she put the flowers into a vase, they went out the back door of the house and she used the remote on her key ring to open the garage door. When Romare saw her sleek little Chrysler Crossfire with the top down he could feel his jaw drop.

"You have a convertible," he breathed reverently.

"You bet your life I do," she answered with a grin. "Let's go!"

Romare was enjoying the ride so much he wasn't concerned with where they were going. He would have been content to just tool along with her until they ran out of gas, and if they ran out in front of a secluded luxury hotel, so much the better. She looked so fine with her ponytail flying in the breeze and the light glinting off her classy sunglasses. This woman was full of surprises, and he loved every minute of her company. When they pulled off the expressway and headed to Santa Anita Raceway he was all but done in. A woman who liked ragtops and horse racing was his kind of woman. This was going to be a great day.

6

Afterward, Romare couldn't decide which part of the day was his favorite. The drive to the racetrack was perfect, as was the day of racing with lunch in the restaurant. They had a table that overlooked the track, and the food had been surprisingly good, although it could have been hotdogs and sauerkraut as far as he was concerned. Anything would have tasted good with Raquel. They'd made a couple of small bets and won, increasing their enjoyment of the day. After leaving the track they went to an artist's colony and visited a gallery, then had dinner in a quaint café. Good company, good conversation, a snappy convertible, which she let him drive on the way home, what was not to like?

He finally decided that his favorite part of the day had been when they drove up to the hills far above Hollywood and looked down at all the lights. He could still remember the warmth of her hand as he held it, the faint fragrance of her very feminine perfume, and the softness of her lips as he'd kissed her. It was the most wonderful torture he could ever remember. It was like being a teenager again, experiencing the bliss and agony of wanting to be closer than close with the object of his desire. It was sweetly innocent, but at the same time it was a form of punishment because he wanted her so badly he could literally taste it. After their tongues entwined the first time, he knew he'd never get her flavor out of his mouth and he never wanted to. It was crazy, feeling such intensity for a woman he'd just met, and on a dating show of all things, but no one ever said passion was logical.

He was standing in a florist shop picking out an arrangement of colorful and exotic blossoms he thought would please her. According to the rules of *Meet Your Mate*, they weren't supposed to call each other, they weren't supposed to e-mail each other or speak in any way between dates. But there was no way he could go an entire week without contacting her in some way, and there was nothing about not sending flowers in the regulations; he'd checked them thoroughly. So he was sending her something earthy, fragrant, and lovely, just like she was. He had a dreamy expression on his face as he thought about how pleased she'd be to receive them. The irritating chime of his cell phone snapped him back into reality.

"Oh, it's you. I hope you jokers have my money ready because you're about to lose this bet big time," Romare gloated.

"So you're telling me this is the perfect woman for you? This is the one woman you can find no fault with, the one who meets those ridiculously high standards of yours?"

"Look, I never said she was perfect. And I keep telling you fools I'm not that particular, I just like what I like. And she has everything I like. I can see spending a whole lot of time with this lady; she's just that special," he admitted. She was special to him in a way he couldn't articulate to his brothers. He could talk to her for hours, which was what they'd done high in the hills that night. Between the kissing and the touching and the yearning, they'd had a real conversation, and the intellectual exchange was just as arousing as the caress of her lips.

"Yeah, man, she's special," he repeated thoughtfully. "She might be the one." His face contorted as he held the phone away from his ear to protect himself from the raucous laughter on the other end. *How did I wind up in the same family as those fools?*

Liz was one big mass of nerves. All week long she'd received one wonderful gift after another from Romare. He'd figured out a way to circumvent the rules of the game and let her know she was constantly on his mind. He'd sent beautiful blossoms, imported candy, and a wonderful gift basket containing scones and shortbread from Scotland, a porcelain teapot, a jar of lemon curd, and Devonshire cream from England along with a box of fantastic breakfast tea. The basket was decorated with a jaunty little teddy bear wearing a monocle. Every single thing he sent put a smile on her face, so much so that Fletch had a new nickname for her.

"Okay, Perma-Grin, what's up? I see you cheesin' like a field mouse again. What have you and Mr. Perfect been up to? Are you sure you're not violating some bylaw of the show?" Fletcher accompanied his words with a mocking smirk. He was leaning against the door of Liz's office, watching her closely.

With a guilty start, Liz hastily shoved the card she'd been addressing to Romare into the top drawer of her desk. Trying for a coolly disinterested expression, she countered, "I have no idea what you're talking about. I'm fulfilling my part of the bargain, that's all. No one said Romare Alexander is Mr. Perfect," she said haughtily. "He's a nice guy, and the ordeal isn't as painful as I thought it was going to be, that's all."

Fletcher gave a short, loud laugh. "Save it, girl. You can't kid a kidder. Remind me not to let you play bid whist with my cousins and me because we'd destroy you. You can't bluff anybody, Liz. Who do you think you're fooling?"

Her eyes dropped to her hands, which were toying with a pen. She wished with all her heart that Fletcher would go away; it was too hard to keep up this façade of disinterest. He moved from the doorway and brought his long legs in front of her desk.

"So, what's next? This is your last date, right? What's going to happen after that, when you're free to do what you want? How are you going to tell him that you're really Elizabeth Walker, executive producer, and not Raquel Taylor, production assistant? Or do you plan to keep up the charade forever?"

Liz's hand clenched the pen and her head jerked up. Fletch was looking at her with a raised eyebrow and an expression that told her resistance was futile. He had her there; she couldn't avoid the inevitable much longer. At some point she was going to have to tell Romare the truth about her deception and the illogically inane reasoning behind it. She dropped her head into her upraised palm and sighed deeply. "I don't know, Fletch. I just don't know. Maybe I'll just run away and forget any of this ever happened," she mumbled.

Fletcher sat down, his face both guilty and concerned. "Lizzie, I didn't mean to push you so hard, I was just having fun at your expense. It's not that serious; just tell him you were trying to prove a point to me and you went a little overboard. He'll understand, I know he will. He really cares about you," he said earnestly.

Instead of looking reassured, Liz looked even glummer. She shook her head and started playing with the pen again. "You don't get it, Fletch. This is like the nicest man I've ever met in my life. He wouldn't deceive anyone; he's just too honorable for that. Don't ask me how I know, I just do. And I also know he's not going to be able to deal with the fact that I tricked him like this. He's going to hate it, and me, too, probably." She brooded silently for a few seconds, and her face went from despondent to red with embarrassment.

She was thinking about the gifts she'd sent him that week to reciprocate his thoughtfulness and to show her own interest in him. The first one was a gift basket full of the kind of old-fashioned candy he'd remember from his youth like Mike & Ikes, cinnamon red hots, Squirrel Nut Zippers, Now and Laters, and the like. There were also a few miniature versions of kid games. They'd had a long conversation about that kind of thing, and Liz knew he'd love the gesture. She'd also sent him a wonderful book called *Sweets*, written by a woman named Patsy Pinner from Saginaw, Michigan. It was a fascinating cookbook and memoir she knew he would enjoy, given his passion for cooking. Those things she was okay with, it was the last gift that gave her pause.

She'd been in a bookstore buying a birthday gift for one of her brothers when she saw one of her favorite books entitled *This is My Beloved* by Walter Benton. It was written during World War II and was considered extremely racy because of the deep sensuality of the poetry, which depicted a love story from its inception to its end. One of her older sisters had introduced her to it when she was a romantic teenager, and she'd loved it ever since, but she'd never thought about giving it to a man before. She walked around with it in her hands for a while and suddenly the matter resolved itself when she spied a CD of the poem recorded by the legendary Arthur Prysock. Several versions had been recorded, but this was widely considered to be the best. This was the version that could make underwear levitate across the room by itself; it was just that sexy. The lush music, the sensual sound of Arthur Prysock's voice... Of their own volition, as if she had no control at all, her hands picked up the CD and she went straight to the checkout counter with the goods. In less than an hour they were gift wrapped and on their way to Romare.

That was two days ago, and she hadn't stopped wondering if she'd gone overboard with that gesture. Would he think she was being too forward, or would he just enjoy them? Liz bit her lip as she mulled it over. Tonight was the big date, their last official *Meet Your Mate* outing. Liz was thrilled to have the whole ordeal over with; but on the other hand, she was dreading tonight because it might really mean the end. What would she do if Romare didn't ask her out again? She had to tell him the truth about her little charade, and once it was out he could very well tell her to take a hike. She frowned and stood abruptly, startling Fletcher, who was still sitting there looking fatherly.

"You okay, Lizzie? You look kind of...out of it," he said.

Liz nodded curtly. "I'm fine, Fletch. Really. I'm leaving early; I have a couple of errands to run. She got her purse out of the credenza behind her desk and gave him a good imitation of her usual smile. "I'll talk to you tomorrow. Everything's fine, I promise it is."

She took her blue funk over to Tasha's salon, where she got much less sympathy than she had from Fletcher. All she got from her friend was a stern look and some tough love while Tasha applied setting lotion.

She combed the fragrant liquid through Liz's thick hair as she lectured her. "You made this mess all by yourself, and now you've got to clean it up. I told you this was a bad idea," she fussed. "Now you've met this wonderful man and you've told him a pack of lies. And there you sit, looking like someone stole your puppy."

Liz was amused by her friend's frankness, but her candor stung a little. "Hey, you're supposed to be on my side, remember? *My* side, *my* side, *my* side! Through thick and thin, whether I'm right or wrong, that's part of the girlfriend's creed," she said indignantly.

"Liz, hush. I *am* on your side, even though you're wrong as two left shoes. I want you to be happy. I want you to land this man so I can be in the wedding. Shoot, he might have some fine brothers or cousins for me," she laughed. "But you need to handle your business, chick. Quit whining, put on your big girl panties, and take care of this mess," she advised as she placed Liz under the hair dryer.

A few hours later, Liz faced her reflection in the full-length mirror in her bedroom. *Big girl panties, hmmm?* Despite her inner turmoil, she managed a short laugh. These were itty-bitty panties, but they were only for big girls. She was wearing a delicate and very sexy pair of thong panties with a silk butterfly perched at the top of the thong, right at the juncture of her firm, rounded butt. It was a beautiful shade of mint green, purchased solely because she knew Romare liked the color. The matching demi cup bra made the most of her breasts without padding or inserts; it was sheer with delicate embroidery and a tiny butterfly appliqué that disguised the front clasp. Liz turned to the side, then put her back to the mirror and turned to see her reflection over her shoulder.

There was only one reason a woman as practical as Liz would buy expensive, impractical underwear like this; it was because she wanted Romare to see her in it. She wanted his hands on her body, his mouth, his tongue... The phone made her jump and she hurried to answer it, smiling when she heard Romare's sexy voice.

"Are you sure you don't mind driving over here?" he asked for what must have been the tenth time.

"Not at all, Romare. And I have to tell you, I haven't eaten all day because I want to really enjoy the meal you're making for me," she confessed. She could sense his smile through the phone, could see the look of delight on his face as he spoke.

"You poor baby. You must be starving. Well, get in your car and come on over. I'm waiting for you."

"Maybe I should put on some clothes first. I'm in my

underwear," she said mischievously. Her eyes got big when she heard a crash on Romare's end of the line.

"Woman, don't say things like that to a starving man. I'm getting off this phone right now. Drive carefully, get here quickly, and clothing is strictly optional. I'm waiting for you."

She disconnected the call, giggling.

When Romare opened the door to his apartment some forty-five minutes later, he stared at Liz for a long time, then took both her hands in his and kissed each one. "You look gorgeous," he said quietly, bending down to take her in his arms. Still standing in the foyer, they began a long, slow kiss, exploring each other's essence and savoring each minute sensation. Romare finally forced himself to pull away from her and looked down at her with sweet, tender eyes. "I'd better feed you while we can still eat," he said.

He stepped back and looked at her, his eyes full of admiration. "You really do look fantastic."

She could feel herself blushing, but she was pleased by his compliment. Her hair was in its most conservative style, yet still in a ponytail, but a shorter one that Tasha had curled so it looked full and natural. The lashes also had disappeared; she wore only her own with a thick coat of mascara that was all she needed to make their natural length stand out. She was wearing a simple summer dress, a silk faille wrap dress with cap sleeves and a deep V-neckline. The skirt was mid calf length, but it moved when she walked and exposed her long, bare legs, since it fastened with one thin tie at the left side of her slender waist. It was a deeper shade of mint green than her big girl panties, and she didn't have to be told that Romare liked the way she looked in it, but he did anyway.

"You look absolutely fantastic, Raquel. Come on in and I'll show you my temporary abode." He turned to the living room, missing the look of dismay on her face as he said her name.

Hearing him address her as "Raquel" just compounded her guilt. She wanted to tell him her name was Elizabeth; she wanted to hear his voice caressing those syllables, just once. If it was going to happen, she had to do something she was dreading, she'd have to tell him the truth. She took a deep breath and squared her shoulders. This wasn't going to be easy, but it had to be done.

7

Handing him the bottle of champagne she'd brought, Liz looked around the living room with great interest to see if she could detect Romare in the details. He excused himself to chill the champagne and in his absence Liz walked around the space, noting the colorful, impersonal abstract paintings on the walls, the thick peacock blue carpeting, the royal purple leather furniture, and the black lacquer tables. A faux stone wall was host to a fireplace with a narrow mantelpiece that held a row of thick, square glass votives, each with a white candle burning brightly. There were large tropical plants flanking the wall-to-wall glass door that opened onto the balcony. Huge peacock blue, purple, and emerald green pillows were scattered on the long sofa and piled on the floor near the fireplace.

Romare returned with a large tray. "Please don't think this is my taste. This is my cousin's place; he has a bunch of rental properties. I think this is the work of a woman he was dating who claimed to be an interior decorator. Either that or she hated him and he didn't know it," he said with a grin.

Liz returned the smile. "That's actually good news. I was hoping these weren't your things. They just don't look like you," she said, taking in the brash colors and harsh modern furnishings.

Romare opened the sliding glass doors and stepped out onto the balcony. He put the tray on a built-in server next to a bistro table. "No, it's not me at all. It looks like the waiting room of an old-school dentist, the kind who puts in the serious gold teeth with diamonds and stuff."

Liz laughed at the notion and asked where she could wash her hands. Romare directed her to a lavishly decorated bathroom done in marble with purple and gold accents. *Either this guy is a Que or he played for the Lakers, because he does love his purple*, she thought in amusement.

She rejoined Romare on the balcony and looked around with a delighted expression. What seemed like thousands of tiny white lights were all around them, in the potted ficus trees and other potted plants, across the awning covering the balcony and the railing. Candles flickered on the table, and everything looked so romantic she impulsively kissed Romare on the cheek as he seated her. "You're a wonderful host," she said softly.

"You might want to wait until you've tasted the food before you start heaping praise," he said with dry wit.

He sat down across from her and took a small glass plate from the server, filling it from an electric chafing dish. He put the plate in front of Liz. "Try these," he urged. After saying grace, Liz did as he asked.

The plate held small crab cakes, perfectly browned and smelling heavenly. There were also silver dollar-sized corn cakes. There was rémoulade sauce to go with the crab cakes and crème fraîche and red caviar for the corn cakes. Liz's eyes shone with appreciation until she took her first bite; then they closed in utter bliss. They were light and crisp, deliciously seasoned and tastier than any she'd had before. She tried not to make disgusting noises, but a soft moan of contentment escaped. "Romare, this is wonderful. Your restaurant is going to be such a success," she said dreamily.

Romare smiled with pleasure. They had talked at length about his plans to become a restaurateur, and he was pleased she'd remembered. "Thank you, Raquel. It's going to take a lot of hard work, and nothing is guaranteed, but I'm going to give it my best shot."

Liz put her hand on top of his and looked at him without smiling. "Romare, anything you do will be a success. You're brilliant, talented, and you have real vision. I know without question that you're going to be a fabulous chef and restaurant owner. In fact"—she raised the glass of champagne he'd just poured for her—"let's have a toast to that."

They touched their glasses together and kissed briefly to seal the toast. They continued to sip champagne and talk while enjoying the first course; then Romare suggested they go inside for the main course. "I think it's going to rain tonight. Can you smell it?"

Liz rose gracefully and went to the railing to lean out a little. "I think you're right, I do sense that nice moist rain scent."

Romare stood behind her and surrounded her with his strong arms. "And I detect that incredibly sexy fragrance that's all you," he whispered in her ear. Liz was both surprised and aroused by his words and leaned into him, trembling.

"Listen, baby, we need to eat while we still can," Romare said frankly. "Let's go inside." He led her into the apartment and they walked into the dining room, where Liz stopped short in the doorway, struck by the effort Romare had put forth for her. The dining room looked seductively inviting. A turquoise runner in silk duppioni was the middle of the table, with matching emerald green napkins in the same fabric. A thick oval mirror with beveled edges was in the center of the table; it held a shallow glass bowl half filled with water on which several rosy camellias floated. There were tiny tea lights and votives scattered strategically around the table, as well as beeswax tapers on the black lacquer sideboard.

Their two place settings were also on mirrored chargers, the delicate plates and crystal glassware reflecting in the mellow candlelight. It looked like something out of a dream. Liz blinked rapidly; she could feel moisture gathering in her eyes. She always cried when she was really happy or really sad, and right now she was elated. "Romare, this is so wonderful. I feel so special," she breathed.

Romare was pleased with the look of enjoyment on her face. He put his arms around her and kissed her forehead. "You *should* feel special because you are. Now sit down and I'll serve you a meal I think you'll enjoy."

Liz's eyes were slightly glazed with satisfaction, and she tried not to purr from contentment, but a small expression of delight escaped her lips. They were in the living room, sitting on the sofa, relaxing after the sumptuous meal Romare had prepared. Romare had started a fire in the fireplace and arranged a low table for the dessert Liz swore she couldn't consume. "Romare, that was the best meal I've had in a long time. I can't believe you went to all that trouble just for me. It was wonderful," she said with warm appreciation.

Romare had made her a real Southern feast. It was, in fact, Liz's favorite meal, something he'd determined from their previous conversations. He'd made smothered chicken, fresh green beans, baked tomatoes with garlic breadcrumbs, cucumber salad, and yellow rice. Best of all, he'd made homemade biscuits, small, fluffy rounds completely unlike the giant soggy ones served in most so-called soul food restaurants. He had really outdone himself, as Liz had told him over and over while she enjoyed every morsel. Romare was pleased by her compliments.

"I like to mix new techniques with old favorites, which is why I use basmati rice and put a pinch of saffron in the rice and the chicken. I use low-fat milk instead of cream and smoked turkey instead of some form of smoked pork for the beans, that kind of thing. I try to cook healthy, but what I'm really aiming for is the best possible flavor."

Curled up in a corner of the sofa, Liz smiled at him. He looked so handsome in pleated slacks, bare feet, and a blue linen shirt with the sleeves rolled up. His forearms were very sexy, hard and muscular, just like the rest of him. "You're an amazing man, Romare. Creative, intelligent, and gorgeous. And very personable. We hardly know each other, but I feel like I've known you forever," she admitted.

Romare gave her a tender look that almost made her slide off the sleek leather couch. "I think you're wrong, baby. I think you know me very well, indeed," he said quietly. "Come on over here and let's have dessert." He patted the pillows next to him, and like a woman under a hypnotist's spell she rose and walked to where he awaited her. While Liz freshened up after dinner, Romare had put a blanket on the floor for her comfort. When she sank down on its soft surface she made a noise of surprise.

"Romare, this is so soft! I've never felt anything so soft in my life. What is it?"

"It's called a mink blanket, although I don't know why. It's not fur at all; it's some kind of synthetic fabric from Korea. My cousin was on tour over there a few years ago and brought some back. Nice, isn't it?" He leaned over and kissed her cheek, saying he'd be right back.

In minutes he returned from the kitchen with a tray holding a deep bowl, a carafe of espresso, and two small cups. He put the tray on the table and brought the bowl over to Liz. She stared at its contents in curiosity, opening her mouth when Romare offered her a spoonful of the delicious confection. It was homemade vanilla ice cream flecked with tiny seeds from the vanilla bean. The topping was like a fantasy for a sweet lover. It was sliced bananas cooked in melted butter with small amounts of brown sugar, rum, cinnamon, and more vanilla. The slow cooking made the bananas mellow, sweet, spicy, and heady all at once, and the combination of cold ice cream and the warm sauce was sublime. This time Liz didn't bother to control her reactions; she closed her eyes and let out an *ooh* that was both sexy and earthy.

Romare laughed out loud at her uninhibited reaction to the sensational taste. He was smiling at her as he picked up the remote for the stereo and changed the music from the jazz that had been playing through dinner to something that made Liz's eyes widen. It was the Arthur Prysock CD, something she'd almost forgotten about. She felt heat surging up her neck and was about to get really flustered when his words calmed her.

"That's what I mean about knowing me better than you think. How could you have possibly known this was one of my favorite CDs? How could you have known that unless you really knew me? I can't explain it, but I accept it totally," he said.

"You really like it? I got a bad case of regret right after I sent it; I was afraid it would unnerve you or something, that you'd misinterpret the gesture entirely," she admitted.

"My favorite uncle, who was more like a big brother to me, turned me on to this when I was just going off to college. He told me this was what being in love was all about, and unless I was with a woman who could understand and appreciate this CD, I was with the wrong woman. You're the only woman I've ever shared this with," he added softly as he offered her another spoonful from the bowl.

She opened her lips again and licked the corner of her mouth as she accepted the spoon. Taking it from her mouth with a final long, slow lick, she dipped it into the bowl and brought it to Romare's waiting lips. As he filled his mouth, she felt strange, hot and restless and tight. She leaned toward him and put her mouth on his to sample the sweetness of his tongue. He obliged her at once, pulling her into his arms for a long, drugging kiss. His mouth was cool and sweet, and she savored every stroke of his tongue, returning the favor thoroughly. They shared the dessert and the kisses like greedy children, their hunger for each other growing with every caress.

Finally, the bowl was empty, but they weren't nearly satisfied. The dessert had only heightened their desire for another kind of sweetness. The seductive music and the sound of Arthur Prysock's voice were mesmerizing, as captivating as the fire licking the ceramic logs. The promise of rain had come to fruition, and the fresh smell of it filled the room and cooled it at the same time. Liz shivered against Romare, who drew her closer to him. "Are you cold, sweetheart?"

She shook her head and trembled again at the nearness of him, the smell of his skin, the sound of his voice. It was all too familiar, too disturbing, and she blurted it out without realizing what she was saying. "I dreamed this," she whispered so softly he had to put his ear next to her lips. "I dreamed about being in a room filled with the smell of rain and a fire and a blanket as soft as this one. I was with a beautiful dark man, with big shoulders and hot lips, and he knew me better than I know myself and we made love."

Romare got even more aroused by her passionate words; his body reacted almost violently to the soft voice, telling him what he wanted to know, needed to know. He knelt before Liz and drew her into a kneeling position. Cupping her adorable face in his hands, he kissed her again, deeply and sensually, sliding his big hands down her neck, across her shoulders, down her arms, lifting them and placing them around his neck. They looked at each other, staring deeply into each other's eyes, devouring each other with impassioned eyes. He put his hands on her breasts, stroking them gently at first, then squeezing firmly, rubbing her nipples in firm circles with his thumbs. He could feel them tense and harden, then blossom under his touch. "I want you, baby. I want all of you," he whispered.

"I want you, too, Romare. I want you now," she told him.

They kissed again as his hands found the thin tie that held her dress in place. The front of the dress parted to reveal Liz's body in the pretty underwear she'd bought only for him. He put his hands on her shoulders and gently slid the dress down her arms so it puddled around her knees. He moved it to one side and took both of Liz's hands in his before standing up. He kissed her forehead and looked at her reverently, adoring her beauty. "Turn around for me, please," he asked her softly.

Liz looked at him with her heart in her eyes and turned around slowly, waiting for his reaction when he saw the little butterfly on her thong. She was gratified to hear the sharp intake of his breath and the long whistle that followed. "Okay, that's enough of that; come here, woman, before I die from wanting you," he growled.

Liz looked over her shoulder and refused to move. "Not until you show me some skin. I feel like I'm putting on a show for you," she said with a mock pout.

Romare didn't answer her with words, he took off his shirt without even unbuttoning it, he just pulled it over his head and tossed it across the room. Before it landed he had his slacks off and was standing before Liz in his silk boxers, looking like the cover of a steamy romance novel. His body was as beautiful as his chiseled face; it was sculpted and hard, and his dark skin gleamed in the firelight. He looked like he'd been carved from a mountain of extra-fine semisweet chocolate. After staring at his long, muscular legs and the other long muscle that was bulging in his boxers, Liz couldn't wait to take a bite.

"Now you seem to have on more clothes than me," he said softly. "What are we going to do about that?"

Liz covered her breasts with her hands. "You mean this little thing? I can take it off, if you like." She was about to unfasten it when Romare closed the distance between them, embracing her and putting his hands under her derriere to pick her up. She expelled a breath of surprise and braced her hands on his shoulders for balance as she wrapped her legs around him.

"Don't even think about taking that off, that's my pleasure." He walked over to the blanket in front of the fireplace, and they slowly sank onto its soft, inviting texture.

"You're *my* pleasure," Liz whispered, then let out a tiny, satisfied sound when Romare unhooked the front clasp of her bra and touched her bare breasts for the first time. His big hands caressed them and his tongue paid them a sensual tribute that made her tremble and cry his name as the thrill from his lips rocketed through her body to her pleasure center, which throbbed with every pull of his mouth. Every time his lips gently tugged the exquisitely sensitive nipples a shock resonated through her body and she was inflamed with desire like she'd never felt before.

"Romare, oh, *Rom*...oh, please," she moaned.

Romare looked down at her, loving the look of abandon and passion on her face, aroused beyond belief at her uninhibited response to his lovemaking. "Is this like your dream, baby?"

She could barely get out the words as she felt the hot length of his erection on her legs as he kissed his way down her body. "It's better than my dream," she gasped as he began to pull off her thong with his teeth. "Oh, yes, baby, it's better than anything."

8

Romare finished taking off the thong with his hands so he could have the pleasure of stroking Liz's long legs. The silky texture of her skin was delightful to the touch, as was the fragrance that assailed his nostrils. It wasn't just her perfume, it was the smell of her womanhood that drew him unerringly to his target. He knelt before her as she lay on the blanket, her hands grasping the soft folds and her hips undulating as she reacted to his loving. He stroked her feet, kissing and caressing her ankles; then he spread her legs apart gently as he licked and sucked his way up her strong, slender calves. As he rubbed his face along her soft inner thighs, he could feel her trembling, a sensation that grew more pronounced as he neared the apex of her femininity. He slid his hands under her bottom and pulled two of the big pillows under it to elevate her hips.

Gently pushing her legs apart even wider, he began the intimate kiss of ultimate passion. He loved the taste of her, the feel of her body, the closeness he felt to her. His mouth paid her an erotic tribute that would have gone on forever, but he couldn't forestall his own arousal much longer. Every time her body exploded in an orgasm he felt it as strongly as she did, and it made him want to give her more; he wanted to satisfy her like no one ever had. He could feel her body's response, he could hear it in her cries of ecstasy, and he wanted to be inside her so they could experience the wild ride to paradise together. He finally began to work his way up her body, licking away the perspiration as he removed his boxers.

At last they lay in each other's arms, naked, moist, and shaken from the loving they'd shared; but there was more to come. Liz kissed him, while she wrapped her limber arms and legs around him, sighing his name. "Romare, *mmm . . .*" she whispered.

"Yes, baby?"

"It's your turn."

He turned so that she was on her back, all the while continuing to stroke her from her breasts down to the silky curls at the apex of her thighs, savoring the touch of her soft skin. "I have to go get some protection, baby. I'll be right back." He was about to go to the bedroom to get condoms when Liz wrapped her leg around his waist to stop him.

"You don't need those just yet," she purred.

Now she was in control, turning him onto his back and using her hands and her mouth to bring him to a dangerous level of arousal. Using the palms of her hands, she rubbed his nipples in concentric circles, over and over while she kissed his throat, licking and sucking his collarbones, and finally replacing her hand with her lips on the most sensitive part of his chest, treating it the way he'd treated hers, with the same results. She could feel his body convulse as the sensations spread to his manhood, already thick and straining with need. She continued her journey, sliding her hand down until she had him firmly in hand while she kissed his navel, lavishing her tongue around the opening until he called her name hoarsely.

She finally relented, taking his hard, engorged penis in both her hands, moving them up and down while her tongue caressed the tip, licking it like an ice cream cone before covering it with her lips. Pumping it with her hands, she applied a sweet suction that caused Romare to start losing control so quickly he had to put an end to it. Before she knew what was happening, he was carrying her to his bed, making a primal sound that sounded like a soft roar.

"I'm sorry, what did you say?" she asked teasingly. He tossed her onto the bed and braced himself over her body, staring down at her, his eyes fierce and serious.

"I said you're not going to drive me crazy, woman. You'll have me outside your door howling like a wolf every night," he grumbled as he turned his attention to the nightstand where he retrieved a box of condoms. He relented a little as she smiled up at him; she looked too beautiful and too sexy to resist. "I should have known you'd get to me like that," he sighed. Collapsing onto the bed, he blew out a long breath. "Now I'm too weak to put these on," he teased her.

"Oh, really? I think I have the cure for that," she answered pertly. Taking the box from his hands, she took one out and returned the box to him. She made him lay on his back, then opened the packet and unrolled the latex sheath onto his erection, which she noticed hadn't flagged one bit. Once the protection was in place, she opened her mouth but didn't have a chance to get the words out. Romare grasped her hips and put the crown of his hardened sex at her opening, still juicy from their lovemaking. He pushed once as she positioned herself on top of him, and when she leaned forward to brace her arms against his shoulders, he pushed again, joining their bodies.

"Hold onto me, baby, I've got you," he said, his voice rough from emotion and heat. As her muscles clenched him, he moaned with pleasure and started pumping in and out of her yielding flesh, thinking, *She's got* me. *Who am I trying to kid? She's got all of me.*

It was impossible to pretend that nothing had changed; everything was different the next morning, and they both knew it. They awoke tangled in each other's arms and neither one moved; they were too content to be where they were. Liz was cuddled close to Romare's side, her hand moving idly in circles over his warm, smooth skin. Romare sighed in contentment, kissing her forehead every so often. Finally, he spoke.

"So, now what happens?"

Liz wanted to pretend she didn't know what he meant, but they had shared too much, and she had enough to explain as it was. She bought herself a little time by putting the question to him. "What do you want to happen?"

"That's easy. I want to make love some more, then fix you breakfast. Then I want to go to your house so we can pack your things and go for a drive up the coast and stop at a little inn and make love some more. I want to take you to the wine country, I want to meet your family, I want you to meet my family, I want to see your beautiful face every single day; I want to love you. That's all."

Liz, despite the rapid pounding of her heart from sheer guilt, was enchanted. Laughing, she said, "You mean *make* love to me," she corrected.

Romare looked at her without a trace of a smile. "I know exactly what I said, Raquel, and I meant it."

Some time later, Liz was sitting in the middle of her bed in total misery. Her eyes were still swollen from the buckets of tears she'd shed, and she was pretty sure she looked like a Muppet. When Romare had declared himself to her so sweetly and unexpectedly, she felt her heart shatter. There was no way in hell he was ever going to understand why she'd concocted the ludicrous persona she'd adopted to go on *Meet Your Mate*. It didn't even make sense to her anymore; she couldn't justify it in any kind of articulate fashion because in the bright light of the morning it made no sense. It was just incredibly lame. How was she supposed to tell him the truth now? Why hadn't she told him the truth before they had made love? She hiccuped and felt the tears coming again, interspersed with a harsh laugh that bordered on hysteria. All her life she'd been levelheaded, sensible, and responsible. Why when she had decided to do something loony did she have to blow the biggest thing that had ever happened to her?

Before she could start going full blast with the tears her doorbell rang, followed by pounding. With her box of tissues under her arm she went to the door and looked out the peephole, frowning when she saw Fletcher. Holding a tissue to her nose, she opened the door and snapped, "What are you doing here?"

Fletcher let out a low whistle as he stared at Liz. "Good Lord, what happened to you? Are you sick? You look like you got the plague or something." His concern was evident in the expression on his face, but Liz couldn't have cared less.

"Go away. I'm not sick, my heart is broken," she said bitterly.

Ignoring her command, Fletcher walked past her to the living room, grabbing her free hand and dragging her behind him like a sulky child. He sat her down on the sofa and sat next to her with his arm around her shoulder. "Come on, it can't be that bad. Tell Uncle Fletch all about it," he said soothingly.

Liz tossed the box of tissues into Fletcher's lap and gently patted at her swollen eyelids with tentative fingers. He noticed the move and shook his head. "Yeah, you look pretty bad," he said frankly. "You need to tell me why you look like this so I know if I have to go kick somebody's ass." He was dead serious, too, but Liz wasn't impressed.

"Can you kick your own behind? Because this is your entire fault, you know. I met the most wonderful man I'm ever going to meet in my life, and I've blown the whole thing because I was trying to prove a point to you. It's all your fault because you blackmailed me," she said with a loud sniff.

Fletcher had to work really hard to conceal a smile; she looked so forlorn and so bedraggled it was kind of cute in a perverse way. The infamous ponytail was gone at last and her wavy black hair sprang out like it was escaping from slavery. Her eyes were puffy slits, her nose was bright red, and her lips were swollen, too; but despite it all, she was still beautiful, even clad in a raggedy Michigan State sweatshirt and Western Michigan University sweatpants. He took his life in his hands to probe at her even more. "It sounds like you really like this guy, Lizzie."

Liz looked at him with unconcealed disgust in her puffy eyes. "Did we just meet? Of *course* I like him. I'm crazy about him," she sniffled. "And he's going to despise me once he finds out what a big liar I am. Especially since we...well, especially now." Her eyes shifted to her toes, which suddenly became the object of her intense scrutiny.

Fletcher knew evasion when he saw it and raised both his eyebrows as he turned Liz's face to his. "Since you what, Lizzie? Did you and this guy, umm, have sex?"

Liz's lip trembled and she looked more miserable than before. "It wasn't sex. It was better than sex. It was incredible, it was fantastic, and it was beautiful. And I'll never have it again because you manipulated me. I hate you, Fletch," she said fiercely. "And I hate me even more because I'm so stupid," she sobbed as the tears started again.

"Okay, Lizzie, dang, please stop doing that," Fletcher mumbled as he put his arm around her and tried to hold her to make her stop crying. "Why didn't you just tell him the truth, sweetie? If he's as wonderful as you say he is, he'd understand, wouldn't he?"

Liz sat straight up and snatched a handful of tissues out of the box. "Yeah, right. That would've been a great conversation. 'Okay, Romare, see what had happened was I was tryna make you look stupid 'cause I have a really low opinion of men and I was tryna, you know, do my thang.' Oh, that's a great explanation. I'm sure he'll go for that," she said with acid irony.

Fletcher gave her a gentle shake and insisted she go take a shower. "Stand under some serious hot water and don't come out until you've calmed down. You startin' to scare me, girl."

Liz blew her nose inelegantly. "That's right, it's all about you," she grumbled. However, a shower did sound pretty good. Without another word to Fletcher, she rose and left the room. She stumbled her way into the bathroom and got in, letting the hot water beat down on her head for a long time before lathering up with the expensive shampoo she got from Tasha. The tension in her neck and shoulders eased away, and the horrid, clogged up feeling that always arrived after a huge cry also disappeared. By the time she was seated at the dressing table in her peach and mint green bedroom, she felt like a new woman. She combed a leave-in conditioner in her air and let it air-dry while she put on a generous application of her favorite scented lotion. By the time she put on a pair of khaki walking shorts and a hot-pink tank top, she was relieved to see she still looked human. Her face flamed up as she recalled the appalling scene in front of Fletcher, of all people. *Maybe he won't use it against me*, she thought. She laughed out loud, knowing Fletcher would dog her about it for the rest of her life.

She left the bedroom and headed for the kitchen. Her little tantrum had roused her appetite, and she was hungry as a Bull Moose. Her hands shoved in her back pockets, she stared at her bare feet as she walked down the hallway, which was why she screamed bloody murder when she encountered Fletcher in the kitchen making breakfast.

"You got some serious issues, woman. Sit down and eat."

9

Liz flushed bright red again and took a seat at the breakfast bar. "I'm sorry, I didn't know you were still here," she said lamely. "You surprised me. And you cooked for me?"

He had, indeed, presenting her with two slices of seven-grain toast with cashew butter, a dish of yogurt with wheat germ, and one of her favorite things in the world, a smoothie. This one was made with blueberries and strawberries blended with ice and black cherry concentrate. "Fletcher, this is amazing. Thank you so much," she said warmly. After saying grace she tore into the food like the starving woman she was.

He watched her while she wolfed it down and waited until her intake slowed somewhat. "That must have been some night," he said dryly.

Liz was now calm enough to truly regret opening her big mouth to Fletcher. She eyed him warily as she ate the last bite of toast, slightly encouraged by the benign look on his face. "It was," she said in a small voice.

"So how did you leave things?"

Liz sighed as she reached for the smoothie. She stared into its icy and fragrant depths as she began speaking. She was reliving the quiet, tender moments she and Romare had shared that morning. "We decided we were going to honor our commitment to stay away from each other for the week before the final taping. And after that we'd start seeing each other for real. We thought the week apart would prove that we had something worthwhile, something to build on," she reported glumly.

"Sounds like a good plan to me. Makes me think this guy is serious about you, Lizzie. And it also gives you a good week to come up with a coherent explanation for your lame behavior, so quit looking like you lost your best friend and get busy. Surely a woman with your skills can come up with a way to tell the truth, apologize, and ask for his forgiveness while you're letting him know how much you love him," he said quietly.

Liz gave him a radiant smile and her face lit up. "You're right, Fletch. For once you're absolutely right. I can do this, I know I can," she said with a burst of her normal animated energy. "And I do love him, you know. Wait until you meet him; he's an amazing guy. I think we're perfect for each other, just wait and see."

"Just wait until you meet her. She's the one," Romare said with a big smile.

"Look, man, I've known you all my life and I've never seen you like this. Are you sure you're not just trying to win this bet?"

Romare gave the man across the table an evil look. "If you weren't my blood, I'd pound you. Cousin or not, you're coming real close to disrespecting my lady, and I'm not having it. Not today, junior."

His cousin raised both hands in surrender. "Damn, I struck a nerve, huh? I meant no harm, but when you bet us that you could go on *Meet Your Mate* and go out with a strange woman without any of your usual extra-picky criteria, we were pretty sure you were gonna be handing over some serious money."

Romare made an impatient gesture before picking up his glass for a deep swallow of iced tea. "Forget the stupid bet, would you? I'm trying to tell you I've met the woman I've been looking for my whole life, and you're talking about some moronic jackassery you and my thickheaded brothers roped me into. I want to talk about Raquel," he said impatiently.

"By all means, let's hear about your dream girl."

"She's a *woman*, not a girl. I thought she was a typical self-absorbed Hollywood hoochie when I first met her, but she's nothing like that. She's funny and smart and fearless. She can talk about anything, she's well-read, and she has a great appetite. Raquel will eat anything, and she never says she's on a diet or any of that junk." Romare stopped and glared at the burst of laughter from across the table. "You think that's funny but you don't know how irritating it is to me to watch a woman pick at her food and pretend to eat. I'm a chef, man; I need someone in my life who can appreciate a good meal. Eating is like making love, if you know how to do it right. It's sensual, sexy. You can tell a lot about how a woman is in bed by the way she eats," Romare said with a faraway look in his eyes.

"T.M.I., T.M.I., that's *way* too much information for me. I don't need to know about your sex life."

Romare felt a little heat along his cheekbones. Revealing his night of exquisite passion was the last thing he intended to do, even to a close relative. That information was much too private to be discussed. He had too much love for Raquel to dishonor her in any way.

"Yeah, well, I just love the way she eats, the way she smiles, and I love her eyes. She has the most incredible eyes I've ever seen. Big, black eyes that look right through you," he said thoughtfully. "She has the most honest eyes I've ever seen. Just beautiful."

"So what are you gonna do now that the show is over? Are you gonna stay in touch or what?"

Romare gave his tablemate a look of disdain. "*Hello?* Have you heard nothing I've said? We're going to be together, you idiot. We're going to finish up our commitment to that stupid show, which is basically to show up and say we had a wonderful time. Then it's just us. I want to take her to Napa Valley for a long weekend, and then who knows. We start the rest of our lives together."

He stopped talking to inspect the steaming entrée placed before him, eying his tilapia filet, green beans, and rice pilaf hungrily. He completely missed the look of speculation he was getting from across the table.

As they ate the conversation veered from one thing to another and the afternoon passed pleasantly. Romare ended up picking up the check because his cousin had to answer the call of nature and got stopped by a couple who remembered him from his L.A. Lakers days.

As the two men were leaving the restaurant, a hand on his arm startled Romare.

"Hey, that was supposed to be on me. Let me give you some money," his cousin offered.

Stepping out into the bright sunlight, Romare refused the money, saying it was no big deal. "Since you and my brothers are already in my debt, don't worry about it," he said with a smug grin.

Stung, his cousin pulled a couple of fifties out of his wallet and handed them to Romare. "Just take this as a down payment. You ought to be glad we made the bet; you never would have met your dream girl otherwise. And when do I get to meet her anyway?"

Romare took the money and stashed it in his money clip. "She's my woman, not my girl. And unless you can act like you have some home training, you don't get to meet her. Thanks, though, I'm sending her flowers with this money. I'm outta here. Call me later." The two men shook hands as they parted company, and it was plain to anyone who might have been observing them that they were very close, the best of friends.

Tasha looked around the trendy restaurant and had to smile; there were so many wannabes and wish-they-weres in the dining room it wasn't funny. "Thanks again for lunch, Liz. I told you it wasn't necessary, but I sure am enjoying it."

"You deserve it for putting up with me. I've been a total idiot these past few weeks. Now that I've had time to chill a little and assess my situation, I've calmed down. A *lot*," she assured her friend.

Liz really did look like her normal self. Her shining hair was back in its usual stacked bob, she was wearing her regular chic but understated attire, and she was fairly shimmering with happiness. She dug into her chilled avocado half stuffed with crab salad and closed her eyes in bliss. "This is delicious, but Romare can make things that taste way better than this. He's an amazing cook," she said dreamily.

"You don't say," Tasha murmured wryly. "I'll bet he can leap tall buildings in a single bound, too," she teased.

Liz waved her hand at Tasha and her eyes crinkled in acknowledgment of Tasha's joke. "Go ahead and make fun of me, I don't care. I'm madly in love and I don't care who knows it. Romare is truly a man worth loving. He's so smart and well mannered and ambitious and talented. He's thoughtful and kind, and despite the fact that he's extremely handsome, he's genuinely sweet. He's everything I ever wanted in a man, and I'm so lucky to have found him," she said softly. She stared at the bite poised on her fork, then put the fork down to look Tasha full in the face.

"I'm not afraid to tell him anymore, Tash. I know exactly what I'm going to say and I know he's going to understand and forgive me because that's the kind of man he is. I can't wait for you to meet him; I know you're going to like him, I just know it."

They talked for another hour as they finished their leisurely lunch, and then they both had to leave. "I've been gone all day; I was taping a summit meeting with other minority television and movie producers. It should be interesting; it's going to be on CNN tomorrow. I need to get back to the studio to see what chaos has ensued since I've been gone. And I need to start a production schedule for my series. Since I did Fletch his favor, he has to grant me my wish," she gloated as they walked toward the entrance of the restaurant.

Tasha smiled wickedly. "Hmm, that makes him your fairy godfather, doesn't it?"

Liz grimaced. "Eww, if all fairy godmothers looked like that there would be no fairy tales."

They were on the sidewalk now and turned to give each other their customary hug good-bye when Liz saw something across the street that made her turn statue-still while all the color drained out of her face.

"Honey, what's the matter?" Tasha cried, startled by the change in Liz.

"That's Romare across the street. And that's Fletcher he's with. What are they doing together?" Liz said in a dead voice as she watched them shake hands.

"Liz, what does that mean? I didn't know they even knew each other," Tasha said, staring at the two men.

Liz laughed, a hollow and painfully bitter sound. "Don't you see? I've been played, Tasha. They got me good."

10

Romare was clad in his usual towel sarong, standing in his favorite spot on the balcony of his apartment, sipping his morning coffee. Two days had passed since the final *Meet Your Mate* date with Raquel, two very long and lonely days. He had no idea it was possible to miss someone so much, but he hated not seeing Raquel, not hearing the sound of her voice, not feeling her warmth or smelling the beautiful fragrance he now associated with her. He stared out at the scenery, but it all looked like Raquel's face. He laughed at his overheated imagination and went back into the living room. He had a couple of hours to kill before leaving for his class, so he picked up the remote control to catch some CNN before it was time for him to get dressed.

Adjusting the towel around his waist, he took another swallow as he watched the big-screen TV. It looked like a panel discussion of some kind, and it was intriguing to him because all of the participants were people of color. Focusing on the words of the moderator, he sat down on the sofa, making sure the towel stayed between his skin and the leather. He brought the cup to his mouth while the moderator introduced another participant.

"It is now my extreme pleasure to introduce a person who really needs no introduction to this panel. For the benefit of our viewers, however, I'm more than happy to cite just a few of her accomplishments. For several years she's been responsible for some of the most respected and innovative programming in the industry. She's won several prestigious awards including two Emmys, a Trumpet award, an Image award, and a Peabody. Now she's breaking new ground in her role of executive producer of Net Productions, owned by none other than Fletcher Raymond. Please welcome Elizabeth Raquel Walker."

Romare dropped the coffee cup and his jaw in the same instant. The camera was trained on a stunningly beautiful woman with a brilliant smile and a fantastic head of hair worn in a tousled style that set off her perfect features, especially her eyes. Those eyes belonged to Raquel, but there they were in this Elizabeth woman's face. Raquel or Elizabeth, or whatever she was calling herself today, that was *his* woman on the television screen. He forced himself to listen to the discussion and was grimly amused at how brilliantly articulate she was. She was insightful, cogent, and totally fascinating. *Production assistant, hunh? I got your production assistant right here*, he thought angrily. *She works for Fletch, my own cousin. This was a setup from start to finish. I don't know who they think they're playing with, but playtime is over, starting right now.*

The anger, pain, and humiliation Romare felt was equaled only by the rage Liz experienced. One of the first things she did was to put Romare into her Chain of Fools file, placing him front and center. It didn't really help, though; she was still full of pain and fury at his betrayal.

She was so undone by what she'd witnessed at the restaurant that Tasha thought she might become ill. Even after two days, her reaction was still the same, she showed no signs of calming down. Tasha tried to reason with her, but it was out of the question.

"Liz, what did Fletcher say when you asked him about it? I mean, when you asked him how he knew Romare?" Tasha asked in a concerned voice.

Liz stopped her pacing to turn on Tasha with an ugly grimace on her face. "Ask Fletcher? I didn't ask him anything. Questions you know the answers to you don't need to ask, do you? Besides, he's out of the country until the end of the week."

Tasha looked at Liz reproachfully. "That's a lame excuse and you know it. You could get hold of him if he was on Jupiter, so saying you can't get it touch with him is a bunch of...of...*stuff*."

Liz had to smile then. Using the word *stuff* was as close as Tasha ever came to swearing, so Liz knew her friend was running out of patience. She couldn't blame Tasha, though; Liz had been acting a true prima donna since they'd seen Romare and Fletcher together. "Tasha, you're right, I could call Fletch if I wanted to, but I don't want to. I don't want to know why he did this to me, I don't want to hear him try to lie his way out of this, and the bottom line is, I don't want to see his face again, period. Besides setting me up and tricking me in the worst way possible, he broke my heart. Fletch was more than my boss, he was my friend, a true friend, or so I thought. I can't even stand the thought that someone so close to me could deceive me like that," she said sadly.

Because Tasha was also a good, true friend, she had to push Liz a little more. "Okay, so you don't want to talk to Fletcher. But what about Romare? Liz, even as mad and hurt as you are, you can't deny you love him. You also can't make me believe he doesn't care about you. Doesn't he have the right to tell his side of the story?"

The two women were in Liz's kitchen, indulging in Liz's favorite cure for whatever ailed you, a smoothie. She was making a lethal mixture of watermelon, frozen Bing cherries, strawberries, black cherry concentrate, lime juice, and pomegranate juice. While Tasha was making her case, Liz had just added some ice to the mixture and put the top on the blender container. She curled her lip and turned it on, the loud motor masking the steady stream of profanity that she muttered under her breath. Finally, she turned off the blender and poured the bright red icy contents into two huge glasses. She stuck long, brightly colored straws into the concoctions, offering one to Tasha.

"No, he doesn't get to tell his side of the story. What could his side possibly be? He and Fletcher set me up, I'm telling you. You saw it yourself, Tash. There they were as big as day. It was obvious they knew each other, and it was just as obvious that Fletcher handed Romare money. It doesn't take a genius to figure out they were up to something," she said furiously. "I may have been a big enough fool to fall in love with him, but that's all over."

Tasha stirred her smoothie with the straw and stared at Liz, who was looking more wrought up than ever as she cleaned the kitchen. Her movements were quick and aggressive, and she looked ready to attack someone.

"Liz, are you telling me that you're willing to let this man walk out of your life just because he happens to know Fletcher? Come on, Liz, you can't throw away a chance at happiness just because you *think* he did something wrong. You owe it to yourself and to him to find out what's going on. Besides, how are you going to avoid discussing this with Fletcher? You work together every day, and he'll be back in town in a couple of days. You'll have no choice but to talk it out with him," Tasha reminded her.

"Oh, but that's the beauty part," Liz said with a bravado that didn't quite reach her troubled eyes. "When Fletcher gets back, I'll be gone. I've handed in my resignation, although he won't see it until he gets back. I'm going to go on the stinkin' *Meet Your Match* show so I can tell Mr. Romare Alexander what I think of him in front of the whole country, and then I'm leaving California for good. I've had enough of Fletcher, enough of his manipulations, and enough of this place. I'm outtie," she said, raising her smoothie in a weak salute before wiping at the unexpected tears that gathered in her eyes.

Romare's bad mood echoed in the tone of his voice when he answered his cell phone. He fairly barked a hello into the mouthpiece, not caring what the caller thought of the sound. The caller, however, was his brother Adrian, who knew when his brother was bent out of shape about something.

"What's wrong, Rom? Don't bother to say nothing because I know you too well. What's up?"

"Aww, don't play like you don't know what's going on," Romare shouted. "I had no idea you idiots were this pathetically eager to win one of these simple-minded bets, but I should have known. You all sold me out for chump change. Are you proud of yourselves?"

Adrian's confusion was plain in his voice. "Romare, man, what are you talking about? Yeah, we always like to win a bet, but we didn't do anything underhanded. What makes you think we did? We'd never sell out our own brother. We may not like you all that much, but we do love you, you big ape. What's going on out there?"

"Okay, I'm gonna take your word for it. But when I tell you what's been going on out here, you'll see why I had my doubts. Fletcher was the one who arranged the bet, right? He's the one who arranged for me to go on his new reality show *Meet Your Mate* and told me that I was going to be hooked up with someone I would have nothing in common with, someone I would try to dump at the earliest opportunity, remember?"

"Of course I remember, that's why we took the bet. We knew we were gonna win because you're impossible to please. It was easy money. As picky as you are, there was no way you were going to meet someone you really liked on the show; all we had to do was sit back and wait. So what happened with the show? We can't wait for the premiere; we plan on bootlegging copies at the family reunion," he cracked.

Romare gave a short, harsh laugh. "That's about par for you jokers. Whatever, man. Anyway, I go on the show determined to make the best of the situation no matter who I'm paired with. And I have to tell you, I wasn't too thrilled with what I pulled. She was one of those music video-lookin' chicks with the fake hair and fake-looking boobs and clothes that look like something an out-of-work hooker would wear, right? She was just this side of looking cheap; real sexy, but no substance. But she did have a good personality and she seemed to be able to understand big words, so I was encouraged. Then we went on our first date and had a ball."

"So where did you take her?" Adrian inquired.

"We went to Disneyland, believe it or not. She even changed clothes, put on jeans and a T-shirt, and we stayed all day and had a blast, just like two school kids. On our next date we went to Santa Anita Raceway in her car. And get this, she drives a ragtop," Romare said reverently.

Adrian was impressed. "So what's the problem? Sounds like she's really a match for you. What's the problem, is she on a weird diet or something?"

Despite his mood, Romare laughed. "No, man, she has a great appetite and she really enjoys eating, which makes her incredibly sexy. She's funny, adorable, pretty, smart; she's everything I ever wanted in a woman."

"Dang, man, I never thought I'd hear you say that," Adrian said after a long, low whistle. "You still haven't told me what the problem is. Everything sounds like it's all good."

"Well, it isn't. She went on the program as Raquel Taylor, a production assistant for a TV station. I found out this morning her name is really Elizabeth Raquel Walker and she's the executive producer for Fletch's company. I was set up, Adrian. It was all a fake, every bit of it."

"Fletch set you up? I can't believe that, Rom. He's always been one of us; he's like our brother, I can't believe he'd do that."

"If it hadn't happened to me, I wouldn't believe it either. It was just too smooth, Adrian," Romare agreed.

"So how did you find out? And what are you going to do about it?"

Romare explained about seeing the panel discussion and his reaction upon realizing that Raquel and Elizabeth were one in the same. "And yeah, I plan to get my own back, don't even worry about it. Fletcher's sorry tail is out of the country, so you don't have to worry about me wringing his neck just yet, but come Friday when the final show is taped I plan to get mine. Nobody treats me like a play toy and gets away with it."

"Yeah, Rom, I get that, but suppose it wasn't a fake? Suppose the woman really cares about you?"

Romare gave a short laugh that was more like a cry of pain. "She'd have to be the world's best actress to pull that one off. She's good, but not that good, and I'll prove it on Friday."

11

Friday morning came much more quickly than Liz anticipated. She'd put the few days into good use, though; she had packed up her personal belongings at Net Productions so that she could make a clean getaway after she told Fletcher off for old and new. She planned on letting him have it after the taping of *Meet Your Mate*. The first thing on her agenda was to excoriate Romare on the air, letting him know exactly what she thought of the cruel practical joke played on her. Then she was going to rip Fletcher Raymond into a million pieces with the sharp side of her tongue and walk out the door a free woman. As much as she loved her job, there was no way she could work for a sleazy creep like him.

She was sitting in front of her dressing table, trying to figure out how best to conceal the dark circles under her eyes. They looked bruised and pulpy, like she hadn't slept in days, which she hadn't. She'd been tortured by memories of the tender love she'd shared with Romare, and she would wake in tears and toss and turn the rest of the night.

Sighing deeply, she dipped her washcloth into the small container of water and ice she'd been using to draw the puffiness out of her face. *Get it together, girl. You can't go out there looking like a waif. You have to look powerful and in control, so cut out the sniveling. Put on your big girl panties and get it over with.*

Liz hadn't had many serious relationships, and she always knew that when she gave her heart away it was going to be powerful, all-consuming, and forever. That's why she was so hurt by Romare's betrayal. He was the first man she'd ever wanted in her life for always, and he turned out to be a jerk. And as for Fletcher, well, when this was all over it would be a long time before he tried to play someone again. *Yeah, right. I can cuss him until I'm blue in the face and it won't mean anything to him because he's a heartless monster. I'm better off without him in my life.*

She finally put down the washcloth and patted her face dry to begin to repair the ravages of the past few days. She carefully applied moisturizer, a special undereye treatment to reduce puffiness, and a very light coating of foundation. A little concealer and a dusting of powder made her face look normal, even to her own critical eye. She took longer than usual with her eye makeup and was satisfied when they stood out, large and luminous, although lacking their normal sparkle. She lined her lips and blended it in, although the gloss wouldn't go on until after she was dressed. The outfit she selected was laid out on the bed, and anyone could see it was more a uniform than a dress; this was what a woman wore when she went to war. And there might be a thin line between love and hate, but the line between love and war was even thinner, and as far as Liz was concerned, this conflict was to the death. She was taking no prisoners.

Everything about the studio looked the same to Liz, but everything was different. The smarmy host, Wes Bradley, was the same, with his capped teeth, his expensively bland outfit, and his lacquered hair. The boringly decorated set was the same, as was the politely robotic studio audience who seemed to find every single world Wes spoke captivating because they laughed in an annoyingly chipper manner after each of his lame quips. Everything felt different to Liz, though, because of what she had to do. She had come to the show with but one purpose in mind, to rip into Romare and expose him for the conniving heel he really was. She was shaky inside and out as it came closer to the time for her to say the words she'd rehearsed over and over, and she was determined not to let her nerves show. And if Wes was to be believed, she'd succeeded.

"Well, Raquel, you certainly look beautiful this evening. That dress is something else," he praised.

She was wearing a seafoam green dress with wide-set straps that met behind her neck, a tight bodice, and a body-skimming skirt with a slit on the side. This dress meant business; it was a dress one wore to attract and hold every man's attention and to hell with what anyone thought. When she'd slithered onto the set wearing it, the audience went wild, which was what she'd intended, but now she despised the scrutiny.

"So, you and Romare have had three dates and no contact between the dates or after the last one. Now we get to hear your side of the story. Were you successful? Did you meet your mate, or did you have three horrible dates? What say you, Raquel?"

She took a deep breath and was about to deliver the speech she'd rehearsed when suddenly she caught a glimpse of a very tall, very dark, handsome man waiting to come onstage. Their eyes locked and the world fell away. No one else existed except Romare, the man to whom she'd given her heart, the man who'd turned her life upside down and taken her to a place she'd never been before, a place she thought didn't exist. She forgot where she was, forgot the silly little man next to her, forgot everything except the moments she'd spent with Romare.

"Raquel? Whoo-hoo, we're still here, honey, where'd you go?" Wes said with a nervous giggle.

With a little sigh, she turned to Wes. "I had an incredible time with Romare. He was kind, attentive, and a total gentleman. He's brilliant, talented, and has a way of making a woman feel like a queen. I...I..." Her voice faltered and she tried to continue speaking over the lump in her throat.

"My goodness, someone had a good time, didn't they?" Wes sounded like his usual gossipy self, but there was genuine concern in his voice as he looked at Liz. "Here, honey, have some water," he urged her, handing her a glass of ice water heavily beaded with moisture.

She tried to express her thanks, but it wasn't necessary because by now Romare had joined them onstage. He didn't speak, he just held out his hands to Raquel, who rose to accept his embrace.

"I'm so sorry," she whispered so only he could hear.

"You don't owe me an apology. I love you," he whispered back. Heedless of the noise from the audience, he bent his head to hers and took her mouth in a long, sweet kiss.

They might have gone on kissing for a lifetime but Wes's insistent voice finally penetrated their haze of passion. "Well, Romare, I take it you feel the same way," he said loudly and jovially.

Romare and Liz looked at him with slightly dazed expressions until they remembered where they were and what they were supposed to be doing. Flustered, they sat down next to each other on the long sofa, and Romare put his arm around her protectively. He kissed her cheekbone one more time, then turned his attention to Wes.

"I'm sorry, what did you say?" he asked politely.

"I asked if you felt the same way about Raquel, and I can see that you do. Why don't you tell us about your dates?" Wes asked gamely.

Giving each other ravishing smiles, they did indeed describe their dates, at least the part they could share with the world. A lot of things were just too private to be discussed. Finally, Wes asked them what was next on the agenda.

Romare smiled at Liz and kissed the back of her hand before answering. "What's next? Marriage, family, happily ever after."

The audience *oohed* and *aahed* while Wes said a reverent "wow." "You two met about three weeks ago and you've basically had three dates and you're ready to walk down the aisle? I'm impressed, but a little skeptical. Raquel, we haven't heard from you on the subject. Are you ready to make a commitment like this?"

Liz touched Romare's cheek and kissed him lightly. "Yes, I am. Big wedding or small?"

"Huge, and my cousin Fletcher is paying for it," he said with a grin.

"Your *cousin* Fletcher?" Liz's eyes grew wide.

"Yes, *Elizabeth*, my cousin. You and I have a lot to talk about, sweetheart."

Some time later, they were in Liz's living room, their arms around each other as they kissed and talked about the events that had led to so much misunderstanding and unhappiness.

"My brother Adrian was the one who had sense enough to call Fletch and get everything straightened out. See, my brothers and Fletch have a habit of making bets on anything and everything. And my love life is one long joke to them; they think I'm doomed to being the eccentric bachelor uncle because they say I'm too picky. So with Fletch's help, they thought of this brilliant idea to scam some money out of me," he admitted.

Liz was more interested in tasting Romare's skin than talking, but she wanted to hear the whole tale, so she forced herself to listen. "So you were determined to be nice to whoever you were matched up with just to win a bet, is that right? And then I came out looking and acting like a chickenhead," she laughed. "You poor thing, I must have scared you half to death."

It was Romare's turn to laugh as her fragrance wound its way through his senses, arousing him to a dangerous level. "No, you didn't scare me, and that's what was so scary. You didn't look like the kind of woman I usually go for, but you were so smart and funny I couldn't resist you. And you were so much fun to be with. That day at Disneyland was still one of the best dates I've ever had." He kissed her thoroughly then, pulling her into his lap and tangling his hands in her hair for the very first time. When they pulled apart he groaned in pleasure as Liz boldly straddled him and leaned into his warmth.

"I love this hair, Elizabeth. It's so sexy and natural; it's just like you. And I love the name Elizabeth. Very regal and feminine," he murmured.

Liz rubbed her face against him and sighed. "No one calls me Elizabeth. Everyone calls me Liz or Lizzie."

"I like Elizabeth, but I'll call you anything you like as long as I can make you Mrs. Alexander," he said in a deep, sexy voice that made Liz's eyes fill with tears.

"Are you sure, Romare? Really sure? Are we crazy to think this is the real thing? I mean meeting on that stupid show, of all things. How do we know we're not just caught up in the whole thing?"

Romare smoothed his big hands up and down her thighs and didn't answer for a moment, he was too busy looking into her astonishing eyes and loving what he saw reflected there. Finally, he spoke. "I know this is right, Elizabeth. The fact that you're concerned about this being true love convinces me. You want this to be real and you want it to last as much as I do. And by the way, the show was a fake. Fletcher has been wanting to introduce us for a long time because he knew we were perfect for each other. That show was just a ruse; it's never going to see the light of day."

Liz pulled away from Romare and stared at him with huge eyes and a wide-open mouth. When she could finally speak, she sputtered, "That moron! Why didn't he just introduce us like a normal person?"

Romare had to kiss her again before he could answer her question. "Because he said we were too hardheaded to meet like regular people. And he has a point, because if he'd told me he had the perfect woman for me, I'd have run with the speed of a thousand people in the opposite direction."

Liz lay against his hard chest and giggled. "This is true. If Fletch had tried to hook me up with someone, I'd have gone into the Witness Protection Program to get away from him. Have you ever met some of Fletch's friends?"

Romare didn't answer, he was too busy savoring the softness of her skin, relishing the warmth of her body, and enjoying the sexual need that was building in his loins. Finally, he spoke. "It may be crazy, but it's right, baby. You're the one for me and I'm the only one for you. We're going to have a wonderful life together. And we're going to have some beautiful kids. You do want babies, right?" He looked at her, suddenly anxious.

"Yes, I want babies, a ton of them. Do you plan on staying in California?" It was her turn to be anxious.

"No, I plan to go back to Chicago and open two restaurants. Do you mind?"

A sigh of relief issued from her lips as she settled back on Romare's body. "I love Chicago. I can work from anywhere. And I'll be closer to my family in Michigan." Liz planted another in a series of kisses on the smooth, dark skin of his irresistible neck. "I do love you. I'm going to love being your wife and having your babies. But you have to promise me one thing, sweetheart."

Romare was trying to figure out how to unfasten her beautiful green dress and smiled triumphantly when the straps came apart in his hands. "I love you, too, Elizabeth, more than I thought possible. And you can have anything you want. What would you like, baby?"

Liz raised herself up and placed her hands on Romare's broad shoulders, ignoring his pleased smile when the dress slipped off her shoulders and slid down to her waist, exposing her pretty breasts with the nipples blossoming just for him. "I want him to pay. I want to get Fletcher good," she said with a wicked smile.

The smile turned into a gasp of pleasure as Romare bent his head to a nipple, stroking it with his tongue before pulling it into his mouth with a tender but intense suction. Before he turned to the other one, he managed to agree. "Oh, Fletch will get his. But first, we're going to get ours. Come here and quit talking, woman, we have work to do."

With a long, soft moan that ended with a very sexy giggle, Liz agreed with all her heart. "You're absolutely right, baby. Let's get busy," she sighed as he carried her into the bedroom.

To My Readers

I hope you enjoyed Liz and Romare's story. I had a lot of fun writing it, because the subject matter is so timely. Modern dating is definitely not for the weak of heart! But sometimes taking a chance on love pays off, as they both find out.

Thanks for your continuing support. The last few months have been really challenging for my family, as some of you know, and your prayers and words are encouragement have meant the world to me.

Stay Blessed!

Melanie
I Chronicles 4:10
MelanieAuthor@aol.com
P.O. Box 5176
Saginaw, Michigan 48603

ABOUT THE AUTHOR

Melanie Woods Schuster currently lives in Saginaw, Michigan, where she works in sales for the largest telecommunications company in the state. She attended Ohio University. Her occupations indicate her interests in life; Melanie has worked as a costume designer, a makeup artist, and admissions counselor at a private college, and in marketing. She is also an artist, a calligrapher, and she makes jewelry and designs clothing. Writing has always been her true passion, however, and she looks forward to creating more compelling stories of love and passion in the years to come.

TO HAVE IT ALL

Kimberley White

*For everyone trying to make sense of this
relationship thing*

1

A $2,000 dress designed by Antonio Marras adorned Lacey Montgomery's slender figure, making her feel as elegant as Grace Kelly. Made in Italy, the fine silk revealed the smoothness of her chocolate milk-colored skin with its V-neckline and scoop back. The floral design patterning the asymmetrical bottom was mostly brown with beige highlights. Black ribbon trimmed the edges. As a child, Lacey dreamt of wearing dresses as dainty as this. Her shoes were Versace—smart slingbacks made of black suede and leather. She'd paid $650 for the privilege of balancing herself on the four-inch heels.

Lacey had it all! This evening she planned on sharing her happiness with her friends in a grand housewarming celebration. She'd invited her friends, including her agent, who, in turn, used it as a promotional springboard. Before Lacey realized what was happening, her guest list included Atlanta natives Spike Lee, Chris Tucker, and Brittany

Murphy. Director Nino Del Padre was expected to drop by, too.

Lacey was the ideal hostess, greeting each guest personally and making sure everyone had a good time. The caterers prepared the food to perfection. The wait staff was efficient and professional.

Lacey's multimillion-dollar mansion was designed for entertaining. People milled around the enormous banquet-size dining room with bay windows overlooking the two-acre backyard. Once night fell, the grounds glowed with strategic lighting, illuminating the pool and tennis court. Many of Lacey's guests were drawn outside to sit by the pool, sipping exotic drinks in the sticky heat. Others awaited her in the tremendous film room. The extensive entertainment center included all the necessary home theater equipment, a bar, and accent lighting. It had been the selling point for Lacey. Once she saw the theater and envisioned a private showing of her screenplay, *The Next Step*, she was sold.

She deserved to splurge some of the $2.5 million advance she'd earned from the sale of her first screenplay. She had waited tables and sold stories to magazines that had folded before they could pay her. She had given so many free writing workshops in an attempt to build her name in the industry, she thought people would start calling her the Goodwill Lady. She'd lost hundreds of dollars entering contests where she never even placed in the top hundred. She searched for three years before she found an agent who agreed her work was commercial enough and well written enough to sign her. Her agent had pitched the script hard, hoping the sale would propel her into the big league, too.

People started talking. The buzz spread from coast to coast until somebody who knew somebody who knew Steven Spielberg heard about it. Seems Spielberg was looking to produce and direct a big drama. Lacey's agent was on a plane to La-La Land the next morning. She pitched the script, and a handshake later, the deal was made. When heavy hitters Harrison Ford, Morgan Freeman, and Hilary Swank signed to star in the project, Lacey knew success was only a box office away.

The movie opened to rave reviews. There were whispers about Morgan Freeman being nominated for an Oscar. *The Next Step* made $50 million in its opening weekend, which made Lacey a big, fat, seven-figure bonus. Eight weeks later, the film had dropped only three places—to number four—in overall weekly ticket sales. With such phenomenal success, the offers began pouring in for Lacey's next screenplay. Her agent giddily announced Ron Howard and Martin Scorsese were both expressing interest in working with her. HBO had been calling, asking her to develop an eight-week dramatic series in the tradition of *Soul Food*.

Lacey had gladly quit her job as a waitress, hired an accountant to manage her newfound wealth, and began living the good life. Her parents kept her grounded, reminding her to stay in church, cherish her family, and remember the people who helped her get where she was. Knowing Hollywood could be fickle and the screenwriting business schizophrenic, she'd decided to purchase a home in Atlanta, where she'd been living since graduating from Clark Atlanta University seven years ago. Her mother had griped about her oldest child throwing away good money on a lavish new lifestyle, *after* Lacey had purchased her parents a home in Tampa, of course—a good distance from the suburbs of Atlanta where she'd chosen to live. She'd purchased her two younger brothers a condo in Ohio, near the campus of Wilberforce University, where they both were majoring in engineering. Her brothers were a year apart, and they had the tendency to use their superior intelligence for luring women instead of academic achievement. The brats had made her teenage years a disaster, but she loved them dearly.

Lacey joined her best friend, Joel, in the film room just

before the credits rolled. "Did I tell you how gorgeous you look tonight?" Joel whispered in the darkness. Of course he was in the front row, always her greatest supporter.

"I still can't believe this is really happening to me." She was the star of her own fairy tale. *The Next Step* had propelled her into the top echelon of the film industry.

"You better start believing it, sister."

"Do you know what else I can't believe?"

"What?"

"I can't believe you wore a suit."

"Had to make an impression. You never know who you might meet at one of these things." Joel was struggling as an actor, but with his latest television commercial running around the clock, the offers were beginning to trickle in. "This movie is great. I can't believe the writer is my best friend." He hugged her close, kissing her cheek. "You did good."

Lacey pushed him away, ending the sentimentality. They shared mud pies as kids and dating war stories as adults. They didn't hug and kiss and get mushy with each other. "Are you staying over?" she asked. Having all the celebrities mingling in her home, offering congratulations, was wonderful, but she needed sincere, quiet time with her friend. She needed him to help it all sink in.

"I have to get up early to make my flight."

"Flight? Where are you going?"

"I have a flight to New York in the morning. There's a good part in a new off-Broadway stage play I want to audition for. I'm going to stay with some actor friends for a few weeks while I try to get *my* big break." He never begrudged Lacey her success but was hungry for his own.

"But you'll stay tonight?"

"Sure." He pulled his eyes away from the movie screen. "Hey, are you all right?"

"Tired." She rubbed her eyes. "It's been a long evening."

"We'll kick everyone out after the movie."

"You can't ask *famous* people to leave your home."

Many of the artists appearing on the film's soundtrack had stopped by, including Angie Stone, Harry Connick Jr., and Outkast. The party was peppered with writers such as Gary Apple and Lynn Barker. The evening had been interesting, with an eclectic mix of big stars and Lacey's friends—workers from the diner, struggling actors, and not-yet-published writers.

"Lacey, *you're* famous now. You can do whatever you want."

She smiled into the darkness, sinking into the comfort of the plush velvet seat. "I can, can't I?"

When the film ended, Lacey accepted congratulations, thanked everyone for coming, and began ushering her guests to the door. The Southern girl remaining in her didn't like huge crowds and noisy parties. She much more enjoyed a quiet evening of sipping wine and laughing with her closest friends.

After the better part of an hour, everyone had finally gone home. Lacey shed the expensive silk dress and got comfortable in an oversized tee.

"This was the best party I've ever been to," Joel said. They lay next to each other across the bed in one of Lacey's seven guest rooms, staring up at the vaulted ceiling. They'd been holding these private discussions since they were young enough for it to be all right for a girl and boy to have an overnight in the same bed. They'd been heartbroken when their parents announced it wasn't proper for boys and girls to have sleepovers together in the same room. They had followed their parents' rules, but as soon as they were old enough to leave home, they had begun retreating into their private world again.

Lacey turned to him. "I've got it all."

"It would seem so." He turned his head to meet her gaze. "Too bad you're not happy."

"What are you talking about?"

He screwed his mouth to the side, mocking her with his doubt. "I know you, Lacey."

"I'm very grateful for what I have. I've achieved so much, and at such an early age. There aren't many twenty-nine-year-olds with a blockbuster movie on their résumé."

"Your career has taken off."

"Yes, it has."

"This house is unbelievable."

"It's beautiful," Lacey agreed.

"*You're* beautiful, intelligent, and one of the kindest people I know."

"Thank you. Like I said, I have it all."

"Who are you trying to convince: me, or yourself?" He turned onto his side, facing her. He propped his chin on the heel of his hand and stared down at her. "Why are you alone?"

She laughed. "Is this about getting married and settling down? My mother put you up to this, didn't she?"

"No, she didn't. Lacey, I love you. You know I only want the best for you." He tweaked her nose. "You shouldn't be one of those women who declare their work is their life. It's what you're trying to do, and it doesn't fit you."

Lacey rolled over, propelling herself off the bed, and crossed the room. "There's nothing wrong with devoting time to my career."

Joel sat up, drawing his legs onto the bed. "There's something wrong with devoting every minute of your existence to your career." He paused, clearly trying to decide how far to push his point. "What happened with Terrence?"

"Terrence decided he didn't want to be involved with me when I wouldn't agree to help him sell his manuscript. I told him I'm not an editor, or a publishing house. I don't buy manuscripts, and I don't have any clout with anyone who does." She dropped down on the ottoman at the foot of the bed. "You don't even ask me for career favors, and we're best friends."

"Obviously, Terrence was a loser, but—"

"But enough is enough. How many times can I put myself out there? Exposing my heart, only to have it ripped apart over and over again."

"If you keep looking, you'll find the right person, and the only thing he'll want for you is the best."

"Every time I get involved with someone and start to care about him, it ends the same way."

"Anybody who has ever dated has a story to tell. You don't let the losers win. You keep looking for the right person."

"What if there isn't a 'right' person? There's no law that says there's someone for everyone. If I were in one abusive relationship after another, I'd walk away. Emotional abuse is just as bad. It's too hard to open yourself up, thinking you've finally found someone who's real, only to be hurt again. I can't keep letting men abuse my emotions."

"So what're you going to do?"

"Work."

"Give up? Lacey, you're not a quitter. We've been through too much together. I can't let you give up on living." Joel was referring to his brief addiction to cocaine while they were in college. She'd stood by him during that time, fighting the addiction as if it were her own. They'd managed to keep his problem from their parents. It had been a long, grueling battle, but Joel had overcome his addiction and refocused his priorities; now he was living a healthy life again.

"This isn't the same thing."

"You stopped me from throwing my life away. I'm watching you throw yours away. I can't let you give up. You're Rapunzel in the tower." He opened his arms to encompass the mansion. "You've locked yourself inside this mansion, and now you're withering away. We're getting too old for sleepovers."

"It must be the actor in you, because you're being

overly dramatic. I've chosen not to date anymore. It's no big deal."

"You're not taking a break from dating. You've decided writing is your lover—and you're content. It scares me."

"Don't worry about me. I'm living a very fulfilling life."

He twisted his mouth in disagreement again. "I'm looking in your eyes, and I see you're lying to me. Wendy and I are getting along really well—"

"This is about you and Wendy. I should have known."

Joel was beautiful with dark, curly locks, pale skin, and blushing pink lips. Living in Atlanta, where a beautiful man was presumed to be gay, caused him to have to fight off more men than Lacey did. He fell fast when he emotionally connected with Wendy, his Narcotics Anonymous sponsor. For once it wasn't about his boyish good looks. She respected his feelings and supported him through the emotional muck he'd had to wade through to fight his addiction.

"I'm thinking about getting serious with her," Joel announced. "I don't want to leave you out there alone when I do."

"I'm not an emotional cripple. What do you think is going to happen when you get serious? And what do you mean by 'get serious'?"

"I haven't figured out the details, but I'm in love with her and I want to be with her for a very long time."

"Good. I'm happy for you. Don't worry so much about me, Joel."

"Lacey—"

She abruptly changed the subject. "Are you sure you don't need a ride to the airport?" She stood and moved to the door.

"I don't need a ride."

"Wake me up before you leave in the morning."

"Lacey—"

"Joel, I'm fine." She left, closing the door behind her before he could continue. She had everything, after all. A dream career, a fabulous house—How could she not be happy? Joel had her best interest in mind, but he was wrong about her life. She didn't need a relationship to make her happy. She was fine. Women like her defined their lives differently than most. She was a career woman. Years from now the tabloids would write stories about her having a new boy toy on her arm for every red carpet appearance. She'd go through them like Kleenex. While Joel grew old with Wendy and a bunch of kids, she'd be legendary.

But she couldn't lie to Joel, and she couldn't lie to herself. Being fine wasn't good enough.

Joel had succeeded in making her question her new lifestyle. She couldn't sleep with the memories of old boyfriends flooding her dreams and turning them into nightmares. She tried to remember the last time she'd felt the loving embrace of a man. As she rehashed past romances, she couldn't recall one man who had honestly loved her. She remembered the ones who needed a convenient sex partner and had no qualms about lying about their feelings to get one. She thought of the men who cared for her in direct proportion to how much they needed her to do something for them. She pushed away tears for the down low, undercover brother who needed a front to hide his homosexual "experimentation."

She left her bed and made her way to the computer. She had an office downstairs where she did a great deal of her writing, but she most enjoyed having a computer in the sitting room of her bedroom. She did her best story development when the suburb was quiet. When an idea hit her in the middle of the night she could jump up and jot it down quickly.

As she stared at the computer screen this evening, she faulted Joel for stamping out her muse. She always insisted on being honest with herself. She examined her new fame and plentiful blessings and uncovered an emptiness she had been fighting to conceal. Wealth and a successful career hadn't made her happy. It meant nothing without someone special to share it with. No matter how many celebrity parties she'd attended, at the end of the night she came home to an empty house—alone.

Terrence was one long, lonely year in her past. One evening he'd stepped into the diner where she waitressed, dressed in a dark suit that showcased his perfect behind. He flirted, smiling at her with perfect teeth. His arrogance was just enough to get her attention, but not too much to turn her off. At the end of the night, he carried her heart out of the diner in his briefcase. After a while Terrance's arrogance proved to be major overexaggeration. His job in the entertainment business turned out to be as a stagehand at the local children's theater—not a director, as he had led her to believe. Like so many others, he carried a movie script in his briefcase, shoving it in front of anyone who would sit still long enough for him to hand it over.

By the time Lacey had found out how Terrence had deceived her in describing his lifestyle, she'd already developed a fondness for him she couldn't shake—no matter how many warning bells went off. Car repossessed—*ding*. Borrowing money for rent—*ding*. Fired from the children's theater—*ding*. Finding his clothes hanging in her closet—*ding*. Coming home after a long night at the diner and discovering him passed out on her bed after a night of partying—*ding, ding, ding, ding!* Somehow, he'd always managed to convince her with loving touches and sensual kisses that he was a man down on his luck, but that he was trying hard. He needed a good woman to stand by him until he could pull it together, because once he got his break, he'd take her with him into the land of luxury.

When *The Next Step* was optioned, Terrence's touches proved to be opportunistic—not loving. She'd tried to bring him into the business with her, hoping that exposing him to the right contacts would pay off for him. Terrence would dress in his best suit and play the role of supportive boyfriend—until she turned her back. How many times had she found him pinned in a corner with a wannabe starlet? She couldn't count the number of times he'd embarrassed her with some off-color joke. He became the person everyone avoided at parties, until finally, her agent insisted she find another date for publicity events. Terrence didn't take the news too well, but she refused to let him blow her big chance.

Then came the threats. "If you love me, you'd help me make it in the business. I've always promised to take you with *me*." It had worked for a while, and she'd actually tried to casually pitch his script at parties, but once read, it was always rejected. She'd sneaked a peek at it one day— he'd never let her read it because she might subconsciously use his ideas in her own writing, he'd said—and understood why it had been rejected numerous times. It was terribly written, but there was a good underlying story, so she'd offered to help him get it into shape. That's when everything fell apart. Terrence began barking at her during their critique sessions. Women started openly calling her apartment. He began pushing her to use her advance to produce his movie. It all spiraled out of control, but she'd stayed as long as she could because somehow she'd fallen in love with him.

Terrence made her the victim one too many times. She hated being helpless or dependent. When he shattered her heart, she'd realized she didn't do dating well, so she best not do it at all.

In one evening, Joel had made her revisit the need to be needed. He'd made her remember how important it was to share intimate moments with a lover. She was full of love, bursting from it because she had no one to give it to.

Lacey *Googled*, doing research for her new script, but before she knew it, she was browsing online dating services. Maybe the key to finding the right person was remaining anonymous. If the man didn't know about her success or wealth, she could be certain he was interested in her as a person. She wouldn't have to disclose the truth unless something serious came of their dating. Getting to know a man over the Internet could help to eliminate the losers and users, without her first investing her emotions.

Exploring the dating sites became addictive, and before she knew it, she'd been jumping from one dating service to another for over an hour. Finally, she came across ultimatemates.com. Joining this service came with a hefty fee, but she chose it because of its safeguards. Every member was required to complete an extensive personal history, which was used to run a credit and criminal background check before membership was granted. There were also financial limitations. All members must have a verified source of yearly income of no less than six figures.

She hesitated only a moment before deciding to apply for membership. Clicking on the "Successful Matches" page instantly convinced her of the value of Internet dating. Handsome couples, staring at each other with love in their eyes, filled the page. Some had gone on to marry and have children. Many more gave testimony to the professionalism of ultimatemates.com. Letter after letter asked why they had waited to join the exclusive club. Lacey labored over completing the profile, wanting to project the right image. After she submitted her credit card information and completed her profile, she would be notified within twenty-four hours of her acceptance or denial as a member. She perfected the profile, falling asleep at the keyboard.

"Lacey," Joel whispered, gently shaking her shoulders. "It's time for me to leave."

She jerked awake, having the presence of mind to shield the computer screen by putting it on Standby. "I fell asleep." She did that more often than she liked to admit.

Joel grinned. "Get into bed. I have to go, or I'll miss my flight."

"Fly safe."

"Always do." He kissed the crown of her head. "Get some rest." He took long strides to the door. "By the way, you didn't have to turn to the Internet. I could have hooked you up with one of my struggling actor friends."

2

Mikel Bauer was everything to his clients: agent and attorney by contract, but also publicist, career planner, friend, and nurse. As he sat at his desk for the eighteenth straight hour, he realized how tiring being anyone's everything could be. The early morning sun sluiced over his broad shoulders. He wheeled his chair around and propelled himself up. He stood at the expansive window of his office and watched the city wake up, lording over Atlanta's Central Business District skyline, his chest swelling with pride. He put himself in check, remembering to remain humble about his successes. He had worked most of his thirty-two years to reach this point in his life. Being one of the country's top entertainment attorneys came with the hefty price of giving up his personal life. With that one exception, he loved the luxurious world he had created around him.

It wasn't as if his personal life was nonexistent. He dated

so many pretty women that physical appearance was no longer important to him. A beautiful woman had to have more than a flawless face and a perfect body to catch his attention. He'd dated too many starstruck women, only interested in his wealth and his connections. He continuously encountered women who wanted to know exactly what he planned to spend in order to keep her in his life.

He never wanted for physical companionship. He only needed to consult his Palm Pilot if he needed a warm body in his bed. He couldn't deny sex without commitment sometimes fit his needs, but it always left him cold and empty in the morning.

As Mikel waded through memories of his dating career, he came to the sad conclusion that at thirty-two, he had never been in love with a woman. He'd been infatuated. He'd had women infatuated with him. These lopsided relationships always ended in disaster. He'd remained on good terms with one or two—the one or two who hoped an occasional romp in his bed would encourage him to help her become a starlet.

He had grown sick of the dating games and retreated into the world of entertainment law full time—twenty-four hours a day. The first reaction of his friends and employees was to help him snap out of it by introducing him to every pretty, available woman they could find. None satisfied him, so he'd begged off, refusing to be set up anymore. As he increased his hours at the office, his client list grew, helping him to become a wealthy man. He moved his office into the downtown Atlanta high-rise. He currently leased five floors of the building, including the apartment suite on the twentieth floor. He could get more work done if he eliminated the office commute. He buried himself in work, signing top movie stars, athletes, and singers. Everyone he touched turned to gold. He had it all!

It had been one of his staffers who pointed out depriving himself of his manly needs resulted in a grumpy boss not many could tolerate working with. He'd refused to accept any more blind dates, and he seemed to attract only gold diggers, so he shied away from random meetings. Harry, his legal assistant, had turned him on to ultimatemates.com. At first, Mikel had been very happy with the Internet dating club. The women were beautiful and successful. He received a great number of hits and found it hard to answer them all. It worked well with his crazy schedule. He was at his computer most of his waking hours and ultimatemates.com was only a click away.

It hadn't taken long for him to tire of the boring, unimaginative conversations. The chats always went the same way. Get the demographics out of the way, check the income, and then the pornographic sex talk began. He enjoyed sex as much—maybe more—than the next man, but at this point in his life, he needed an emotional connection.

Harry reminded him ultimatemates.com had a good track record of matching up couples and suggested Mikel change his approach to Internet dating. "Instead of answering e-mails, why don't *you* choose who you want to meet?" A novel idea, Mikel had agreed to give it one last shot.

"Were you here all night again?"

Mikel turned away from the window as Harry entered his office. "I finished up those endorsement contracts for the Atlanta Falcons' players."

"I'll get the guys to come in as soon as possible to sign."

"Or you could fly out and meet them after the game in Dallas."

"Sure thing." Harry saluted with a broad smile. "I love my job."

"I'm going to get a couple hours of sleep. What's on the books for today?"

Harry used the stylus to pull up Mikel's calendar on his Palm Pilot. He rattled off a list of unimportant tasks. Together they delegated the meetings among the six attorneys and agents on Mikel's payroll.

"I'll come in for the signing of Tandy's contract," Mikel said as he packed his briefcase. He liked to greet every new client, especially musical artists with the extraordinary talent Tandy promised. New to the jazz scene, Tandy had a voice as stunning as her attractive face. Several record companies wanted to sign her to lucrative contracts. The agent who had discovered her was in for a big bonus. "You're in charge," Mikel said as he left the office.

His humor was lost on Harry. Harry always thought he was in charge—even when Mikel was in the office. He had finished law school last year but hadn't passed the bar. Failing couldn't discount his practical knowledge. Harry was a quick study, and they worked well together. He correctly read Mikel's moods and understood how important delivering quality service with ethical standards was to him.

Mikel collapsed across his bed, fully clothed. He had to stop working so hard. He needed a healthy diversion. That was the last thought on his mind when he drifted off to sleep, the first when he awoke, and it nagged at him as he met with his charming new client Tandy later in the evening. By the time he ended his day and returned to his apartment, it was all he could think of—finding a plush diversion to cure his distraction. He briefly considered making a call to someone from his past, but he understood it would come with strings. If it hadn't worked out the first time, it wouldn't work out just because his body was screaming for a female's touch.

Mikel settled in for the evening with a cold beer and his favorite easy-listening radio station. He typed in ultimatemates.com and took Harry's advice. He ignored the fifteen messages sitting in his mailbox awaiting replies. This time he would be the aggressor. As he scanned the profiles on ultimatemates.com, he acknowledged Harry's wisdom in being the *chooser* instead of the *choosee*. He thought himself a good man, not a perfect man. The women he dated often complained he was too aggressive. He hadn't decided if being aggressive was a positive or negative quality—he had built a very successful business from his aggressiveness. If he wanted to find the right woman, he couldn't suppress his natural personality traits. The woman for him would accept him, faults and all.

There were tons of beautiful, successful women profiled on the site, all ages, shapes, and hues, searching for someone with whom to share their lives. He quickly scrolled past those he'd had encounters with in the past. Those women he knew were not searching for a real relationship, but rather a meal ticket, or a sucker to fleece. He had bluntly explained to them he wasn't that guy and ended their association before it could get going.

He needed fresh faces. He learned how to navigate through the profiles, narrowing his search to women who had joined ultimatemates.com within the past week. He was quickly pulled into a sea of pretty faces. He read each profile as if conducting a life-saving research study. If he chose the wrong woman, he could only blame himself. And then he would have to face the fact that he was inept at dating, and that was not something he wanted to admit. Becoming obsessed with his search, he lost track of time. Finding plenty of beauty, but not making a connection, he reversed his methods. He read the written profiles before looking at the photos.

Once he moved beyond the superficial, he found the perfect woman with one click. Perhaps it was the screen name Brown Sugar that enticed him, her name being as corny as the one he had selected. Her profile was snappy and concise, no flowery language to pad the truth. He could best describe her as "sassy." She described herself as confident. A bit of a loner, but she didn't shy away from a good party. Didn't smoke, and only drank socially. He'd dated a woman who could drink him under the table, and it hadn't been pretty. Brown Sugar enjoyed exploring new territory and sought a match who would be open to introducing her to new experiences. She called herself a passionate but sensible lover. That statement alone made Mikel want to get to know more about her.

She had never been married, and wanted a serious relationship. When she described her perfect match, she didn't mention any physical requirements. She used descriptors such as professional, intelligent, self-assured, and conservative. She preferred a nonsmoker with a good sense of humor. If he had any doubts about contacting Brown Sugar, they were put to rest when he read her final note: I need a man who is confident enough to take charge and gentle enough to surrender.

She worked in the entertainment business. She didn't specify what she did, but one look at her photo told him she had to be a model. A successful model because she met the income requirements of the online dating club. Her hair was stylishly cut into short mahogany curls. She had a bright smile framed by two deep dimples. Her brown skin glowed golden against the dark background. Thick lashes could not hide her big, brown eyes. She portrayed a woman who was strong, intelligent, and loving.

He, admittedly, was a difficult man to love. He worked far too many hours. He could be stubborn and opinionated. He wasn't always politically correct in his relationships, believing being the man carried certain privileges—and responsibilities. These faults he could live with. They had been useful in building his business. Women didn't share the sentiment. The few serious relationships he'd been involved in hadn't survived because of his headstrong personality.

Brown Sugar seemed tough enough to handle a virile man.

Mikel penned an e-mail introduction, swallowed his apprehension, and pressed the SEND button.

Lacey doubled over in laughter. Whatever had possessed her to try Internet dating? Chocolate Dream!

Yeah right. How dare he use the word *chocolate* in vain? He probably was a toad of a man who would be her nightmare. She'd joined ultimatemates. com three days ago, and every inquiry she had received was a joke. Each one began with crude flattery of her looks. Lacey was sure she had enough material to write a bad B movie. She vowed to remove her profile at the end of the month, but for now writer's block had derailed her, and she found herself reading each comedic e-mail. The anonymity of conversing over the Internet allowed her to have a little fun at—she scanned the screen— Chocolate Dream's expense. She rolled her eyes. Chocolate Dream!

Lacey opened Chocolate Dream's e-mail, and a slow smile spread across her face. He certainly wasn't a toad. He was Taye Diggs dark, a rich, mocha cream. Handsome in a brooding way, he hadn't smiled for the picture in his profile. His full lips slanted downward with sulky seductiveness. His jaw was covered with a five o'clock shadow, as if he were too busy to labor over his appearance. But he was wearing a designer suit—a direct contradiction. He looked like a man who took life seriously. He looked like her fantasy man—dangerous, sexy, and sophisticated.

Chocolate Dream started his e-mail by describing himself as a leader, protector, and political rebel. Becoming more intrigued, Lacey sat forward on her elbows, bringing her face closer to the monitor as she read: I have never surrendered to a woman, but I'd be interested in finding out if you were the woman who could make me. He'd actually taken time to read her profile. He scored points for his effort. She read on: You seem the type who doesn't like to waste her time. I can appreciate that. I'm looking for a good woman to have a serious relationship with. I'm not interested in one-night stands, or a quick sexual encounter. I'd like to find a woman who can challenge my mind. I'll honestly tell you I'm a good man, but not perfect. Interested in learning more?

Lacey studied his picture. Of course she wanted to learn more.

Hi.

The dialogue box popped up in the middle of her screen. She had an instant message from—

It's Chocolate Dream. I e-mailed you yesterday on ultimate-mates.com.

Lacey watched the screen, a little freaked out by a stranger contacting her.

Are you there? he asked.

Yes. She hit the SEND button and waited.

Did you receive my e-mail?

Yes.

After a long pause, Am I disturbing you?

No. Lacey punched her thigh. She was a screenwriter who couldn't come up with two good words to put together under pressure.

What are you doing?

Working, she finally typed into the message box.

Me, too.

Lacey stared at the screen unblinkingly.

There?

Yes, she answered without hesitation.

How's this computer dating thing working for you?

You're the first person I've met.

Chocolate Dream didn't respond.

Lacey retyped the message.

I'm your first? he asked.

Yes.

I'll try to make it a good experience for you.

Have you been at this long? While she waited for his reply, she took another look at his photo.

Dated a few. Sarah was the last. She wasn't anything she said she was.

Why not? Lacey found herself asking, truly curious about how and why he'd decided to date a stranger he'd met on the computer. "Computer dating? Instant messaging? Does this guy live on his computer?" she asked aloud.

Got time?

She glanced at the clock and ignored the fact that she should be writing. She told him to spill. An hour later, Lacey was still sitting at her computer typing messages to the man known as Chocolate Dream. She had laughed and laughed as he told her about his blind date with Sarah. He had a strong presence even over cables and wires. *Sarah must be somewhere kicking herself*, Lacey thought. She ate chips while they debated who had the busier work schedule. He'd won hands down. They discussed politics and religion, and surprisingly, had many of the same views. She hadn't had such a stimulating conversation with a man since—since ever.

OK, Chocolate Dream typed. Keep your end of the deal.

She shot forward to reread the message, crushing the bag of chips to her chest. Caught up in good, humorous conversation, what had she promised this stranger?

What deal, Chocolate? she typed.

Forgot so quickly? Or backing out?

Not backing out. Remind me.

I tell you about the blind date, you meet me here tomorrow to chat.

A little while ago she had decided to pull her membership with ultimatemates.com. Now she was actually considering making a computer date with one of the members.

Hellooo?????

He was impatient and she told him so. My, my, afraid I might cancel?

Hell yes. Been chatting for 2 hours. Want to continue this conversation.

Tomorrow...same time.

He replied with a goofy picture of a man salivating, and then signed off.

3

Lacey welcomed any interruption she could get while working on her next screenplay. Matching the success of *The Next Step* would be difficult, and she was letting the pressure get to her. Joel was still in New York auditioning. Her other friends had real jobs and worked during the morning hours. She wandered to the kitchen for a snack, and much needed break. She hadn't typed a decent word in hours. As she stared out at her pool, she found herself wondering what Chocolate Dream was doing. Their chats had been getting longer and longer. They'd moved beyond the superficial and were really getting to know each other.

She knew more about his likes and dislikes than she had ever learned about Terrence. She liked online dating. She could get to know Chocolate without the superficial interfering. Sexual attraction didn't have the chance to overpower her common sense. Without the temptation of sexual exploration, they were free to have real conversations.

She found herself thinking about him a lot during the day. When her characters weren't speaking to her, she would daydream about Chocolate. She was always anxious to find out how his day at work had gone. He was an entertainment attorney and always had an interesting or funny story to tell. Who did he meet with today? Was he negotiating any big deals? Was he aggressive like the D.A. on *Law and Order*? Or was he more subtle and clever?

She longed to pair mannerisms with his photo. Did he look as handsome in person as he did in his photo? Did he have any nervous habits? Her lashes floated downward. What cologne did he wear? How did he dress for a casual date? Would his shirt collar be soft beneath her fingers?

Lacey's eyes popped open. "Am I fantasizing about a guy I met on the computer?" She scolded herself, forcing her mind to become focused and return to work on her screenplay. When she sat down at her computer, Chocolate Dream was there.

Brown Sugar?

I'm here.

Thought you weren't talking to me.

No, away from the computer. How was your day?

A client gave me passes to a movie. *The Next Step.* Great flick. Have you seen it?

Lacey battled the obvious questions, such as who had given him the passes. Who had he gone to see the movie with? And why did she feel so jealous about him sitting in the darkened theater with another woman? She hadn't told Chocolate she was a screenwriter. She certainly hadn't told him she was the writer of the biggest box-office smash since *The Passion of the Christ*. She was enjoying their conversations. She didn't want to find out Chocolate Dream was like the other men in her past: all smiles when they realized she was in a position to do great things for them. The biggest pleasure in online dating was anonymity.

Yes, I've seen it, Lacey answered.

Did you enjoy it?

Yes.

We should see a movie together. When she didn't reply, he added, Some day.

It was the first reference of them meeting in person. Somehow, online dating seemed safe. Lacey could excel at a relationship this way. Meeting Chocolate meant making it too real, and right now she was enjoying the fantasy.

What do you think about that? he asked. Us getting together.

She watched the screen, frozen with indecision.

Didn't mean to push you. Maybe we could start with a phone call...

A phone call? How had she not considered he would want to advance their chats to real, live interactions? The security of communicating over cables and wires would be obliterated. This was usually the time in the relationships when she discovered the guy she believed was honorable was really deceptive. She had to decide how to handle merging her online fantasy world with her real world. She could keep Chocolate Dream at arm's length—or keyboard length. Or she could take a leap, hoping that this time it would pay off, and agree to move their relationship forward.

Truth was, she really did enjoy chatting with him. Their conversations were fresh, and never boring. His intelligence was obvious as he related his dealings with famous clients. But she had been deceived before. Once he learned she was a successful screenwriter, he'd probably want her to introduce him to celebrities so he could build his business off her back. Suddenly, an attraction of minds would turn into an instant opportunity for him. She'd been the woman men adored because of her connections. She knew what it felt like to be loved because of her status. She understood why men hated gold diggers. She didn't want her newfound connection with Chocolate shattered.

When you're comfortable, Chocolate Dream typed. Sorry. Didn't mean to spook you.

You didn't.

Our conversations have been going so well, I forgot we're strangers. You don't know anything about me. You have to be safe. You have to feel comfortable.

Lacey wondered if she had overreacted. She certainly wasn't afraid of Chocolate Dream. She would take the same precautions in dating him as she would if she had met him at a party or the video store. Her fear lay much deeper—within the protective shell of her heart.

A clear compromise popped into her head. You could give me your number.

And you can use it when you're ready.

When Joel returned from New York, he made arrangements to meet Lacey at her favorite laptop café. She often took her work there and contemplated story-lines over an American Club sandwich and vanilla milk-shake. Her new script was progressing, but too slowly. She would not meet her self-imposed deadline. Her agent's telephone calls were coming more frequently and sounding more frantic. She could smell another financial windfall.

Lacey wasn't ready to consider any other offers until she got a handle on the current script she was writing. Instead of the industry leaders seeing it as what it was—she needed time to write—they felt she was being elusive. Had she already signed with another production company? Were actors seeking her out in hope of making their first feature film? Did she have her eyes set on Cannes? Nothing makes Hollywood hungrier than unavailability. The more offers she refused, the more that poured in. If she refused a meeting, they wanted to fly to Atlanta to meet with her. The constant pressure was taxing, making it harder to write.

Lacey enjoyed speaking at the local colleges and universities. The students were hungry, and appreciative. Hollywood hadn't tainted their visions yet. Plus, speaking helped stimulate her creative process. She gladly accepted all the speaking engagements her agent could arrange.

"Guess who?" Joel's hands covered her eyes.

They greeted with a long hug. Joel wore a pair of beat-up jeans slung low on his narrowly thin waist. His tight tee had an obscene word splattered across it, bringing attention to the tight definition of muscle. Unlaced, ratty sneakers completed his ensemble. His hair showed signs of not having been combed for days, curls spiked every which way. His thick eyebrows were too bushy. His face was clean-shaven, cheeks flushed, and lips blushed. He looked as handsome as ever.

All the women, and half the men, watched, transfixed as they said their hellos. Having received this treatment his entire life, Joel hardly noticed what effect his pretty-boy-gone-bad appearance had on the opposite sex. It still unnerved Lacey. To her, Joel was Joel—her best friend. The guy she'd made mud pies with in her backyard. The mooch who slept more nights at her mansion than in his ratty old apartment. Not a sexy lady-killer. Not an actor who could read a tuna label with such emotion he'd have an entire audience crying.

"How was your trip? Tell me everything," Lacey demanded.

He slouched into the chair across from her. "I'm starving. I'll share my sandwich with you," he said, taking half of her club.

"So what's this big audition you called me about?"

In between bites, Joel explained, "I was leaving an audition—I bombed. I don't know what was wrong with me. I couldn't get any of the lines right. I refused to sleep with the director—"

"You didn't."

"I know. I know. Never refuse to sleep with the director until—"

"Until you have the part," Lacey finished for him.

"You know"—he swallowed—"your agent might be a jerk." She had been the one to give him the rules for auditioning for a gay director, which is why Joel never pursued her for representation. "Anyway," he continued, "I was standing outside, feeling down, when I overheard two actresses talking about a new big-budget movie in need of extras. I took a walk to the audition. If I got the part it would cover the cost of my airplane ticket to New York." He paused in the middle of the story to give the waitress his order. "I was standing in line, and the director walked by and pulled me out of the crowd. She had me read a pretty juicy part."

"What's the movie about?"

"Futuristic sci-fi. They wouldn't tell who was playing the lead. Said they were still in negotiations."

"Sounds promising."

He nodded. "Got a callback." He smiled, wide and bright. "And I wouldn't mind sleeping with this director." He used his fingers to outline a perfect hourglass shape. "Nice body, pretty face."

Lacey laughed. "Liar. You only have eyes for Wendy."

"Busted."

As she listened to Joel talk about how great Wendy did everything—cooking him dinner, cleaning his apartment, making love—her mind wondered to Chocolate Dream. After he gave her his telephone number, she pretty much started avoiding him. Cold feet, nerves—she didn't know. She only doubted her sanity. He had become a major distraction in her life. When he sent an instant message, her heart raced. It had become her routine to log on the Internet before she started writing—in case he tried to reach her. She missed him during the day, often pulling up his photo and staring at it for long minutes, fantasizing about what their relationship might become. Somehow, she had started to have genuine feelings for him.

"How's the screenplay coming?" Joel asked, bringing her back to reality.

"I'm stuck, and I'm sweating." She told him about how the offers pouring in had a strange reverse effect on her creativity, stifling her writing.

"You have fear of success," he told her. "You've always been that way." The waitress placed his sandwich in front of him. "You don't really want me to repay you the half of your sandwich I borrowed, do you?"

"I knew you would weasel out of it," she chastised.

His eyes dropped, and his face split into a boyish grin. The women in the restaurant took a collective sigh. The waitress beat it to their table with his drink and a complimentary piece of pie.

"She wants you to have her pie," Lacey observed.

"I have Wendy. I don't taste anyone else's pie." The grin slid into place again.

Lacey gave him a dramatic eye roll. "What do you mean I have a fear of success?"

"You do," he answered, his mouth full. "Remember when you almost won Project Greenlight two years ago? You sabotaged your chances by withdrawing when they named you one of the ten finalists."

"I couldn't take off work to compete in a screenwriting contest."

"I had no idea waitressing called for so much commitment. You were a finalist in Matt Damon and Ben Affleck's screenwriting contest! Even if you didn't win, it would've opened doors for you. You got all artsy-fartsy, saying your writing shouldn't be commercialized."

"Exactly, artistic integrity."

"Exactly, fear of success. Whenever you're standing on the cusp of greatness, you take a step backward. If it weren't for the pit bull agent you have, *The Next Step* would still be sitting in a box at the top of your closet. Do me a favor, let go of the fear and grab the fame with both hands."

Something he said—she refused to admit he was right—punctured a hole in the bubble encasing her creativity, and a scene popped into her head. She started typing frantically, going to the place in her head where she couldn't see anything but her computer screen. She couldn't hear anything but the keys clacking on her keyboard. Joel sat silently, eating his meal. He had been with her before when these fits of creativity hit her. She could go for hours, never budging from the computer until every ounce of ingenuity was wrung out of her.

"Was it good?" Joel asked when she stopped typing.

She pressed back against her chair, gripping the edges of the table. "Better than sex."

"Then we need to get you laid immediately." He chomped on a fry. "Speaking of grabbing opportunity with both hands." He easily picked up the conversation where he had left off. He knew her better than anyone, and he had learned to adjust their friendship to her creative moods. She knew him as well, and she had embraced her role as his rescuer many years ago. "How's the relationship search going?" he asked.

Her mind slid back to Chocolate Dream.

"Any luck?" Joel gestured at the laptop.

She tried not to smile, but when she talked about Chocolate and some of their conversations, she couldn't help it. They were playing the traditional mating game, learning each other's moods, likes and dislikes. They were devoting too much time to their attraction, distracting Lacey from her writing. She enjoyed his pursuit. He made her feel warm, and feminine, and appreciated.

"Chocolate Dream?" Joel's mouth twisted.

"I shouldn't have told you." He would tease her to no end.

"What's his real name?"

Lacey was stunned. She had never asked. She frowned. "I don't know."

"You've been talking to this guy every day since I left for New York, and you never bothered to ask his name? Stick to dating the old-fashioned way. You could be chatting with Ted Bundy, but you wouldn't know it because you *never asked his name*."

"Ted Bundy is dead."

"You know what I mean."

"Asking his name has never come up. When we chat our conversations are much deeper."

"Deeper than knowing his name?" He screwed his mouth to the side again. She hated when he did that.

"Deeper than demographics."

"You're kidding, right?"

"He's smart. Whatever the topic, he can speak intelligently on it. He's a workaholic, like me. He has never asked me what I do or how much money I make. He's never asked me *for anything*—except to call him."

Joel watched her across the table. Worry tugged the corner of his mouth.

"What?" she demanded.

"You like this guy. For real."

"Didn't I start this conversation by telling you how interested I am in him?"

"You don't even know him."

"Don't think I haven't doubted the logic, but there's something about him." Her cell phone rang, saving her from defending a position she wasn't sure she should be taking. It didn't make sense for her to fall for a guy over the Internet. On the other hand, it felt too right to discard without deeper investigation.

"What's going on?" Joel asked when she disconnected.

"My agent wants me to fly out to L.A. She thinks the change of scenery will motivate my writing."

"What's she up to?"

Lacey smiled. "She's throwing a party. She says a few industry people will be there. She's been wanting me to meet with some directors and producers to discuss future projects."

"Gotta give it to her. She's making you successful despite yourself."

Lacey shot him a look at his fear of success reference. "I leave this afternoon." She started packing away her laptop.

"I'll drive you to the airport." Translation: He wanted to borrow her Mercedes while she was gone. "Get this, will you?" He pushed the check across the table.

"The man is supposed to pay," she called as he sauntered to the door.

"I'll repay your kindness when I'm as rich and famous as you are."

Their last Internet conversation had gone something like...

What's wrong? Brown Sugar had learned to read his moods from the rhythm of his typing.

Lonely, he didn't bother to deny.

Why longly? She corrected her mistake, Sorry...can't type... Why lonely?

As Mikel ambled around his apartment, not having heard from Brown Sugar in days, he regretted being so honest. Women *did not* want to hear a man complain about being lonely. Being lonely in a city where women outnumbered the men by double digits was a sign the man had real problems—legal, emotional, or otherwise. His confession didn't encourage relationship development. But he had thought Brown Sugar was different from most women. She would appreciate his honesty. Apparently, she hadn't, because she hadn't returned his last few e-mails or been available for their nightly instant messaging marathons. He should have gotten a dog. Wasn't that what lonely people did, buy themselves a dog? Or a cat, if he were a little old woman.

He'd been living the celibate life of a little old woman

since he first chatted with Brown Sugar. Whenever a woman as lonely as himself called requesting a "date"—code word for one-night stand—he graciously declined, making up an excuse related to work. Although he had never even spoken to Brown Sugar on the telephone, going out with another woman felt like cheating in his mind. He could be called a lot of things, but cheater wasn't one of them. He'd witnessed the drama cheating caused his friends, and he wouldn't be sucked into that vile vat of misery.

Mikel poured himself a drink—gin and juice—to mellow his mood. He grinned around the rim of the glass. Ordinarily, he was too much man for one woman to handle, but Brown Sugar's fiery conversations hinted she was up to the job. He shed his black silk robe and climbed into bed with his drink. The reflection from the screen of the 42-inch flat-screen plasma television hanging on the opposite wall brightened the room but did nothing for his mood. As he sipped his drink, flashing through the channels with lightning speed, the devil in him surfaced. He hadn't chased a woman since losing his virginity. Why did Brown Sugar have him tied in knots, distracted, and in a foul mood? The next time they chatted, he would lay down the law. He would take charge of their relationship. It was progressing entirely too slow for his tastes. He was a busy man. They needed to step it up, move beyond the computer screen.

He fell asleep planning his mission. He awoke the next morning with a thunderous headache he refused to attribute to stressing over a woman. "Must have drank too much," he said, climbing out of bed, but one gin and juice had never been enough to give a man his size a hangover.

Lacey's agent lived in a cozy apartment in a modest neighborhood near the beach. Lacey had discovered everyone lived near the beach in L.A. Her agent insisted Lacey spend the weekend at her apartment—Lacey recognized it as a subtle way to monitor her writing. Lacey griped to Joel about her agent, but truthfully they had fallen into an easy relationship fueled by business but held together by mutual respect. The agent, as Lacey called her, pushed when needed, pursued at the right time, and didn't mind holding the hand of the talent. In return, Lacey gave her wide latitude to make demands on her time. When she could get her tortured writer's soul in gear, she delivered a quality product the agent always seemed happy with. They built their careers together, and they found loyalty to each other based on that fact.

The agent had been right. Lying on the beach under the bright, warm sun had motivated Lacey to concentrate on her writing. She had churned out the first two scenes of the screenplay, edited to a fine point.

"Tell them about your new screenplay," the agent said as she flitted off to converse with her other guests.

An actress Lacey vaguely remembered from her guest appearance on a sitcom sipped at her wine, waiting to hear the details. Two writers from Lacey's favorite medical show surrounded her on the sofa. A director ambled over, perching on the arm of the sofa, pretending to be only mildly interested.

"I haven't worked out the entire plot," Lacey said, "but it's about the survival of a black family at the onset of slavery."

"Another gut wrencher?" the actress asked, already salivating. "Any juicy parts for someone like me?"

Lacey rarely discussed her work in progress, giving only vague details when asked. Actresses and other writers didn't realize she had absolutely zero clout. She could not get them acting jobs—if she could, Joel would be a huge star, because he truly was the best actor she'd ever seen. She didn't have any connections to help other writers get published or establish themselves in Hollywood. The only information she could share was what had worked for her, and this she did in her seminars and speaking engagements. Directors and producers always pushed for more information on her screenplay—What was her vision? What motivated the main character? Who did she see directing? Would it be as big a hit as *The Next Step*? She couldn't answer these questions, which they found confusing, choosing to believe she was trying to shut them out instead. The agent had lectured her about being more sociable and learning to play the game. Lacey had reminded her she was a writer, conjuring up all the stereotypical beliefs about the anguish of the craft.

The vaguely interested director handed Lacey his card. "So, you're thinking this will be a generational piece?"

She smiled as she accepted his card, glancing down to read his name. The agent had mentioned him in passing but was courting bigger players. This man had directed a few indies that had gotten good critical reviews, but they had not been box-office smashes.

"I haven't worked out the details yet. I know where I want to go, but I don't know what path the characters will take to get me there."

He nodded, fully understanding the schizophrenic thinking of writers. "Can't remember the last time a slave picture stormed the box office."

"I suppose it's time."

His face shifted, as if he hadn't considered breaking the mold and introducing something new to Hollywood. Giving them what they wanted would pay the bills, but writing a screenplay with meaning had made Lacey an overnight success. She understood why the agent had discounted him. Never get involved with anyone who can't share your vision.

The agent signaled from across the room, saving Lacey from the uncomfortable conversation with the director. She knew where it was going, and she didn't want to promise him a first look when she completed the screenplay. It would be unprofessional for him to try to bypass her agent, but she got the feeling he had done many unprofessional things in his life.

"Stay away from him," the agent whispered in Lacey's ear. "I have someone I want you to meet. He's been after me all night to introduce you."

She blew out a long sigh. "Is this business?"

"No." The agent tossed a broad smile across the room before waving.

Lacey followed her eyes across the apartment to where a man of average height, and average weight, and average looks stood nursing a drink. He pushed away from the wall and strolled across the room to join them. The agent quickly ducked out, leaving Lacey to have an average conversation with the average man. He bored her quickly, his discussion a smoke screen to determine her interest in dating him. She tried to get away several times, but her flimsy excuses of needing a drink or wanting some air only encouraged him to help her meet her needs. She found herself out on the balcony, cornered while he gave her the dirt on the industry. She soon learned this average man held a spectacular position at NBC. She mentally rolled her eyes. The agent always had a motive connected to business.

Lacey tolerated the average man with a smile, but her mind swiftly drifted to a not-so-average man. She listened to him babble, trying to picture Chocolate at work. She calculated how many days it had been since she got so wrapped up in writing that she hadn't chatted with him. As the average man made his move, asking her out before she left L.A., she questioned why she hadn't picked up the phone and called her Chocolate Dream. Politely, she declined the average man's offer of dinner, an unforgettable night of sex, and expensive gifts.

The conversation had been enough to make her slip into the bedroom where she was staying when the average man finally left her alone. There were so many people crammed in the apartment, it would take a while for the agent to notice she was missing.

She lay on the bed, staring up at the ceiling and debating. Without further hesitation, she picked up the phone and made a telephone call for which her agent would later be billed over a hundred dollars.

4

"Hello?"

Lacey clutched the phone to her ear. She needed to hear it once more—

"Hello?"

She would never, ever forget the first time she heard his voice. Sleep roughened, deep, and dripping with sexual innuendo, Chocolate Dream's timbre vibrated through her ear canal, spread through her chest with heated purpose, and exited her body with an explosive flourish.

"Hello? I'm hanging up," he said with edgy resolve.

"Chocolate Dream?" Her voice was small, and she felt silly calling a man with the masculinity of his voice by such a corny name. Joel made sense—she should've asked his real name a long time ago.

"Who is this?" The annoyance was slipping away, replaced by curiosity.

She hadn't given him her name either. "Brown Sugar."

He was silent.

"You gave me your number…"

"I know."

She heard rustling. "Is this a bad time?"

"No, I was sleeping, and I'm surprised by your call."

She glanced at the clock. With the three hours West Coast time difference, it was two in the morning in Atlanta. She apologized. "I'm in California on business. I'll call you another time."

"No!" His voice shot across the line, whipping the side of her face. "Don't go." His voice dropped to a seductive octave. "I've been waiting for you."

Her stomach dropped. Her head swirled. She closed her eyes and pictured the grainy Internet photo.

"You called," he said, his voice causing her fantasy to dissipate. "You made me wait so long I didn't think you would."

"I've been really busy with work."

His voice slowly lost its sleepy resonance. "Are you a model?"

She wondered why he would think she modeled. She hadn't told him anything other than she worked in show business. "No, I'm a writer."

"And you're in California for work?"

"Yes."

"What do you write?"

"Scripts, but I don't want to talk about my work."

"What do you want to talk about?" A deep chuckle crossed the phone line. "Why don't you tell me about all the noise in the background."

Upon hearing his voice, Lacey was transported into a dark, warm, isolated place where only Chocolate Dream and Brown Sugar existed. "I'm staying at my agent's place, and she's having a party."

"And no one is occupying your time?"

"I've made the obligatory rounds. Now I'm hiding out."

He chuckled again, and then his voice became sultry and suggestive. "How about me being your date at this party?"

She smiled, and her voice reflected it. "And how do you plan on being my date with us being thousands of miles apart?"

"Close your eyes," he instructed.

"They're closed."

"Hold me close."

She complied, squeezing the receiver and pressing it against her ear. "Okay." She was suddenly breathless.

"Shut out all the other noises around you and only listen to my voice. I'm going to hum, and we're going to dance."

Chocolate Dream hummed a slow, provocative song she couldn't name. She lay in the center of the bed, eyes closed, gripping the phone receiver, and no one else existed. She pictured his face and imagined his physique. She felt his arm slide around her waist and pull her close. He rested his face in the crook of her neck...and they danced.

5

Lacey observed herself in the full-length mirror of her walk-in closet. She had changed her outfit four times and refused to procrastinate any further by changing again. She'd settled on a white Dolce & Gabbana blouse with pearl buttons and exquisite lace trim outlining the flaps. The color flattered her brown skin. The blouse slimmed her waist and provided a peek at her cleavage through the sheer material. Not wanting to be too dressed up, or down, she paired the ultra-sexy blouse with dark blue denim jeans with two pockets on front and the D&G logo on the swell of her behind. She completed the look with silver Giuseppe Zanotti python leather slingbacks. With sharply pointed toes and metal buckles at the ankles, her feet looked scrumptious. The hot pink transparent details on the shoes bought out the subtle details of the blouse. The matching purse added the shining touch.

Happy with her wardrobe decision, Lacey fluffed her

short curls, freshly snipped that morning by her chattering hairstylist. She brushed mascara on her thick lashes but did not paint over her dimples. She added a neutral gloss to her lips and surveyed the finished product.

She was finished dressing.

Her hair and makeup were complete.

The Mercedes was parked out front, the tank full of gas.

There are no more excuses, she told herself. She couldn't find another reason to delay leaving the mansion. She looked over her shoulder at the clock on her dresser. Forty-five minutes before Chocolate Dream would be craning his neck around the restaurant, searching for Brown Sugar. A thousand doubts ran through her mind. She should have suggested another meeting place. Maybe she should change into something more casual. Had she stared at his photo long enough to recognize her date? *She never should have agreed to meet Chocolate Dream.*

Their phone calls had been going so well.

He was so persistent.

And she couldn't keep him off her mind.

After fifteen days of extra-long telephone calls—and very little sleep—Chocolate had insisted they go on their first date. Of course she was reluctant, always considering her safety, but something about Chocolate tugged at her heart and pulled her toward advancing their relationship. Today would be the true test. Could their bond transcend computer cable and telephone wire, sealing their connection with real-life chemistry?

The phone rang, startling her.

"Don't tell me you're backing out on me."

A slow smile spread across her face, and all her doubts disappeared. "What would make you think I'm backing out?"

"You're still at home and not on the way to the restaurant."

"I was just leaving."

Thirty minutes later, Lacey paced nervously near the door of the restaurant Chocolate Dream had selected. Near Underground Atlanta, the restaurant served a variety of foods sure to fit anyone's taste. Diners' attire ranged from business to casual, encompassing all styles of dress. Chocolate had chosen a place eclectic enough for any personality to be comfortable. After his phone call, her doubts had shifted, and she wondered if he would be happy with her once they met in the flesh. She gave herself another round of pep talks, remembering she was a dynamic woman with much to offer.

All doubt melted away when Chocolate's black Chrysler 300M pulled into valet parking. He emerged from the car with long, muscular legs that could not have possibly fit inside the interior of the vehicle. His full lips slanted downward, and his eyes were narrowed in annoyance. He waved to the valet, hurrying him over. He said a few quick words, and then stepped into the restaurant. An aficionado of fine clothing, she appreciated the fit of his dimgrey Armani suit. The three-button jacket was of classic length, stretching over the strong haunches of his behind. The darkness of his skin radiated against his cream shirt. The brooding handsomeness portrayed in his photo could never capture his commanding presence. When he entered the restaurant, a little disheveled because of his late arrival, everyone took notice. Without him muttering a word, all eyes swiveled his way, subconsciously acknowledging his presence. It was overwhelming to Lacey to know all his intensity would soon be focused on her.

Chocolate searched the lobby. Their eyes locked, a moment of shared recognition. A bright, seductive smile slashed through the five o'clock shadow covering his jaw. His hurried steps became liquid smooth as he approached. All the stress plaguing him moments ago disappeared, taking any doubts she ever had in meeting him.

He offered his hand. "I hope you're Brown Sugar."

His palm swallowed her hand. "Chocolate?"

"Mikel. Mikel Bauer."

Her skin reminded him of cappuccino cheesecake—rich, brown, and creamy. Lacey Montgomery—the name screamed power—was far more than Mikel could have wished for. He couldn't stop grinning. The outfit she wore, he shivered internally, sexy, sexy, sexy. Their conversation flowed easily, and they talked for hours as if they were old friends recently reconnected. The more he learned about her, the more he wanted to know. He fired questions at her just to keep her talking. The matching dimples on either side of her mouth winked when she spoke. In every way, she was captivating.

"Who is your agent?" he asked. "You said you stayed at her place when you traveled to L.A."

She answered with a name. "But I call her 'the agent.'"

He did a quick scan of his memory. "I don't know her."

"You're an entertainment attorney?"

He nodded, taking a drink from his coffee. "Attorney–agent would more accurately describe me." He fished a business card from the inside pocket of his suit and slid it across the table. "I thought I knew everyone in the business—at least by name or reputation." Her fingers brushed his when she reached for it. He looked up quickly, catching her gaze. "If you ever tire of 'the agent,' give me a call."

The waiter visited their table, checking their needs.

"We've been here for hours," Lacey said when the waiter walked away.

Mikel looked at his watch. "Four." They had finished their lunch many hours ago but lingered in the restaurant over dessert, coffee, and conversation. He pinned her with his smile. "And still, I'm not ready to end our date." Thinking quickly, he asked, "Would you like to take a walk? The Underground is only a few blocks over."

She hesitated only a second. "I'd like that."

Mikel paid the check and met Lacey out front after her detour to the ladies' room. "Should we move our cars?" she wanted to know.

"They know me here. Our cars will be fine." He knew from past experience he could leave his car overnight and it would be safely secured until he could retrieve it. Frequenting the restaurant with superstar clients, and leaving large tips, afforded him special consideration with the owners.

Mikel boldly pressed his hand into the small of her back. The soft silk of her blouse was shockingly arousing as his fingers rode the fabric back and forth across her skin while they walked. He was considerably taller than Lacey, but she didn't seem intimidated. She gravitated to him as they walked, her taking two steps to match his long stride. His hold on her felt *natural*.

They made their way through the early evening shadows to Underground Atlanta. A three-story, underground shopping mall built on the original streets of old Atlanta, the Under-ground seemed a perfect setting to continue their date. As they walked the cobblestone streets window-shopping, Mikel let the old-world charm of the mall transport him back in time. He held Lacey's hand with gentlemanly tenderness as they strolled from shop to shop, with Lacey seeking discount prices on exclusive purses. From the fine fit of her clothing he could tell she wasn't a woman who skimped on pseudodesigners.

"I've never had a man take me shopping on the first date," she said. "Usually men avoid shopping with women at any cost."

"I'm not most men," he answered with a cocky smile. For his arrogance, he paid penitence, knowing most women couldn't resist a good sale on dresses. He lined up against the wall at the front of shops while she scoured clothing racks. He hated shopping—it was difficult to find a good suit to fit his broad shoulders—but he enjoyed watching Lacey, knowing the rest of the men standing on the wall were watching her, too.

Their conversation never lagged, discussing everything from current events, to politics, to the entertainment business. They stopped to enjoy the street vendors' magic tricks and fortune-telling. As the hour grew later, the corridors filled with tourists wanting to experience the shopping, dining, and history for which the Underground was famous.

"We've been out all day," Lacey said a bit later as they made their way through the growing throng of people.

He didn't want to end their date. Being with Lacey was easy and arousing and interesting and fun. He wasn't ready to let her go. It had been too long since he felt so drawn to a woman. And there was so much more to learn about her. He wanted to know everything. Like how she managed to keep him so engaged. How she became so irresistible? Most importantly, how did she feel about him?

He hadn't forgotten how they'd met. Many more men were probably sending her sweet promises wrapped in e-mails. Letting her go, without making an impression, might result in this being his last opportunity to enjoy her company.

"It's getting late." Her voice had that "time to end the evening" tone to it.

"You should be hungry again. It's been hours since we had lunch."

She stopped in the middle of the crowd and smiled up at him, her dimples deepening. "Are you trying to keep me out with you?"

He turned to her, fighting the urge to stroke her beautiful face. "Yes."

"For how long?" The slant of her eyes told him she was toying with him.

"Until."

Her thick lashes dropped. "Until what?"

"I don't know. I can't imagine when I'd be ready to let you go."

She straightened her shoulders and looked up at him. "We could grab a bite."

Now he smiled. "What would you like?"

"I know where we can get a great hamburger and shake—"

"Johnny Rockets," he finished her thought.

This delighted her. "Just what I was thinking."

Mikel managed to snag them a table, and they settled in to eat burgers and fries. "I like your diversity."

She laughed. "What do you mean?"

"You went from a chic restaurant to a fast-food burger joint in under twenty-four hours. Any other woman would have complained about me being cheap."

"I expected you to demand I pay for the burgers."

Her comment made him wonder what type of man she usually dated. Sounded like she'd encountered her share of gold diggers—hustlers—too. "Why ultimatemates.com?"

"Too busy, and uninterested in trying to meet someone in a bar. Those things never seem to work out."

"And has this worked for you? Internet dating?"

"You're the first guy I've met, remember?" She lifted her milkshake and sipped from the straw, watching him with insightful brown eyes. "It's working pretty well so far, don't you think?"

He wanted to be a strawberry, floating past her lips and over her tongue. He wanted to be consumed by this woman. "Damn good."

"How many women have you met this way?"

He'd wanted to ask her the same question all day—right before forbidding her to ever log on to the Internet again. Being the first man she'd met at ultimatemates.com didn't mean he'd be the last. "A few. Most have been Sarahs."

She smiled with recognition of their first chat conversation. "I'm not a Sarah."

"No, I don't think you are." He braced himself. "How many men have you met?"

"One. You."

He took comfort, bursting with pride. "I'm honored."

"I was getting cold feet about meeting you today." She did the thing with the straw again, and this time Mikel's body responded. "I am *so* glad I didn't back out."

"Then you would do it again? Go out with me, I mean."

"Definitely."

"Good to know."

Lacey Montgomery was addictive; the more he had of her, the more Mikel wanted. After finishing their dinner, he persuaded her to accompany him to the Event Loft. An upscale nightspot with urban appeal, the club featured an inviting dance floor. Reminiscing about their first telephone conversation, they joined the crowd on the dance floor to make new memories. The fast tempo of the music didn't allow Mikel to hold Lacey as close as he would have liked. He placed his hand in the small of her back, becoming more familiar with her warmth as he guided her onto one of the balconies overlooking Historic Kenny's Alley.

He stood close to her at the railing as they looked out together on Atlanta's skyline. "When I started the Internet dating thing, it was because my assistant thought I should try it. The Sarahs were a disappointment, and I had all but given up on meeting anyone of substance." He eased his arm around her slender waist, testing her reaction to his forwardness. When she didn't move away, he continued, "I'm glad I gave it one last shot." He leaned into her, bringing her into him by his hold on her waist. "You are beautiful, funny, and vibrant. No matter what happens, I'm happy we met."

She didn't look at him, but her body relaxed, melding with his. "I'm happy you're not a pervert." She erupted into laughter, dissipating the seriousness of the moment.

He joined her. He didn't laugh often—he had always

been a serious person, even as a child—but Lacey brought his lighter side to the surface.

She angled her body into his, looking up at him. "Can I buy you a drink?"

"Yes, you can." He stared down into her eyes and tried to remember when a woman had ever captivated him so completely. They had chemistry. What he'd experienced over the Internet hadn't been a fluke. She tempted him with big brown eyes. Her body teased him, daring him to touch her. She watched him, and her magnetism activated the pull of attraction between them. Her body angled forward one imperceptible millimeter. The surrounding crowd disappeared, leaving them alone on the balcony under a sky filled with stars. He leaned down and placed a gentle kiss on her lips. He pulled away slowly, hoping not to overwhelm her, but wanting so much more than a quick taste of her lips.

"Nice," she breathed.

He took her hand and weaved through the crowd toward one of the two bars in the Event Loft. Opening out onto the beautifully bricked veranda, the bar was swamped with people calling out drink orders.

"It's like an auction gone very wrong," Lacey said.

Mikel led her out onto the veranda, away from the chaos.

"It's crazy in there," she said.

They stood together, sharing a magnificent view of the downtown cityscape. Everything was going right on this date. Mikel couldn't have planned it better. "I'll get your drink while you wait here."

She touched his arm as he turned away, stopping him. "How badly do you want that drink?"

"Not so bad." Not badly enough to leave her when she watched him so seductively. He draped his arm over her shoulders, and they watched the lights of downtown Atlanta. "Do you see the building right there?" He pointed, guiding her line of sight to the right.

She pointed, clarifying. "That one?"

"Yes, I run my business from that building."

"You probably have a great view."

"My apartment is on the twentieth floor and it has a wonderful view...and a fully stocked bar."

6

The lobby and corridor floors of Mikel's building were covered with cream-colored marble. Large plants lined the halls, absorbing the sound of Lacey's heels. The luxury of his apartment was equally impressive. She was greeted by a dramatic nine-foot ceiling in the foyer. Vaulted ceilings opened the living areas to exquisite crown molding. She stepped through the arched doorway into the contemporarily decorated living room to wait while Mikel turned on the lights. The ceiling fans in each room whirled to life, covering the nervous thump of her heart. Built-in bookshelves lined the far wall of the living room. She wandered over to find titles written by Trump, Covey, and Martin. Through the adjacent arched doorway was Mikel's large oak desk, securely tucked away in a cubby surrounded by massive windows.

"Lacey," he called for her. She found him standing behind the bar in the formal dining room. He had shut off the ceiling fans but opened the French doors leading out to the covered terrace. Sweet, late-night Atlanta breezes wafted over Lacey, making her feel at home. She joined him at the bar and climbed up into the bar chair with ladylike finesse.

"What would you like?" he asked, placing two glasses on the bar.

"How dramatic can I be?" she teased.

"Go for it."

She considered her mood. "A Pink Lady?" Lacey wasn't much of a drinker—a glass of wine with dinner or champagne on a social occasion was the extent of her prowess. She called out the name of a drink she had heard the agent order while in California.

"I can do better than that. How about a Beauty Mark?"

"Sure, I'll try it."

She watched as Mikel went to work, his concentration shrinking tightly to encompass the task at hand. Methodically, he placed ice, orange juice, sweet vermouth, and dry vermouth in a shaker and gave it a toss. He poured a splash of grenadine in the bottom of her glass and strained the other mixture over it. He handed her the glass. "Sip it slowly."

She did. The drink was sweet and went down smoothly. Mikel poured himself a cognac.

In this, their first moment of nervous silence, Lacey felt the effects of the Beauty Mark. She swayed a bit, noticing for the first time how high the bar stool was from the ground.

"I told you to sip slowly," Mikel said, rounding the bar and helping her down. "I'll take this"—he removed the glass from her hand—"and get you a coffee."

"It's too late for coffee. I'll never sleep."

"Fresh air then." He kept his grip on her arm as he helped her through the French doors out onto the terrace.

"I'm not intoxicated." She sank down, lying on the softness of a lounge chair. "You made my drink too strong, and I took too big of a sip."

"More like a gulp," he teased, the corner of his mouth lifting. He reclined in the matching chair. "I want you fully in control of your faculties."

"I'm always in control." She flopped her head to the side, catching his profile. "It's what I like about you."

He turned to face her. "What do you like about me?"

"You're so composed and self-possessed, I don't have to be."

"Only a writer would use a word like self-possessed to describe someone. You're saying I'm an in-charge kind of guy."

"Yes."

"And you like it."

"Yes."

He sipped his cognac, watching the city lights in the distance. "Meaning I can have my way with you?"

"Only if I let you."

They watched the skyline in serene silence.

Mikel reached for her hand, holding it securely within his. "You said, 'I need a man who is confident enough to take charge and gentle enough to surrender.'"

"You're not interested in one-night stands or quick sexual encounters." She rolled onto her side, facing him. "So if we're intimate tonight..."

He placed his glass on the ground on the opposite side of his chair. He eased out of his seat and knelt next to her. "It's a beginning, not an end."

Mikel leaned into her, freezing an indiscernible heartbeat away from her lips, as if asking permission to kiss her. She watched him and he watched her, neither able to hide the emotions playing across their faces. She let her eyes roam the chiseled planes of his face, wanting to commit this moment to memory.

Their eyes locked, and he crushed his mouth to hers. She pressed her hand against the cottony softness of his five o'clock shadow. He wrapped his arms around her, lifting her slightly and bringing her into him. He smelled contemporary and masculine: coriander and then geranium tickled her nose, but the endnotes of cedar and oakmoss would stay with her long into the night. She inhaled, letting her lashes dip with the pleasure. He moved into her mouth, bringing the heady burn of cognac. His kiss communicated attraction, affection, passion, and lust. With tutored flare, he added, *I'll miss you, baby,* and Lacey knew she never wanted to leave.

He pulled away first, their eyes still locked.

The sensuality of his kiss left her dizzy. She blamed it on the drink. "It's the Beauty Mark." She swayed, and he steadied her in his arms.

"It's my kiss." Mikel was revved up, but his quiet charisma made him fight to keep it in check.

They watched each other for a long time. The Atlanta breeze brushed over them; the moonlight sliced the darkness.

"Are you ready for this?" he asked, as if his body held so much pleasure she needed preparation.

"Are you ready for me, Chocolate?"

He frowned. "Say my name."

"Mikel." It rolled off her tongue with ease, as if it belonged there.

He smiled. A faint shiver ran through him when she used his name. She noticed because he was still perched on his knee next to her chair, inches away from kissing her again.

She toyed with him. "I'll say your name because you think it gives you power over me, but really it gives me power over you."

"Remember those words. They'll come back to haunt you."

She accepted the challenge.

"Are you ready to start something with me? I'm not always the easiest man to get along with, but I'll treat you right. I ask too much and demand even more. I'm too serious, and when I want something, I go after it full throttle."

"Is there something you want now, Mikel?"

"Definitely. You. All of you."

"How long are we going to discuss this?"

"Have you decided if you're ready for me? Ready to go into this understanding it's a relationship and knowing I want to take it to the max?"

Lacey searched his face for sincerity and found it clearly displayed in the intensity of his gaze and the harsh set of his jaw. He wanted her. Not just for sex. He wanted her in his life. He didn't know how far it would go, but he had an idea where he'd like it to end. She saw something different in him. There were no games. There were no false pretenses. He wanted this, and he openly displayed his cards. She had found someone special. She didn't know how she knew him so well, so quickly, but she did.

"Lacey? Did I scare you?"

She inhaled him, long and deep. "Where's your bedroom?"

Lacey looked up at the 9-foot ceiling, watching the blades of the ceiling fan rotate. The drapes were still open, and the moon cast a sliver of light across Mikel's bedroom. The carpet was neutral. Everything else was black. Very contemporary. Very male. Mikel was perched at the foot of the bed, slowly slipping her silver Giuseppe Zanotti python sling off her foot. She heard it drop to the floor. He caressed her other foot, moving over the leather and releasing the metal buckle at her ankle. It thudded against the carpet.

He used his teeth to open the pearl buttons of her blouse while his fingers caressed the lace edging. He pushed apart the flaps, exposing her brown skin. He gave her a break from his overwhelming sensuality and kissed her neck, ears, and eyes. She synchronized her shallow breathing with his deep inhalations. If he touched her, she would ignite in flames. If he didn't touch her, she would explode.

His hands slipped into the front pockets of her dark denims. He outlined her curves, tracing the D&G logo on the swell of her behind. His massive hands hooked the jeans and raked them down her legs, tossing them to the floor.

She was fully exposed, her ivory-colored lace bra and panties glowing in the darkness. He blew out a long stream of air, washing her in cognac. "*You are beautiful*," he said slowly. He cupped her breasts, moving his hands down her body, into the indention of her waist and over the flare of her hips. His touch was light and gentle, leaving a heavy and rough impression on her body. Her breathing quickened. "Hurry," she told him.

"Help me," he said, standing next to the bed and pulling at the buttons on his suit. Later, he would tell her, "Show me."

She swung her legs to the side of the bed, reaching for him. He stepped closer, and together they removed his clothes. It was dark, but Lacey made out his flat abdomen, rounded behind, and broad shoulders with her fingers. His legs were so long, they went on and on—lean and muscular and strong. He kissed her, pushing her back as he climbed onto the bed. She hadn't had time to explore *there*.

He straddled her waist.

His fingers outlined the lace swirls in her bra. He dipped a finger inside the cup, finding his target and mercilessly twirling it. His other hand removed the opposite strap from her shoulder. He bent his head and latched on to the newly exposed peak.

Lacey moaned, unable to coordinate the various movements of his hands, fingers, mouth, and tongue. His thumbs hooked her panties, and he discarded them with a flourish.

"Where?" she panted.

"Top"—he kissed her belly—"drawer."

She wiggled out of his grasp to the head of the bed and slid the drawer open. She fumbled in the darkness, finding a new box of latex armor. She handed Mikel the package. He ripped it open. She pushed him onto his back, catching him by surprise. He realized she was serious when she'd told him to hurry. Frantically, he unrolled the sheath. He sat up, grasping her arms in an attempt to switch positions. She brought her arms up, breaking his hold. He mumbled a curse that sounded more like an endearment in anticipation of her next move. She placed her hands against his broad shoulders and pushed.

Mikel fell backward. His hands went to her hips, but he let her lead. She straddled him. She washed his chest and abdomen in kisses, building his frenzy to match hers. His grip tightened. His legs jerked. She climbed on board. They moaned in unison as she took him inside. She rolled her waist, riding him to a funky-cool beat only she could hear. He found her rhythm and rolled his hips in unison. She locked her fingers behind her head. Perspiration poured between her breasts. He licked it away. She locked her thighs against his waist. He palmed the moons of her behind and pulled her deeper onto him. He gyrated his hips, angling his erection at just the right spot. One thrust and she screamed.

Mikel continued the assault with excruciating patience. When she collapsed against him, her head sagging on his chest and her arms wrapped around his neck, he flipped their positions. She lay on the bed, open to him. He climbed between her legs and used his hand to guide himself deep inside. His hips rotated with shocking thoroughness. He braced his hands on either side of her head. She explored his body with her hands, pressing her feet into the mattress and offering herself by raising her hips off the bed. His stroke accelerated, deepened, and then he erupted with an ear-shattering, thunderous cry.

The garden-style oval tub in Mikel's master bath was made for soaking after a long-overdue session of vigorous lovemaking. Lacey had lain limp as he kissed her from head to toe, taking much longer to recover than he did. He took charge the next time, slowing their pace and filling the act with premature emotion. It was spellbinding. It was amazing.

Lacey left Mikel sleeping afterward while she went to shower. She discovered the huge tub and couldn't resist making herself at home. She ran the water while exploring his medicine cabinet for oil or bath salts. She grinned, recalling a popular television commercial where a woman was going through her boyfriend's cabinet and it fell off the wall. Mikel's apartment was too expensive to have fragile medicine cabinets, but she treaded lightly just the same. She found bath oil she recognized as Mikel's fragrance, and she poured a capful in the tub before getting in.

She was being a bit territorial, but he had been insistent that intimacy came with commitment. She'd clarify just what he meant later. At the time, the cut of his suit, the smell of his skin, and the skill of his kiss had distracted her.

Exhaustion combined with the heat from the tub caused her to become sleepy very quickly. She toweled off, grabbed a black silk pajama top off the back of the bathroom door, and joined Mikel in his bedroom. He hadn't moved. He slept silently, breathing deeply on his left side on the left side of the bed. She climbed in behind him and pressed her front to his back. She drifted to sleep thinking, *Thank God for computers.*

The next morning, which came only five hours after Lacey had gone to sleep, Mikel still lay in his comatose state. She gingerly left the bed and wandered into the kitchen. She pulled breakfast food from the subzero refrigerator and went to work. She didn't cook much at home. She found the kitchen too intimidating to cook for one. Most times she would be up late writing and didn't feel like stopping when morning came to fix breakfast. This morning, she was energetic and starving.

She retrieved the newspaper and sat alone at Mikel's dining room table. She ate a huge breakfast, and then wandered through his apartment, trying to get a feel for how he lived. She saved the master bedroom for last, still finding him asleep.

"This is getting ridiculous," she said, jumping on the bed and shaking him awake.

He awoke to her laughter. Stretching, he pulled himself up against the headboard. "What's funny?"

"Do you always sleep this hard, this long?"

He checked the bedside clock. "Never. I usually work on Saturday." He cleared his throat. "It's been a long time." He shuffled his eyebrows and Lacey knew what he meant. "You took a lot out of me."

"Want breakfast? To replenish?"

"You cook, too?"

She sat with him at the dining room table, and they picked up their conversation from the night before. She read the interesting articles to him from the daily while he sipped his coffee.

"What do you do?" he asked.

"What?" She peered at him over the top of the newspaper.

"For a living? What do you do? You said you were a writer? Is that how you earn your living? The last time I asked you didn't want to discuss it. I should probably know."

She sorted through the newspaper, finding the entertainment section. She folded it open displaying a full-page ad for *The Next Step*. The studio was already making its Oscar bid.

"You want to see a movie?"

"This is my movie. I wrote the screenplay."

He took the paper from her hands and stared at the advertisement for a long time. She was worried he might do as others had done. Told her they were intimidated by her success and leave.

He put down the paper and stared at her across the table. "You're a writer?"

"Yes."

"And you wrote this? The biggest movie of the year."

"Yes."

He remained expressionless. "I saw that movie."

"You mentioned it."

"It was great."

"Thank you."

He mindlessly forked food into his mouth. "You *wrote* this?" He pointed to the newspaper.

She nodded, holding her breath.

"Damn," he said, "you have it all." He smiled. "And I have you."

7

Mikel watched the time tick away. At ten minutes to five, he announced he was leaving for the day.

"What's going on, boss?" Harry asked, watching in amazement as Mikel packed his briefcase.

"Nothing. Call me if you need me, but the other attorneys can handle these simple negotiations."

Harry shook his head. "I'm not referring to work. You've been beating it out of here by five every day for the past month. I remember coming to work and finding you slumped over your desk six out of seven days a week. What has you so distracted?"

A vision of Lacey popped into his head. "I finally took your advice and got myself a personal life."

A wide grin spread over Harry's face. "You met a woman?"

"I met *the* woman."

"Tell me about her," Harry said, following Mikel to the elevator.

"Another time. Right now, she's waiting for me."

He stepped onto the elevator, his workday stress lifting as each floor passed up to his apartment. Lacey was waiting for him, as she had been waiting for him every day for the past month. Their connection was so strong everything had fallen into place once they had made love. They had been together every possible free minute of every day since. Other than to gather clothing and her laptop, Lacey had never gone home. His workday was broken by hourly phone calls. When not on the phone, they were instant messaging. He smiled recalling one particularly randy message she'd sent that had him running out on a very important meeting. He slipped out of the office for long, sensuous lunches with her. They went to restaurants, movies, and shows. They spent a lot of time walking around Underground Atlanta, enjoying being together. They had built their own private cocoon, and it was wonderful.

"I'm home," Mikel called, stepping into his apartment.

"In here," she answered.

He followed the heavy aroma of spices into the kitchen. She greeted him with a smile, and he reciprocated with a kiss. "I wanted to take you out to dinner."

"I don't feel like going out. Besides, I enjoy cooking for you. How was your day?"

He grabbed a bottle of water from the fridge, leaned against the counter, and watched her cook as he told her about his day at the office. "How's the writing going?"

"I finished another scene today. I hope you don't mind, I took over part of your office. I needed to storyboard."

"No problem. I like sharing my space with you."

"Okay. No matter what you do, don't touch the whiteboard."

"Yes, ma'am." He tugged at his tie. "I'm going to change." He headed for his bedroom.

By the time he undressed and started the shower, Lacey

was joining him. Without a word, she peeled off her clothes and stepped behind the glass shower door. Making love in the shower had become one of the activities they enjoyed most. She had shown him how to angle the handheld showerhead to make her climax without ever touching her. Then she took it from his hands and taught him how erotic tiny beads of water could be when they massaged his skin. He hoisted her up, and slid her down onto his erection. It took plenty of practice to learn how to balance their weight in the slippery shower, gyrate his hips until they came together, and keep from falling.

Afterward, they were eating dinner on the terrace when Lacey's cell rang. He listened to the cryptic one-sided conversation. "What was that all about?" he asked when she disconnected.

"My friend is worried. I've been tucked away with you for the past month."

Mikel took her plate away to the kitchen.

Lacey followed, continuing the conversation. "I need to resurface in the real world."

"I know. My friends have been complaining, too. Our already limited time has been obliterated." He placed their dishes in the sink and went to her, slipping his arms around her waist. "Is your friend worried about your safety with the Internet guy?"

She smiled, deepening her dimples. "I'm not usually this obsessed with a man."

"Good to know." He kissed her forehead. "Give your friend my number so she can contact you at any time."

"If I give Joel your number, he'll never leave me alone."

"Joel?" His grip on her waist slipped. "The *friend* you're talking about is a man?"

"Don't say 'friend' with that tone. Joel and I have been best friends since we were kids."

"Is he gay?"

She snorted with laughter. "No."

Jealousy rose, bubbling in his stomach and threatening to reject dinner. "Have you ever slept with him?"

"Mikel!"

"Have you?"

"No, I have never slept with Joel." She tilted her head to the side. "Is this you being jealous?"

"Is Joel a one-legged man with terrible acne and chronic impotence?"

She laughed again. "Of course not. He's an actor."

"Then, yes, this is me being jealous." He released her and went to the living room. She soon followed, standing over him with hands on hips, waiting to be acknowledged. He did. "What does this guy mean to you?"

"He's my best friend."

"I don't like it."

"Why not?"

He studied her body from head to foot. "The thought of another man hitting on you bothers me."

"Joel has never come on to me. We're strictly friends. He's happily involved with Wendy—the woman of his dreams." She moved next to him, draping her leg over his thigh, distracting him to her advantage. "The only man I'm interested in is you, Mikel. Joel and I are friends—get used to it. My relationship with him is not going to change. Not even for you. You should be grateful to him."

"Grateful?" he asked, outraged.

"Yes, grateful. Joel has been taking care of me all these years, guarding my virtue for the when the right man came along. He saved me for you."

How could he argue with such delicious logic? He softened. "I suppose I do owe him thanks."

"Yes, you do." She wound her arms around his neck, and they kissed. "I have to go home."

"Not so soon," he moaned.

"Tonight."

"I can go with you."

"We have to come up for air."

"I don't understand why." Reading her expression, he quickly added, "But if it's what you want."

"Have you completely lost your mind?"

"I missed you, too, Joel." Lacey flung her arms around him, fighting his half-hearted withdrawal, and kissed him.

"What is going on with you? Your mother called me twice, warning me to keep an eye on you."

"She gave you a lecture about taking care of me?" She smiled, motioning him to follow her outside to the pool where she was working. Lacey had always been Joel's caretaker. If her mother wanted him to check on her, she definitely had made the right decision about leaving the warm cocoon Mikel had made. She needed a sign, some encouragement not to pack her bags and move in with him.

Since returning home to this self-imposed cooling off period, she hadn't been able to write a word. She sat in front of her computer night and day, but the words would not come. With Mikel, she had been so inspired. Alone, she was stumped to put three good words together. Knowing she couldn't give Mikel control over her creativity—her lifework—she had forced herself to stay away from him for a week...and it was killing her! She missed his attentiveness, his kisses, and his muscular body.

Lacey tried to explain the significance of her relationship with Mikel to Joel as they sat next to her pool, eating lunch. It was impossible, even for a writer, to put the depth of emotions into words. How could she describe the feeling she got when she looked up and found him watching her with exhaustive intensity? Was it possible to explain the way her heart leapt when he caressed her naked body? Did she know any words that could convey the happiness she felt when he returned from work at the end of the day? As Joel watched her with a bewildered smirk, she knew she could never explain what she shared with Mikel by using mere words and gestures.

Joel stared at her for a long, assessing moment. "You *have* lost your mind. Let me get this straight, Lacey. You went on a blind date with a man you met through ultimate-mates.com. He was so good to you, you kept the date going for hours. And when that wasn't enough, you stayed the night with him? It got so good," he added with the drama only an actor can bring, "you stayed an entire month at his place."

"You've summed it up in a cheap, tawdry sort of way."

"I'm calling your mother."

She laughed. "You were the one who suggested I meet someone. I met the perfect guy, and now you're complaining I'm spending too much time with him? You can't have it both ways, Joel."

"You don't know this guy. I'm a man. Listen to me. Do you realize you just served him every man's fantasy on a silver platter? Meeting a gorgeous, rich woman who is uninhibited enough to jump into bed with you on the first date is right up there with the two-women sex romp."

"I know Mikel better than I've ever known any man I've dated. We took time to get to know each other over the Internet, and then by phone. We used impersonal methods to become intimately connected. I didn't just jump into bed with a stranger on our first date. Our relationship is much more than a one-night stand."

He still wore a look of incredulousness. "Has he ever been here?"

"No, and don't worry about my safety or my money. He's not a maniac, and he's very well established in his own business." Lacey told him about Mikel's practice, dropping some very impressive client names in every aspect of show business.

"It could be a scam." Joel's argument was weakening.

"It's not a scam. He's just a nice guy."

"If he's so great, and so normal, why is he trolling for women over the Internet?"

"The same reason I was! Are you calling me abnormal?"

He looked embarrassed. "Of course not."

"I don't know how to put you at ease other than to tell you to trust my judgment."

The worried look reappeared. Joel was reliving her past dating disasters.

Lacey didn't want to travel through the road kill of her dating career. "I don't want to talk about this anymore. You're just going to have to trust me. If Mikel were danger- ous, I wouldn't be sitting with you right now. Tell me what you've been up to."

Joel grinned. "In all your drama, I almost forgot—I got the part!"

"What part?"

He reminded her of his impromptu New York audition. "I read for an under five, but the director said she could see me in a bigger role. I'm playing opposite an all-star cast. I'm talking Pitt, Cheadle, Roberts, and Sheen."

"Get out of here!"

"Serious. And the big star they didn't want to name at the audition turned out to be Travolta."

"No way." Lacey bounced with happiness. "What's the plot?"

"It's like *Oceans Eleven*, but instead of bad guys versus the casino owner, it's bad guys versus mobsters. Travolta is the head bad guy. Martin Sheen is the aging mobster on his way out. He's planning to put his son in charge of the orga- nization, but Travolta wants to stage a coo. He has this major beef with the mob boss over past territory fights." A wide smile spread over his face. "I'm playing the Italian mobster's son."

"You're playing an Italian?"

They laughed. "My first big role and I'm playing an- other race."

"When you pull it off, you'll be able to write your own ticket."

"The promotion for this film is going to be huge."

"We have to celebrate." Lacey's joy radiated from every pour. "I'll throw you a party. A huge party before you leave for L.A. to start shooting." She stretched out in the lounge chair. "We'll celebrate your arrival on the Hollywood scene, and you'll have the chance to meet Mikel. Meeting him will put your mind at ease."

Late one evening Mikel had been holding Lacey from behind, their naked bodies cooling underneath the ceiling fan in his bedroom, and he had confessed to her he was a difficult man to love. He had whispered his acknowledgment of his faults and how they had been responsible for overwhelming some women and chasing them away. He had tried to temper his stubbornness, but he was who he was.

During their month-long hiatus together, Lacey had seen proof of the truth of his confession. Mikel would try to scramble up something for them to eat if she was absorbed in her writing, but he believed cooking was woman's work. He was very intelligent and kept on top of world news, but she had learned early on to avoid discussions about the death penalty. He demanded organization when it came to his work; however, she couldn't break him of the habit of leaving his clothing lying wherever they were removed. He had a beautiful smile and warming laugh, but he rarely used them, instead remaining too serious. She'd seen him negotiating contracts for his clients—he was tenacious. Of course, his tenacity was welcome when they were making love. He could be obstinate and demanding, but more often he was tender and passionate and caring.

Mikel Bauer wasn't the easiest man to live with, but Lacey found it almost impossible to be without him.

She'd taken a step back from their whirlwind relationship because she didn't want to lose herself, but she missed him terribly. Sleeping at night had become almost impossible. She hadn't written a usable word in the entire week she'd been away from him. Her food was too bland, the sun not bright enough. She missed the spark in her life that Mikel provided.

She did renew her friendship with Joel. He dropped by most days to help plan the party or grab a meal with her. She helped him pack his apartment and move in with Wendy. He'd be in L.A. at least six months working on the film and didn't want to pay rent in two cities. Once *he* was the star of a blockbuster movie, the studio would pick up the tab for his living expenses. For now, he was still a struggling actor—at least until the reviews were in on his performance. She enjoyed spending time with Joel and Wendy, but it made her miss Mikel even more. She had decided to take a week to objectively examine her feelings for him, and at the end of that week, it was clear. She was falling in love with Mikel Bauer—if she wasn't there already.

"Have you found what you were looking for?" Mikel's voice heated her ear and reawakened her insatiable urges even over the telephone line.

"Yes."

"Will you stop punishing me now?" The mild distress reflected in his voice told Lacey he was as miserable as she had been the past seven days.

"I never meant—"

"Is it over between us? I need to know. It's not fair to make me suffer this way."

"I don't want it to be over between us." She didn't want to hurt him, and the thought that he might have misunderstood ignited a panicky flutter in her chest.

"What was this all about? I never meant to imply my work was more important than yours. I tried to provide a place for you here so you could work on your screenplay. I wanted to share my space, not isolate you. I know you

needed to go home to return to your life. I didn't understand I wouldn't be allowed to join you."

"I wasn't trying to exclude you from my world—"

"Then what—"

"Let me finish, Mikel."

Uncertainty about their relationship made him impatient.
She heard his distress in the tremble of his voice. He apologized for interrupting and asked her to continue.

"I needed time to clear my head. Everything between us
happened so quickly I wanted to be sure my feelings for
you were legitimate, and not based on being swept up in a
whirlwind romance. I understand you're taking as big a
chance on me as I'm taking on you. I appreciate you opening your home to me. You have to realize I needed space *for*
me, not *because* of you."

"Now that you've had your space, what does it mean
for us?" His tone said he didn't understand her actions—
soul-searching was a real chick thing to do—but he respected her needs.

"I understand my attraction to you is real."

There was a long hesitation before he whispered, "I miss
you, Lacey. Being apart from you has been unbearable. I revealed myself to you, and you ran away."

On their last night together, he'd held her tight and told
her all his faults. He took responsibility for the disasters in
his past relationships. He'd confessed his greatest fear to her.

She matched his tone. "You told me you're afraid you'll
find the love of your life but lose her because of your
faults."

"And then you pushed me away."

"I shouldn't have."

"No, you shouldn't have. Invite me back now."

"I miss you."

"I wish it were enough," he said teasingly.

"What do you need to come back?" She could play
his game.

He hesitated, humming quietly as if deciding what she would have to do to win him over. "I think I have it."

"Go ahead."

"I'll tell you when I see you."

"Not even a hint?"

"Be naked."

8

Mikel double-checked the address. Having read it correctly, he pulled up to the four-car garage and cut the engine. Lacey's "house" was actually a custom-designed estate sitting on a two-acre lot. The outside of her home was tan European-style hard coat stucco with lavish windows. A nondescript woman opened the door for him. Before he could ask for Lacey, the woman said, "Ms. Montgomery will be right with you. She's on a phone call with her agent. She's asked you wait in the study."

He stepped inside the dramatic two-story foyer with a travertine floor and double-curved staircase and followed the woman to the study. The regal home displayed extensive millwork and gleaming hardwood floors with tile inlay. The travertine floor reappeared, leading them to a fabulous Grand Room with a wall of windows, fireplace, and innumerable architectural niches. Off this room was a deck overlooking a private backyard, pool, and tennis court. There was a billiard room adjacent to the exercise room, which was fully equipped with a massage area.

Did I just pass a home theater with stadium seating? His plan for her to be naked the next time they met seemed blasphemous as he looked around.

Mikel could hardly breathe by the time they reached the private paneled study with built-in cabinetry. He tugged at his tie and sat on the sofa situated to give a view of the fireplace.

"It's a scorcher out today," the woman said. "Would you like something to drink?" She motioned toward a pitcher of pink lemonade.

He accepted the drink. The woman apologized for his wait and left, closing the door behind her. He watched the saltwater fish tank without blinking. In disbelief, he downed his lemonade and wished for something stronger. He poured himself another glass and hurried back to his seat. He glanced around, wondering if Lacey was watching him on hidden cameras. He was happy Lacey hadn't greeted him right away. He needed an opportunity to adjust to what he had just learned. No wonder her friends worried he might take advantage of her—she was rich.

He watched the fish tank while asking himself serious questions. For the first time in his life he wondered if a woman was out of his league. He mentally weighed the pros and cons of their relationship. Lacey Montgomery was beautiful, famous, and loaded. Their relationship began over the Internet—not the best-case scenario. Passion had overwhelmed them, and they embarked on a whirlwind relationship.

The rich and famous were notorious for this type of thing. Grabbing a boy toy, falling superficially in love with him, rushing into marriage, and divorcing twice as quickly. He played the situation over and over in his head, digging a trench of despair. He had come to care about Lacey quite deeply. He dared to admit he was falling in love with her.

To think he might be her hobby—her temporary diversion—made him grind his teeth in anger. He was summoning his courage to confront Lacey, and risk losing what he had with her, when she breezed into the study all smiles.

Every negative thought he had melted instantly when she rushed into his arms. Her face lit up, flashing her dimples when she saw him. He held her tight, swinging her around in a circle. If he had missed her so thoroughly after a week's time, he would never survive losing her forever. They ended their reunion with a heated kiss that made his body shift with tension. He had missed her in that way, too.

"Mikel, I'm so glad you could come early, before people started arriving for the party. Joel and his girlfriend, Wendy, will be here soon, and I—" She caught herself gushing and flushed with embarrassment. Her dark lids dropped to her hands. "I wanted time alone with you first."

He grasped her waist and pulled her onto his lap. She pressed her forehead to his as he smoothed the skirt of her dress. "I missed you, too. Hey," he broke the sentimentality threatening to make *him* start gushing, "I bought you something." He handed her a package wrapped in special acid-free paper.

"For me?" she asked, smiling and ripping into the paper. "I'm a sucker for gifts."

"It was in your profile." He winked at her.

"Oh my…" She glanced at him, surprised.

"I wasn't sure you'd like it. I work with enough writers to know you all can be very particular about things when it comes to your craft. I just thought…" Now he was behaving like a schoolboy with his first crush. "It's the real script. The characters reminded me of yours—from *The Next Step*. Moving. Distressing. Sad." He searched for the right word. She was staring at him unblinkingly. He couldn't label her reaction as happy or offended.

"Mikel, this is great," she whispered examining the

pages. "How did you get your hands on Nicholas Pileggi's original draft script of *Casino*?"

A client had inadvertently made him aware of a charitable auction. The characters reminded him of the effect Lacey's characters had on him. He wanted to buy her a gift, but flowers and jewelry were too ordinary for her. He thought she'd appreciate the screenplay more. He left all that unsaid, and simply asked, "Do you like it?"

"Do I like it? It's the best gift I've ever gotten. I'll cherish it." She thanked him with a kiss that made him want to carry her through the house until he found her bedroom. She stroked his tie. "Can you stay with me tonight?"

"Try to make me leave you."

Chimes rang throughout the house. She bounced up from his lap, leaving him cold and bereft. "That'll be Joel and Wendy."

"Wait." He caught her hand, bringing her to sit next to him. He looked around the room, trying to find the best way to open the discussion. "You live here?"

She giggled. "Yes, did you think I was inviting you to stay the night at someone's else's place?"

"No, I mean, you *live—here*."

Her smile faded. "What are you trying to say?"

He chuckled humorlessly. "Lacey, this is pretty spectacular. You didn't tell me you were rich."

"I didn't think it would make a difference."

"It's—"

"Does it matter?"

"Of course it *matters*."

Angry defenses slipped into place. "You want something from me now? You're getting thoughts about how much I can do for you now?"

His anger mounted, surpassing hers. "I don't use women. I don't use anyone."

She left the sofa and paced to the fireplace. "Then how can it matter?" She whirled around, facing him with heated defiance. "I won't apologize for what I've accomplished, and I won't feel obligated to share with you what I have."

He rose slowly from the sofa. "I didn't ask you to do any of those things, and I resent you accusing me of it."

"I thought you were different."

"What's that supposed to mean?"

"I thought you were successful enough to accept my success and support me in it."

"Are you saying I'm not a man?"

"I'm saying I worked hard for what I have, and I don't want to be judged by it, or used because of it. My having money doesn't exclude you from going out in the world and taking care of your own business. I expect the man in my life to go out and get his own."

He raised his voice, stopping her tirade, "Don't say another word."

She turned her back to him. "I wanted you to be different." There was a hitch in her voice.

His anger softened, and he took responsibility for the misunderstanding. He tried to make it right. "I *am* my own man, and I resent you implying I'm not. Maybe I didn't approach this subject the right way." He stepped around the coffee table separating them. "Maybe you have some history that caused you to jump to conclusions."

She fiddled with a picture on the mantel, but did not turn to him.

"Lacey." He touched her shoulder, encouraging her to face him. "You have to admit it could be shocking to come here for the first time." He made an open-armed gesture indicating her home. "You didn't prepare me for this." He stepped closer, but she remained tense. "I'm looking at a woman who has it all, and I wonder how long before you become bored with me." She started to speak, but he rushed on. "I've told you I'm not the easiest man to get along with. I also don't live in a mansion. My *clients* have recognizable names—my friends don't appear on movie screens. I prefer to be at home, alone with the woman I care about. More so than jet-setting around the country. I look at your lifestyle and wonder how I can fit in it." He stroked her face, lingering over the dimples in her cheeks. "I've been clear from the beginning—I want this relationship to go as far as possible. How far can I go with you, Lacey?"

She watched him intensely, wordlessly.

"Could you give this up for me?"

"No."

He smiled. This was the fire he'd first sensed in her. She would not let him be overbearing, or too demanding. "Would you allow me to share it with you?"

She watched him for a long, assessing moment. "I think I'm falling in love with you."

His heart stopped.

"Lacey, we're coming in!" a man's voice called out as the door to the study flew open.

She pulled away, leaving him in a fog. "Mikel, this is my best friend, Joel."

Joel stepped to him, warily checking him out. He glanced at Lacey, but Mikel couldn't decipher their silent communication. He didn't like another man having a secret language with her. He swallowed his pride and offered Joel his hand. If he wanted a relationship with a woman as dynamic as Lacey, he would have to let go of some of his destructive behaviors. The last thing he wanted to do was lose Lacey because of pride or envy. With their handshake, Mikel and Joel seemed to come to an understanding. For Lacey's sake, they'd hold off character judgments until they got to know each other better.

Mikel enjoyed meeting Lacey's friends. A few of his clients were at the gathering, and from what he could gather, nobody wanted to miss one of Lacey Montgomery's parties, because "Everyone who is anyone shows up."

After wading through the emotional astonishment of

Lacey's declaration, Mikel loosened up and had a good time. There were so many people coming and going, inside and around the pool, he couldn't snag a moment alone with her. He needed to ask her what she meant by "falling in love."

Joel made a point of cornering her off from him. Mikel understood Joel's overprotective stance and tried hard to put him at ease. Once they finished the normal two-men-in-Lacey's-life posturing, they got along well. Business came up, and soon they were discussing the possibility of Mikel representing Joel's career. With a handshake over beers in the billiard room, they agreed Mikel's firm would manage his career.

It was late when the last guests left Lacey's house. Joel and Wendy joined Mikel and Lacey outside by the pool for quiet conversation before ending the evening. Mikel watched Lacey's eyes dance when Joel told her about their agreement.

"This makes me happy," she said, watching Mikel and holding Joel's hand. "I was worried about some shyster signing him." She turned to Joel. "Mikel is great at what he does. You'll be in good hands." She had witnessed his skills during the times she used his home office to work on her storyboard.

"Thank you." He leaned over and gave her a quick kiss. "It feels good to know you appreciate my work."

"We should go," Wendy said, standing up.

Joel stood, too. "I have an early flight."

"I'm going to miss him." Wendy's eyes watered.

"Don't cry. You're going to come out as soon as I get settled, right?"

She nodded, but it didn't seem like enough.

Lacey looked over at Mikel. It was awkward to share their personal moment, but warmth spread through him because he was happy to be reunited with his girl.

Lacey stood. "Can we have a minute?" she asked Wendy.

"I'll meet you in the car." She headed out, leaving Mikel feeling like an intruder.

"I'll be right back," Lacey said, leaning down to kiss him. "I want to say good-bye."

Mikel finished his drink, enjoying the warm weather while watching the sparkling pool.

Lacey said she and Joel had been friends since they were kids. The bond was evident. She'd told Mikel that Joel protected her, and she rescued him. Mikel had been jealous at first, listening to her go on about their adventures, but after having met Joel, he was glad she had someone dependable in her life.

"Chocolate Dream," Lacey's tender voice pierced the darkness a few minutes later.

"Mikel."

"Let's go to bed."

He followed Lacey up a private rear staircase to the second level. She held his hand, taking him to the master suite. The bedroom had a separate sitting room where Lacey worked on her screenplay. It led to an expansive master bath with a black marble floor, enormous corner shower, huge whirlpool tub, double vanities, and double walk-in closets with custom built-in shelves. The elegance of the bedroom immediately put Mikel in a romantic mood. He wondered if she felt the same way—and what she did about it before he came along.

Lacey took him into the bathroom and they undressed each other around breaks for long kissing sessions. He wanted to question her about her feelings for him. He wanted to share his own. Every time he tried to broach the subject, Lacey did something sexy to his body and the conversation was lost. They stepped into the shower under warm water. Double showerheads and body jets caressed their bodies as he made love to her. He had missed her tremendously, and he wanted her to know it.

Mikel knelt on the floor of the shower and lifted Lacey's

leg to his shoulder. Water sluiced over her shoulders as he tasted her readiness. Romance mixed with lust to drive him into a frenzy. Water hit him from every angle, increasing his zeal. He wanted her to feel his affection and his hunger in the strength of the explosion of her climax—and he worked to make certain she did. He let her moans guide his touches. He regulated the speed and depth of his tongue by her groans. He twisted his body until he was perched between her thighs, gripping her bottom and whipping her most sensitive place with blender-perfect precision. He pushed her over the edge with his tongue, steadying her body as her knees buckled.

"Oh my, oh my…" she panted. "Oh my gawd." She clawed at him, urging him to stand up.

"Water off," he murmured next to her lips before consuming her mouth.

The spray subsided.

He pressed her body tightly against his, lifting her and carrying her from the shower. She tied a fluffy towel around herself, and then she wrapped him in a matching towel and dried him from head to toe. He was hard and pulsating, barely able to control the anticipation of burying himself inside her body—inside her heart.

He bent to kiss the top of her head. "Lacey," he whispered, prepared to say the words weighing heavily on his heart.

She looked up at him with bright eyes and a devilish smile full of sensuous intent, and his mouth clamped shut. Her fingers curled inside the towel at his waist and tugged. She whispered flirtatious promises as she led him into the bedroom. She laid him down on the bed, and within minutes he was talking in his native tongue of legalese. She took his mind places he had never gone before. While he was drowning in thick emotion and sticky delight, she controlled his heart and commanded his body.

It did not take long for Lacey to get the response she desired. It became hard for Mikel to breathe. The muscles of his abdomen tightened. His thighs seized in pleasure. His toes stretched wide. He fought to reach the bottom, but resisted finding the end. With the well-timed shimmy of her hips, Lacey made him detonate.

She hovered over him, kissing his shoulders. She showed him her tongue, licking her lips before using it to trace his sternum.

"Chocolate Dream."

"Mikel."

Her brown eyes rolled up to look at him, but her lips didn't leave his abdomen. "I know your name."

"Say it."

She teased his navel, clearly taking her time in meeting his demand. "Mikel." She cupped his manhood. "This is all Mikel."

What could he say when she stroked him with her thumb that way? She'd effectively shut down his male arrogance by using what made him a man against him. She had hardly let him recover before she was making him explode again.

Mikel awoke early the next morning. He had fallen into a comatose state of exhaustion when Lacey finished with him, but her absence from bed immediately startled him awake. He followed the light into the adjoining sitting room. Lacey sat at her desk in front of the computer, wearing a yellow camisole and matching panties. She frowned at the computer screen, highly distressed. He went to her and kissed her cheek. "Did you sleep at all?"

She noticed him for the first time. "Not yet."

"Sugar, it's morning."

She blinked twice. "I haven't been able to write—since I left your place. What I've done is awful, and I have a deadline approaching. My agent is after me to accept some of the offers pouring in, but I can't get this screenplay done."

"Shh." He kneeled on the floor and pulled her chair away from the desk until she was situated in front of him. "You look so sad, and so distressed. Isn't writing supposed to be fun?"

"It was." She shook her head. "It is. It's the pressure." She looked down at him with tears in her eyes. "I'm afraid I won't be able to do it again."

"Do what again?" He spoke to her in a quiet, soothing voice as he stroked her short curls. "Talk to me."

"What if I can't write another screenplay as successful at *The Next Step*? If the next script is a flop—"

"It won't be."

"What if—"

He held her face between his hands. "It won't be."

"But—"

"*It won't be.* You're too good of a writer."

"I don't know if I can—"

"I won't let you do this, Lacey. I won't let you doubt yourself, or your abilities." He smiled. "You're having one of those creativity crisis meltdowns writers are so famous for." He took her hands and stood, bringing her up with him. "You need to step away from the computer for a little bit." He led her back to bed. "You're stressed to the maximum."

They climbed into bed and he pulled her into his arms. "Tell me about your script."

"I don't like to discuss my work before it's finished."

"You're not *discussing your work*. You're sharing your ideas with your lover." It seemed the perfect segue to discuss what they meant to each other. If she didn't want to talk about the script, he'd talk about his feelings for her. He wanted to devote this time to Lacey and her needs, but he desperately wanted to explore her earlier statement. Just as he was about to break the silence by telling her his feelings, she laid her head on his chest and shared her story. He listened intently as she went scene by scene, exploring her characters and their motives.

There was a particularly dicey scene where the heroine had to justify loving a man who was enslaving her. "I can't seem to get past this scene," Lacey told him.

"If you challenge a woman, she fights back. If you open your heart to her, she opens hers to you."

Lacey's head popped up, and she stared at him as if he had called her a dirty name.

"What is it?" he asked.

"That's it!" She jumped out of bed and ran back to the computer. He listened to the keyboard clack until he drifted back to sleep.

9

Lacey finished her lecture at the New York Film School and hopped a cab back to her hotel. She was spending two weeks in the New York area. The agent had arranged speaking engagements and teaching seminars at various venues. Tonight she would be presenting a screenwriter's workshop for local writers. Tomorrow would be a flurry of activity—three talk show appearances in the morning and dinner at an exclusive director's club.

Lacey sighed as she watched the rain-soaked streets inch by. The traffic in New York was too thick. It was too cold and rainy. And everyone she cared about was too many miles away. Her brothers were in Ohio studying. Her parents were in Florida. Wendy had flown out to meet Joel in California because he couldn't stand the loneliness.

A cold ache moved through her chest when she thought of Mikel. He was meeting with Joel in California over the next few days during the prescreening of Joel's movie. He also planned to meet with several of his other clients while in the area.

Their relationship had progressed without a snag over the past nine months, making it extremely hard to be apart from him. She had never felt this way about a man before. She'd been with men who she cared about and enjoyed their company, but never had she felt so bereft when one of them wasn't around. Her body seemed to ache without his caresses. Her writing suffered when he wasn't around to stroke her ego. She'd written about loneliness many times, but never understood the true pain of it until she was separated from Mikel.

The cab came to a complete halt. Cars were parked bumper to bumper in the street. She tried to pinpoint her location by placing the stores lining the street. New York was huge and dense compared with the Atlanta suburb she called home. She'd always enjoyed the hustle and bustle, the crowds, shopping, and restaurants. Her promotional trips to New York had always been a highlight in her writing career—until Mikel showed her the value of quiet evenings alone with him.

Lacey pulled out her cell phone and dialed Mikel.

"Hey," he answered, sounding happy to hear from her.

She didn't try to hide the smile in her voice. "Where are you?"

"Still in Cali. I'm at lunch with some clients. Joel's here."

Joel came on the line. "Lacey, it's me. We're eating lunch in one of your favorite restaurants. Guess which one? We are having a blast! Mikel isn't as stuffy as Wendy and I first thought he was, showing up at the party in a suit and all." He continued to ramble, and all Lacey could do was insert the obligatory chuckle or "uh-huh." She listened to him describe his latest Hollywood adventures. "There are so many stars in this movie, the press can't get enough coverage."

"I've seen the magazine write-ups. You looked good on Jay Leno. You let your hair grow out."

"It was that or makeup, and I'm not wearing a wig for my first starring role. Did you read the script yet?"

She'd read Joel's next script, and it was excellently written. She told him so. "And the reviews for this picture have been exceptional."

"Did I thank you for flying out? I couldn't have handled the whole red carpet thing without you. Anyway, the buzz about the movie is large. The studio is already thinking about Academy Award nominations. And, Lacey, get this! I've been told they're going to push me hard for Best Actor in a Supporting Role."

"Joel, you're a wonderful actor. Of course you deserve the Oscar." Previous nominees for the award included Alec Baldwin, Benicio Del Toro, and Tim Robbins—just being nominated for his first film would skyrocket Joel's career. "Joel," she said.

"What's up?"

She lowered her voice as if those around Joel could hear her. "Are you going to meetings?" He'd received a lot of press coverage after the release of the movie, and it always seemed to picture him at a big Hollywood party.

"Every week," he answered.

"L.A. can be tempting."

"I know, Lacey. I'm going. Wendy and I are going. I promise."

"I worry about you."

"I love you for it."

"I miss you." The cab moved a car-length ahead.

"Here's Mikel," Joel said.

"I have to get going," Mikel said when he came on the line. Everyone in California seemed to be in such a rush these days. When Lacey was there, the atmosphere had always been laid back and carefree.

"When are you coming home?"

"A couple of days. You?"

"Another week."

"I miss you." His deep timbre vibrated in her ear. "I have to go. Call you later?"

"Bye." He disconnected before she could tell him she missed him, too.

Mikel ambled around his apartment, missing Lacey. He had been able to keep busy in California, and at the office when he'd returned to Atlanta, but still her absence in his life was sizable. He hadn't realized the life of a writer could be so hectic. As they grew closer, he dared dream she would be the staple in his life, bringing order out of chaos. Instead, her schedule kept her away from Atlanta for longer periods than his.

His life was getting better and better since meeting Lacey, so he shouldn't complain about her absence. Not only had he met the perfect woman, his business was flourishing. Signing Joel had been beneficial to them all. Lacey had someone she trusted managing her friend's career. Joel could relax and concentrate on his Academy Award performance. And Mikel's prestige increased in the entertainment business. He became distracted from his work, imagining them celebrating the 78th Academy Awards together. It made him miss Lacey even more.

Are you there, Brown Sugar? he typed into his computer.

No response. He thought she might be writing. She had sounded as if she missed him when he spoke to her a couple of days ago. She was in New York, he reminded himself—probably out on the town.

I miss you, he added. Hope you're having a good time.... Hurry home.

While on the Internet, Mikel surfed the Web for a gift for Lacey. He stumbled upon nightygram.com and decided to send her a radiant red, stretch velour gown with spaghetti straps and a plunging neckline. He scrolled the site and added a mouthwatering camisole with tap pants.

He imagined slipping the spaghetti straps from her

shoulders, revealing her luscious breasts for his full consumption. He couldn't wait to open the lace-up front with his teeth, nibbling her tender skin as he worked at the ivory lace trim. He ordered the matching kimono; but if he had his way, she'd never need it. She would want bath salts, and an aromatherapy gift set would help de-stress her during her writing. He added Naughty and Nice fortune cookies and chocolate body paint to the package before having it shipped to her hotel in New York. He would love to be there when she opened the package. He grinned, thinking of the seductive smile that would fill her beautiful face.

Chocolate Dream...

His heart leapt. I'm here, Brown Sugar. Where were you?

Showering.

Alone? he asked, only half in jest.

You were here in my heart.

When are you coming home, Brown Sugar?

Four more days...brb

He waited, impatiently, for her to return to the computer.

The agent is calling to discuss a change of schedule.

Take care of your business. He didn't want to let her go.

Miss you. See you in 4 days.

Those were the four longest days of Mikel's life, and when Lacey returned, he vowed never to be separated from her for so long again. He needed to start planning for a permanent future with her.

She'd bounded off the plane carrying the gift from nightygram. com. "I didn't want to open it without you."

Once they made it back to her place, they'd kissed their way up the private staircase to her bedroom and made love until late into the night. After their vigorous session of love play, he'd fallen asleep, and Lacey headed to her computer. If he were a lesser man, her energy after making love might distress him. Instead of their intimacy tiring her, it seemed to energize her. He was a hard sleeper, so her tapping at the computer never bothered him. It was nice to know she was in the next room, going on with her usual routine as if his presence in her bed was a normal part of her life.

His cell phone vibrated. He'd made a habit of lining up his two cells, his Palm Pilot, and his two pagers on the bedside table on *his side* of the bed.

"Are you awake?" Lacey called from the sitting room.

"Yes," he mumbled, his voice rough with sleep.

"Your phone is ringing. Who could be calling this late?"

"I don't know." He sat up and turned on the lamp. He grabbed the phone and read the caller ID display. "It's Joel."

Lacey stopped tapping at the keyboard and came to stand over the bed while he took the call.

He would wish for many nights he had never answered the phone.

The whirlwind of L.A. overwhelmed Wendy, and she became homesick. Joel didn't admit it, but he needed a break from the endless L.A. hustle himself. The fame quickly inflated one's ego, but it wasn't real. He knew it would only last until his next film left the big screen and hit video stores. And that was assuming this film would receive a reception as large as the last. There were huge stars in the last flick, in this one he had the burden of carrying the plot. The parties exerted phenomenal pressure on his willpower to stay clean. He had seen the look of desperation written on Wendy's face when the drugs called, so he agreed they needed to get out of Hollywood for a while. He secured his apartment and accompanied Wendy back to Atlanta for a long weekend.

"Did you tell Lacey you were coming?" Wendy asked as they departed the plane.

"I want to surprise her."

"Not much chance of that happening." A group of young girls recognized him and made a beeline over. "Hold my bag. I have to use the ladies' room." The girls swarmed around. "I can't handle this right now. I'll meet you out front in the limo."

Joel wanted to protest, but he took her bag and was swept away into a crowd of adoring fans. Security was called when the crowd grew large enough to interfere with the security checkpoint. He was flattered by the attention, but the pushing and shoving to get to him could be frightening. Police with dogs were summoned when the paparazzi came on the scene. He single-handedly turned the William B. Hartsfield International Airport into a mob scene. The police quarantined him in a remote corner while they fought to disperse the crowd.

He was tattered and torn by the time the police and security had everything under control. He was thanking the law enforcement team when one of the dogs became overly friendly. He laughed at first, making an obscene joke that only a few of the cops found funny. Airport security watched him with malevolent scrutiny.

"What's in the bag?" a security policeman asked.

"I don't know," Joel answered. "It's my girlfriend's carry-on."

"Bet they don't search big movie stars when they board planes in L.A.," a burly officer grumbled, his day just made harder.

The police officer handling the dog called him off. "Maybe we should have a little look."

"Boys," the burly officer said, "collect the movie star's luggage. The least we can do is show our Hotlanta hospitality and rummage through his delicates in the privacy of the office."

Minutes later, Joel's mouth hung slack in astonishment as the officers dug bag after bag of coke from Wendy's carry-on. His arms were forced behind the back of the chair, and the handcuffs were eating into his wrists.

"A big star like you will probably get probation with SAI," the burly cop said, slipping into "bad cop" mode rather easily. One of the initiatives to deal with correctional crowding in Atlanta was the development of the Special Alternative Incarceration, or SAI program. Mandated as a special condition to a sentence of probation, SAI required offenders to serve ninety days in prison, and then a period of postconfinement community supervision at a boot camp. "Yep, ninety days in prison ain't a long time." He rubbed his chin. "Of course, that's ninety days in Atlanta time. In Hollywood time, it's long enough to end your career."

"I always thought being busted helped your career in Hollywood. Those are some twisted people out there," the other cop in the room said.

"You're assuming he won't be in prison long enough to lose those pretty boy good looks of his."

"Well, yeah. Let's just wait and see what DEA and Homeland Security have to say before you go promising the movie star an easy trip."

Joel knew enough to keep his mouth shut while they played games with his head. They obviously hated the rich and famous because they were thinking of calling Homeland Security in on the deal as if he were some sort of terrorist. Wait until they found out about his history of drug use. It didn't matter that he had been clean for years, they would use it against him for leverage. He had never been arrested for anything more serious than loitering, but being in the county jail until Lacey could bail him out had scared Joel enough to throw him into detox. He couldn't do hard time in a real prison. He'd heard the stories about boot camp, and going there wouldn't be a cakewalk either.

"Of course," the burly cop said, "if Joel was to work with us, give us some information—that might make it easier on him. We'd get a bigger fish off the streets. He could fly back to Hollywood and save his career. Everyone would be happy." He pulled up a chair and got in Joel's face. "What do you think about that?"

Joel dropped his head. "I want to call my attorney."

Mikel ushered Joel into Lacey's mansion. She grabbed Joel and held tight. "You look terrible. What did they do to you in that place?"

Disheveled and withdrawn, Joel broke her embrace and ambled into the kitchen. He smelled awful. His hair was matted and dirty—*were there bugs crawling on his clothes?* Lacey tried to make eye contact with Mikel, but he kept his gaze trained to the floor as he followed Joel.

Joel rummaged through the refrigerator. "I'm starved."

"Let me fix you something," Lacey said, nudging him out of the way.

"Something quick."

Joel and Mikel sat at the table while she made Joel a sandwich.

"Eat this. I'll heat you some dinner, too." She joined them at the table. "Why wouldn't they let me see you in jail, Joel?"

"The first day there was a fight—"

"What kind of fight?" she wanted to know.

"For every fan I have, there are two big goons who are pissed off because their girls compare them with me."

Lacey tried to catch Mikel's gaze, but he dropped his eyes to the table. Joel had been in jail for a week before she was allowed to post bail. Mikel never offered a satisfactory reason why it had taken so long. After hearing about Joel being attacked, she wondered what else he was keeping from her, and why he found it so difficult to look at her.

"Are you all right, Joel?"

"Physically, yes." He choked down another bite. "Can you believe Wendy would do this to me?" He looked to Mikel. "Have you been able to find her?"

Mikel shook his head.

Lacey threw him an angry look. He needed to be more encouraging. "Don't worry, we'll find Wendy and bring her back so she can explain the truth."

"I *love* her, Lacey," Joel said.

"Did you know she was back on drugs?"

"No, if I had known, I would have checked her into Betty Ford or something. It's partly my fault. I was so busy with work and my career, I wasn't paying enough attention to what she was doing."

"You know better, Joel." Lacey had participated in meetings to cope with her guilt over Joel's addiction. She knew the abuser had to take responsibility for his or her own actions, and he did, too.

"I need a shower." Joel pushed back his chair. "Can I crash here with you for a while? Until I get a handle on all of this."

"You don't have to ask."

He kissed her and left the room, his gait dragging with defeat.

"I can't believe what he's going through. You're awful quiet."

Mikel cleared his throat. "There are some things Joel is going to have to face."

She removed the dirty dish from the table. "Like what?"

"This doesn't look good."

"We have to handle this as quietly as possible before the media gets the story." She rejoined him at the kitchen table.

"He has a lot more to worry about than his career. Joel is facing prison time."

"Prison time…" She let the words fade, refusing to believe it. "We have to keep that from happening."

Mikel cleared his throat. "There's no *we* in this, Lacey."

"What do you mean?"

"I'm not a criminal attorney."

"Neither am I, but we can still help him."

"How?"

She didn't like where this conversation was going.

"Listen, Lacey, the success of my business depends on my reputation. I can't get caught up in a high-profile drug case." He watched her closely as he delivered the next blow. "Joel's contract has a morality clause, and I'm going to exercise it. I no longer represent him, and I have to distance myself from this problem."

"*Problem?* He has a name."

"I've discussed this with Joel, and he's okay with it. Let's not fight about it."

She crossed the room, afraid of what she might do sitting so close to him. "If you plan on dumping my friend at the first sign of trouble, we're going to have one hell of a fight, Mikel."

"It's business, Lacey. You know I like Joel, but I have to think of the business I've built, and my commitment to my other clients."

"*This is Joel!* You have to have some level of commitment to him. He's your client, but he's a friend, too. He's *my* best friend. That should mean something."

"It does. If it didn't I wouldn't be having this conversation."

"We aren't having a conversation," Lacey yelled. "You come in here and announce the fact that you're dumping Joel when he needs you most. A conversation implies a discussion before taking action."

"I had the discussion with Joel. He understands. Why don't you?"

She turned her back on him, slamming pots and pans to work out her anger. Mikel came up behind her and tried to wrap his arms around her middle. She whirled around, stepping out of his embrace. "You can't do this. Acting is all Joel has. Without it, I don't know what will happen to him. The only thing keeping him clean has been his acting career. Without it, I don't know what he'll do."

"What? Joel has a problem? Drugs?"

"He's been clean for years."

"And you knew about this?" he shouted. "And you didn't warn me before I signed him as a client?"

"It wasn't relevant."

"Obviously, it was."

"You can't believe he's guilty."

"He had two grams of cocaine in his bag."

"Wendy's bag."

"Which was packed with his things, and Wendy has conveniently disappeared."

She stepped out of his shadow. "Joel said he didn't do it. His word is enough for me. And it'll have to be enough for you, too."

"What do you mean?"

"If you care about me, you'll stand by Joel and help him through this like I plan to do."

"I care about you more than you know, Lacey; but I have to see the big picture here."

"Yes, you do need to see the big picture. If you can't accept my best friend, you can't possibly want to be with me."

"What are you saying? Be careful here."

She folded her arms across her chest. "Joel has been a part of my life since we were kids. He's my best friend. He's family. I don't know how you could be involved with me and not accept him."

"I don't take ultimatums well," Mikel said through clenched teeth.

"I don't take betrayal well."

"You'd put our relationship up against my business decision?"

"This is about more than business."

"Just answer me!" he yelled.

"Yes, if you can't show any more loyalty than to run when times get hard, I have to wonder what you'll do when times get hard between us."

"I'm going to leave now before this goes too far." He

stepped to the kitchen door. "You're angry and you're hurt. You don't mean what you're saying."

"I mean exactly what I'm saying."

He turned to her. "And what is that, Lacey?"

"If you can't help Joel through this, you *should* leave. For good."

He watched her for a long moment, probably hoping she would break down and blubber and beg him to stay. She wouldn't do it. Women didn't cry over men anymore—they were stronger than that. At least the characters in her screenplays didn't cry when their hearts were smashed to pieces.

Mikel stepped out of the kitchen and charged out of her house, brutally reminding her this wasn't one of her screen-plays—this was her life. And in her real life, she did cry when her heart was ripping apart.

10

Lacey's stomach clenched with despair. She hadn't eaten a good meal in weeks. She reached deep into her gut and extracted the misery, smearing it onto the pages of her manuscript. The agent told her it was her best work yet.

"Why are you so distressed?" the agent asked. "You should be celebrating."

How could she celebrate when her life was teetering between gloom and hopelessness?

Joel received the Academy's nod for his performance in his first movie. Whether he'd be able to attend the event in March was another matter. The media was fanning the flames, reporting on his pending drug charges every day. If there were no new developments, they dug up some low-life from his days of addiction and propped him in front of the camera to tell a sensational, but untrue, story. Joel remained on house arrest at Lacey's mansion, and that opened a whole debate over justice for the rich versus justice for the poor. "Martha Stewart wished she had it so good," one reporter said.

Joel's lawyer remained positive, looking for new ways to circumvent the law. He filed motions and tried to exclude the evidence. He went on television holding Wendy's picture and offering a reward for information about her location. He'd forgotten to say *credible* information, so they were wading through hundreds of bogus tips. Meanwhile, Wendy was going deeper underground. Locating her seemed hopeless.

The parents were calling—both Joel's and Lacey's— spouting the gospel about the evils infecting the entertainment business.

Lacey was supposed to be watching out for Joel, his parents scolded, after all, he would do the same for her if their situations were reversed. Where had she been when he needed her the most? It didn't matter that she was standing by him now. She had thrown away her relationship with Mikel—the best thing to happen to her in a lifetime—because she was trying to save Joel. Didn't that amount to anything? According to Joel's parents, it wasn't enough.

So Lacey tried harder. She pressed the lawyer and came to Joel's defense with the media. She lobbied, using her contacts in local government, trying to pull any strings she could to keep her best friend out of jail. She fought to save his career because he needed to have something waiting for him since the love of his life had run off. She helped Joel hire a publicist, although finding another attorney–agent proved impossible. No one wanted to attach their name to his while he was under such scrutiny.

"Knock, knock." Lacey stood on the threshold of the bedroom where Joel was staying.

"Come in." Immediately, he slid to one side of the bed, making room for her. He was watching a movie from her DVD collection. He seemed to spend all his time with his lawyer or in his room watching old movies.

Lacey lay next to him, grabbing a handful of popcorn from the bowl he placed on the bed between them. "What did your attorney have to say today?"

Joel didn't take his eyes from the television. "SSDD—same sh—"

"I've got it."

"—different day," he finished.

"I'm having lunch with a councilman tomorrow. He has friends at the courthouse, and—"

"Don't get yourself in trouble by offering to do something crazy."

"I just want to feel him out. See if he can give us any information about the case, or the judge who'll be hearing it. Don't you think that will be helpful?"

Joel turned away from the television and looked at her. "I don't think anything will be helpful to me right now except Wendy coming forward and admitting the drugs weren't mine. Since that's obviously not going to happen, I need to think about other alternatives."

"What kind of alternatives?" She grabbed the remote and shut off the television. "What are you thinking of doing?"

They sat Indian-style facing each other.

"My attorney thinks he can get me a righteous plea bargain. I can do SAI standing on my head."

Joel was a pretty boy. No, he couldn't.

"To get a plea bargain, you have to say you did it. You have to go before the judge and tell him you have a drug problem and you broke several drug trafficking laws."

He watched her unblinkingly.

"But you didn't do it. Admitting to a felony drug charge might not hurt your reputation in Hollywood, but your parents would die. I would die. You'd have a record. If you ever got into any more trouble, it could be very bad."

"I don't plan on getting into any more trouble."

"You didn't plan to get into this trouble, Joel."

His gaze shifted away from her. "I'll have to be more careful."

"This is crazy. You can't do time for something you didn't do."

"Maybe it is my fault. I should have been more attentive to Wendy. I could have stopped her, or at least gotten her help."

"The only thing you did wrong when it comes to Wendy is fall in love with her. I'm not going to let you take the rap for her."

"Lacey." His voice was quiet but full of conviction. He had thought about the plea bargain and had already made up his mind without talking to her first. "This isn't about what you want. I have to do what's best for me."

"This isn't the best thing for you, Joel."

"Lacey." He took her hands in his and gave them a shake. "Stop trying to save me. You've been rescuing me since we were little kids. And I've always let you."

"I love you."

He released her hands and left the bed, pacing over to the window. "I'm a man. I should have been standing on my own two feet a long time ago. Well, now things are desperate, and no one can save me but me. I should have put a stop to this right away."

"A stop to what?"

"Letting you take care of me. Needing you to take care of me."

"We need each other." She crossed the room and sat on the windowsill with him. "I can't count how many times you've looked out for me and saved my behind."

"You're a girl. I'm supposed to look out for you. You aren't supposed to be fighting my fights. I should have stepped up when you broke up with Mikel."

A sharp pang pierced her chest.

"I know how much you care about him. I hear you crying over him at night. I stood by and let you choose me over your own happiness. That wasn't looking out for you. I'm so sorry for that. I was so scared about going to jail, I wasn't thinking straight."

"Mikel should have stood by you."

"No agent would let one client bring down his entire firm. No, Mikel did the right thing."

"You're saying I'm wrong?"

"I'm saying you love me too much, and sometimes I don't deserve your unconditional devotion. Sometimes I screw up. And sometimes I have to fix my messes all by myself."

"So I'm supposed to stand by and watch you be convicted for something you didn't do?"

"If it's what I decide to do, yes. If it's what I ask you to do, yes."

They were both momentarily lost in thought. Joel broke the silence. "Have you talked to Mikel at all?"

"Not since the day you came home."

"He's called."

"And e-mailed, but I don't want to talk to him." No matter how much she missed him, this was about her beliefs and convictions. She couldn't be with Mikel when their idea of loyalty was so differently defined. It would cause them problems later in their relationship. She'd spent a lot of time convincing herself that she'd done the right thing—giving Mikel up before he could disappoint her again.

Joel draped his arm over her shoulder. "I'm giving you permission to call him. I won't hold it against you. It won't affect our friendship in the least. You deserve to be happy, and Mikel makes you happy."

She shook her head. "I can't. I feel betrayed by him. I need to know he won't run when the going gets tough. What if the drugs had been planted in *my* bag? Would he have supported me? Or would he have placed his firm's reputation above me? Where's the trust in that?"

"It wasn't you, Lacey. Mikel is mad-crazy for you. I have a feeling he would fight a little harder to save you if you were in trouble."

"I don't know."

"Figure it out. I'd like to know you have someone here watching out for you if I'm not around for a while." He propelled himself from the windowsill and left the room.

Lacey was still sitting there, trying desperately to understand Joel's reasoning, when she heard him splash into the pool beneath the window.

Okay, so he was a fool. Mikel could think of a couple of other choice names, too, but he tried not to use such colorful language. For weeks, he'd been glued to the plasma television hanging on his bedroom wall as the news sliced and diced Joel's reputation. His career was fairing well, but there definitely weren't any new offers on the table. Not knowing Mikel had dropped Joel from his client roster, the few sponsors with outstanding deals called his office to withdraw from negotiations with a quickness. Every day there were piles of angry letters from outraged fans.

Whenever Mikel saw a candid shot of Joel being dragged through a sea of paparazzi, Lacey's could be seen in the background, fighting through the crowds alongside her friend.

Mikel was good at judging character. He knew Joel was telling the truth about the drugs. If he were honest, Mikel would admit he was afraid to get tangled up in Joel's mess. Building his business had come relatively easy when put into perspective, but managing talent was a fickle line of work. Hollywood prided itself on making stars, and then crushing them when they became too big.

Reputation was everything in a business full of shysters and criminals. He couldn't risk losing everything for one client. He had rehearsed this justification so many times he could recite it on cue to his staff's dirty looks. He'd used the argument to explain his decision to his team at the office. He threw in the "I have to consider all the employees here who are supporting their families" rationalization, but his employees weren't overwhelmingly in agreement. The more he justified his behavior, the more he began to doubt it. His clients needed to know he would fight for them as tenaciously for their lives as he did for their contracts.

Mikel still had not slept on a *Lacey's side of the bed*. He rolled on his side and pictured her lying next to him, her mind spinning with ideas while she waited for him to release her to go to the computer. He would keep her in bed sometimes, toying with her body until she screamed his name. When he was done tasting her and caressing her, he'd let her go to the computer and work on her screenplay while he slept.

Out of curiosity, he checked to see if Lacey was online. The yellow icon next to her name confirmed she was.

He typed, How are you holding up?

She didn't answer.

Please try to understand.

Nothing.

I did what I believed was right.

No response.

We can work through this, but you have to talk to me.

Radio silence.

Dead air time.

He could *feel* her at her keyboard, watching him and trying to decide if she wanted to talk to him. He punched the keyboard, I miss you.

She didn't respond.

I'm going to Cali in two weeks on business. Meet me in L.A. I'll send you a ticket. We'll talk. Work it out.

Lacey signed off.

"Breaking developments in the alleged drug possession case with Joel," the television reporter was saying. In Hollywood, he was known as *Joel*. No last name, like Cher.

Mikel stood in front of the television, watching the news unfold.

"Inside sources tell us Joel will be turning himself in to Atlanta detectives tomorrow. It is expected he will plea-bargain..."

Mikel's concentration faded as he thought of the turmoil Joel's actions must have been causing Lacey. Joel had completely duped him. He'd been certain Joel was innocent of the charges.

He went over Joel's initial phone call, seeing him in jail, and their candid conversation as they drove to Lacey's house. Joel had been devastated by Wendy's betrayal, but more upset about the possibility of her using drugs. He had been so worried about Wendy, he pleaded with Mikel to cruise through Drug Alley—a section of the city known for overt drug usage—to look for her. Mikel had refused, knowing Lacey was worried and wouldn't approve.

Joel couldn't be guilty. Mikel was a good judge of character. He hadn't released Joel because he believed he was guilty. He'd done it to save his business.

"Why would he confess to something he hadn't done?" he asked aloud.

Could it be to save Wendy? he wondered. The police didn't even believe Wendy existed. No, that scheme wouldn't work. His lawyer would advise him against it.

Then it became clear to Mikel. "He'd do it to get a lighter jail sentence if his case looked impossible to win." Joel would go to jail to protect Lacey. He would accept a plea bargain if he was afraid a long trial would hurt Lacey. He wouldn't want her suffering alongside him, fighting a losing battle. And he wouldn't want to jeopardize Wendy. He'd never turn her over to the police so they could prosecute her, and from what Mikel knew about the case, Wendy coming forward was his only hope at vindication.

Mikel swallowed his guilt. He had been the first one to abandon Joel. His inaction had set all this in motion. He had to make this right. He couldn't be responsible for an innocent man going to jail, or ruining his career. If he were in any way the catalyst for Joel's decision, he had to step in and do something. He had no idea what. The only thing that would save him was for Wendy to show up at the police station and corroborate Joel's story. Even then there was no guarantee they would believe her. According to news reports, several distraught fans had already tried.

Mikel went to his office and made a long-overdue phone call.

"Yeah?"

"Joel, it's Mikel. Are you hanging in there?"

"It's been rough."

Mikel swallowed his pride and tackled the awkward situation. "I saw the news reports. You're going to turn yourself in?"

"At this point, it's my best deal." He sounded defeated.

"Man, I have to apologize. I shouldn't have canceled your contract, and if I have anything to do with your decision, reconsider."

"I don't blame you for jumping off a sinking ship."

"I'm your agent and attorney. I shouldn't have abandoned you. Especially when I know you're not guilty. I don't know what I can do at this late date, but I'd like to rejoin your team."

Joel was quiet for a long moment. "Does this have anything to do with Lacey?"

"Yes." He didn't lie.

"I don't want you representing me if it's only to get the girl."

"It has everything to do with Lacey because I care about her and she was the only one honest enough to tell me I was out of line."

"I can't help you get back with her."

"I know."

Lacey wouldn't be so easily influenced. If it were that

easy, Mikel would have asked for Joel's help a long time ago. It would take more than apologizing and helping Joel. Getting Lacey back would take endless hours of proving himself worthy to be with her. He'd have to demonstrate in an undeniable way how much he cared for her.

"What can I do to help?" Mikel asked.

"Find Wendy."

Lacey poured the angel hair pasta through the strainer, and then placed it back in the pan. She stirred in the sour cream and was about to add the onion-tomato-ham mixture when Joel walked in and announced, "I just met with your boyfriend."

The mixture fell from her hand; most of it landed in the pan, but some spilled onto the top of the range.

"I don't know who you're talking about," she said once she recovered her composure.

"Hmmm." He grabbed a bottle of water and straddled the kitchen chair.

She resumed her cooking, but Joel's silent insistence was nerve-racking. "Tell me what he said."

A boyish smile spread across his face. It had been weeks since she'd seen his carefree smile. "We have a plan."

"What kind of plan? What are you talking about?"

"He's had a change of heart—or fit of conscience—I'm not sure which." He gulped his water, making her wait for the details. "I signed a new contract with him."

She shook her head. "I don't understand what's going on."

"He's representing my interests again. And as you know, representing me right now also means becoming an active member of my criminal case."

"He's not a criminal attorney." Her mind scrambled to make sense of what Joel was telling her. Her heart was thundering, hopeful an amicable end could come to their argument.

"No, he's not, but he's experienced at speaking with the media. And he can put the right spin on this for the right people, and maybe save my career."

She hadn't heard Joel speak of his career in positive terms since he was arrested. "How did this happen?"

Joel lazily shrugged a shoulder. "Don't know. He called me a couple of days ago. We talked and worked it out."

"You're okay with re-signing with him? You're not worried he might bolt again?"

His expression became serious. "I'm more worried about you. How long are you going to be a martyr for my causes?"

She turned back to the stove and resumed cooking. She refused to discuss her relationship with Joel when she didn't understand her jumbled feelings about Mikel. "What kind of plan did you come up with?"

"It isn't a brainstorm, just common sense. We have to find Wendy. He's going to help me do it."

She looked over her shoulder at him. "How is he going to find her? The police haven't been able to."

"Have the police really been looking? They didn't exactly jump all over my story. They think I'm making it all up—like the one-armed man who killed the doctor's wife."

"Wendy couldn't have gotten far. She left all her valuables with you in the carry-on. You've checked with her family. Where could she have gone?" Lacey asked for the millionth time.

Joel shrugged a shoulder again. "I don't know." He sauntered out of the kitchen. "Call me when dinner's ready."

"Where are you going?"

"To track down Wendy."

She smiled, calling after him, "So you've changed your mind about the plea bargain?"

Joel didn't answer.

"You wouldn't be searching for Wendy if you still planned on pleading guilty," she called after him.

Joel wouldn't have re-signed with Mikel if he planned on going away to prison, or boot camp. There was renewed hope in Joel's life, easily reflected in his attitude.

What had Mikel said to Joel that she hadn't?

"Mikel," she breathed. She missed him. She missed their conversations. She missed their lovemaking. She missed a lot of things about Mikel, but mostly she missed how he made her feel so womanly.

She'd grown up with two little brothers and a dominant but loving father. Her best, and only true friend, was a man. She had to be tough. Growing up, she'd been a tomboy always roughhousing with the boys. With Mikel, she became soft and fuzzy. She melted in his embrace and relished in his strength. She wore frilly nighties, and he appreciated it. She let him open the tops on jars and lift heavy packages. He had been right in his self-assessment: He wasn't an easy man to be with. But being without him was too hard for Lacey.

Lacey climbed the staircase and went to Joel's room for a reconnaissance visit. "Knock, knock."

Joel was at the computer, looking at a street map of Atlanta. "What's up?"

She flopped down on the bed. "You didn't mention your meeting earlier."

"What meeting?" His attention was keyed in on the computer screen.

"In the kitchen you said you met with Mikel today."

He swiveled around in his chair, wearing a teasing grin. "What?"

"I said I met with your boyfriend."

She was busted. "How did he look?"

"How did he *look*? We've been friends too long, Lacey." He turned back to the computer. "I'm not a gossipy female."

She hesitated. "Did he ask about me?"

"No."

She stood over his shoulder as he examined the screen. "Mikel didn't say *anything* about me?"

Joel blew out an exasperated breath. "He asked if you were okay. He said he's been trying to contact you, but you're ignoring him."

"What did you say?"

"Lacey," he said, annoyed. He gestured at the computer screen. "I don't have time to manage your love life right now. I'm trying to stay out of jail."

"You're right. Sorry. Can I help?"

"Yes, go finish dinner."

She turned, her heart lighter knowing Mikel was still thinking about her. "You have been hanging around with Mikel. He thinks cooking is woman's work." She looked over her shoulder to catch Joel's smile.

"He's a good guy, Lacey. And that's all I'm saying about it."

Mikel and Joel scoured Atlanta looking for Wendy. The woman had disappeared. On the surface, it wasn't strange. Of course a woman hiding from betrayal and criminal charges would go underground, but Mikel had been spending enough time with Joel to know the opposite was true. Addicts did not just disappear. They were creatures of habit. They relied on rituals to make it through the day. A huge part of their recovery process was breaking the rituals associated with drug use and replacing them with healthier habits.

"Someone's hiding her," Joel deduced.

"Or keeping her against her will."

Joel's brows knit together in thoughtful consideration. "Do you think she's been hurt?"

Mikel drove in silence for a while, considering the possibility before answering. "Could someone be holding her against her will?"

"If someone was holding her it would be for ransom, and no one has contacted me."

Mikel nodded. "I could be way off on this."

They drove along carefully scrutinizing every woman in the alley who was slumped over a crack pipe.

"Not so far off," Joel said, his tone reflective. "We've been looking at this thing all wrong. Wendy loves me as much as I love her. I know she does."

Mikel couldn't offer an opinion on Joel's emotional affair with Wendy. He hadn't been able to manage his own relationship with Lacey. He wondered how Joel could be so certain of Wendy's love, even after her betrayal, and he asked Joel, "How can you be so sure she loves you?"

"A man knows his woman."

Mikel thought of Lacey. He could feel her love for him, and he knew it was real.

Joel continued, "Wendy brought the drugs on the plane because she's addicted, not to hurt me. She would hide from the media and the police because she's scared. But she's not scared of me. She loves me. She's gone somewhere she knows only I can find her. She's waiting for me to come to her and forgive her."

Mikel watched him with a sideways glance. "Where to?"

Mikel stood in the shadows watching as Joel knelt next to Wendy. She was dirty and disheveled. Joel aroused her from her drug-induced nod. She was crouched in a corner, shaking. She was scared, and she was drugged out. Joel touched her tenderly, speaking in a low, comforting voice.

Mikel turned away from the tender moment, asking himself how he and Lacey had managed to screw up their relationship so badly. Joel and Wendy were battling adversities Mikel could only imagine, yet they continued to act as if they cared for each other.

Lacey had been stubborn, obstinate, and unyielding, unwilling to consider his side of the argument—just what he needed in a woman since he had cultivated the same qualities within himself. He liked not having to walk on eggshells around her. He didn't pretend with Lacey, and she cared for him anyway. She was spunky. She was his equal intellectually. She had a good spirit, obvious by her loyalty to Joel. As tough as she was, she was just as soft. He liked the effect his petting had on her. His pride swelled with the knowledge that he knew how to touch her—the right words to say—to de-stress her.

Mikel watched Joel gather Wendy up in his arms. His heart ached for Lacey. The pain went down to his toes. He had to make things right between them. There was so much he wanted to do with her. They'd gone on the traditional dates—movies, dinners, shows, long weekends—but there was so much more. She hadn't met his parents, nor he hers. When her next screenplay was released, he wanted to sit with her in a crowded movie theater and watch the reactions of the patrons. She said that was a nerve-racking moment for her. He had to be there to hold her and tell her the movie was as wonderful as the writer.

Joel held Wendy tightly around the shoulders, supporting her weight. "I want to get her cleaned up before we do anything. I don't want her to feel humiliated, or ashamed."

Mikel nodded and walked ahead, opening the door to his Chrysler 300M. Joel helped Wendy into the backseat, and then joined her. Mikel watched their interaction in the rearview mirror—a living definition of unconditional love. He wanted a love as strong. He could have it with Lacey—if she'd give him another chance.

11

Lacey watched Joel on the big television screen. He smiled as he answered questions about his recent Academy Award nomination. The drug charges had been dropped, and certain people in the prosecutor's office were being publicly scrutinized for their narrow-mindedness in handling his case. Lacey shook her head. When on top, the world sung Joel's praises, but as soon as things got rough, everyone was ready to persecute him.

Wendy had admitted to carrying the drugs onto the plane. Being a big star, Joel and his companion hadn't been thoroughly checked at security—several people had lost their jobs for being starstruck. With all the negative media coverage, the prosecutor had been willing to give Wendy probation with the added stipulation of drug rehabilitation. Joel immediately had her sent to a swank clinic where the rich go for treatment. The last time Lacey spoke with Joel, Wendy was doing fine and he still loved her as much as ever.

The amount of television coverage Joel was receiving was completely ridiculous, and Lacey would have stopped watching every little sound bite if she wasn't hoping to see Mikel standing in the background. She scoped him out of the crowd once or twice, but it wasn't enough. She asked Joel about him whenever they spoke, but Joel was too happy to pay her relationship troubles much mind. Watching the *Access Hollywood* interview made her miss Joel, and she picked up the phone and dialed his cell. He was in L.A., hanging out with friends.

"Call him already, Lacey. I can't make you trust him."

"Trust?" Their fight had nothing to do with trust.

"It has everything to do with trust. He didn't trust that I was telling the truth. You didn't trust him to make the best decision for his life and his company. It's all about trust, and I can't tell you to give yours to him. Mikel and I have worked out our problems. Do you care about him?"

Joel rarely asked how she felt about the men in her life. It wasn't considered manly to discuss feelings and emotions—even if his best friend was a *girl*. "Well?" he pressed.

"I do."

He made a distressed sound into the phone. "I swear, you're going to end up alone. You know that, don't you? Women make things too hard. If you care about him, call him. Work it out. And you better hurry up about it. I see the way the honeys eye him when we're on the road."

Honeys? Lacey curled her lip, indignant at thinking *other women* were hitting on Mikel. "I can't trust his loyalty to this relationship."

"Why not?"

"Because he turned his back on you so easily."

"Lacey," he sounded more patient, "you shouldn't have made him choose. What was happening to me had nothing to do with his feelings for you, and it doesn't have anything to do with his loyalty to your relationship. He called and e-mailed for weeks, but you never answered. Seems pretty loyal to me. You turned your back on him."

She refused to get mushy and start crying. "I've been hurt so many times in the past. He disappointed me. I thought what we were building was much stronger."

Joel told her to hold on, and the noisy background faded as he moved away from the ever-present crowd around him. "Are you okay?" He was concerned. "If you need me to come be with you, I will."

"No." She tried to sound strong and brave when her chest was constricting from the pain of Mikel's absence. "I'm a little blue today. I'll be fine."

"If you want me to beat up Mikel for you, I will."

She rescued him. He protected her.

She managed a short laugh. "I don't want you to beat him up, silly."

"Seriously, Lacey, call him. I don't like seeing you hurting like this when you don't have to."

"I have to go."

His tried to lighten her mood by changing the subject. "Working on the next blockbuster script?"

"The agent is pushing, pushing, pushing."

"Make sure you write a part for me."

"I will." She already had patterned her male lead after his boyish good looks.

"Love you," he said.

"Me, too."

"Call Mikel," Joel said before he disconnected.

Lacey hung up and sat at her desk, prepared to work on her third screenplay. She'd decided not to immediately pursue the HBO series offer. She had a plot for a screenplay she had to get out of her head, or it would drive her crazy. As she became submerged in the Hollywood scene, she was learning the advantages of multitasking, so she had started a storyboard for the HBO series. The agent was delighted to hear about it.

As she typed, she thought of Mikel. She always thought of Mikel.

Joel's words were harsh but true. She shouldn't have forced Mikel to choose their relationship over his livelihood—and the livelihood of his business. Impulsively, she switched onto the Internet. The icon next to Chocolate Dream's name was dim, indicating he wasn't online. Deep in thought, her gaze wandered to the organza hatbox sitting on the table in the far corner of the room—the gift he'd sent her in New York before everything in her life went crazy. She exhaled sadly, and then typed, I was wrong; she pressed the SEND button before she lost her courage.

She refocused her attention on her manuscript, but her gaze kept going back to the organza box. When the decorative box had arrived at her hotel in New York, she'd read the gift card and decided she wouldn't open it until she was with Mikel. It was torture, because she loved receiving presents, but she wanted to be with Mikel so he could watch her reaction to the gift. Once she'd arrived home, they'd rushed to her bed and made love. And then Joel's call had come, shattering everything. Events had made the time seem as if it were flying by. After their breakup, Lacey couldn't stand the thought of opening the box and finding a heartfelt gift from Mikel. She'd moved the box to her sitting room so she didn't have to stare at it when she should be sleeping. Lacey recognized the rationale for what it was—she lived in a mansion, the box could have been stored in any room other than the one she spent the most time in.

The computer chimed, startling Lacey from her musings.

We both were.

Her lashes dropped and she whispered her thanks for whatever had moved Mikel to answer her message.

Brown Sugar, are you still there? Minutes had passed since Mikel had typed an apology to Lacey. After all these weeks, she'd finally reached out to him and he had been on the phone working at the time.

Yes, Chocolate. A short hesitation before she typed, I'm sorry.

Me, too.

I miss you.

I love you. He put it out there. He loved her. No more dancing around it. He loved her, and he needed her. It was probably more of a surprise to him than to her. They had been typing in rapid session, but it came to an abrupt halt.

Sugar? Did I scare you? He always worried about scaring her when he declared his feelings. She appeared to him a wounded bird when it came to relationships. Brown Sugar, are you there? he asked again.

Yes.

The words *I love you* are too simple to tell you how I really feel.

Nothing.

His heart sank. Sugar?

He had scared her off.

It's all right if you don't feel the same. He was trying to save any shred of their relationship he could. We can build from here.

A minute passed without any reply from Lacey.

Tell me what you're thinking, Mikel pleaded. *Talk to me.*

He stared at the computer screen, unblinking, until it became painfully clear Lacey was not going to answer him. She'd been rejecting him since the argument in her kitchen by not answering his calls or messages, but this was different. She'd reached out first, but he scared her off. Maybe her intention was only to apologize for Joel's sake. He'd made her run by telling her he was in love with her. He second-guessed himself, wishing he could take the words back and answer with something more aloof. He could kick himself.

Mikel sat at the computer for the next thirty minutes.

He pretended to be working, but he was hoping Lacey would respond to his messages. He didn't want to be away from the computer if she did.

The doorbell rang, and he dragged himself to the intercom. "Yes?"

"It's Lacey."

Lacey! His heart drummed. Why had she come to see him? Why didn't she answer his messages? He buzzed her inside, hurrying to the elevator to meet her. He mashed the button hoping she'd arrive quicker if he called the elevator up to him. The doors of the elevator opened and Lacey stepped off. She was holding the organza box he recognized from nightygram.com.

She took one long, bold step up to him. The box was pressed between them. "Chocolate Dream, I love you, too."

"Say my name," he rasped.

"Mikel. Mikel, I love you."

"I love you, Lacey." He took the box from her and ravished her mouth. He pressed their lips together and showed her how much she'd been missed.

"I wanted to be with you when I opened your gift," Lacey said, indicating the box.

"We should go inside, because you'll need to be nude when you do."

She cocked an eyebrow in question. "I have to be nude to open your gifts?"

"You can open my gifts any way you like."

She held his eyes, correctly reading his message. He respected her opinion, and they would never break up again because of their stubbornness.

"But you'd prefer me naked when I do."

A slow smile spread over his face. "You have to be nude so I can make love to you."

"If I make love to you, it has to be our new beginning."

He reminded her, "I don't do quick sex or one-night stands."

"Are you confident enough to take charge and gentle enough to surrender?" Her dimples connected directly to his heart.

"Come inside," he told her. "I'll give you whatever you need."

ABOUT THE AUTHOR

Ms. White resides in metropolitan Detroit. During the day, she's a trauma critical care nurse. At night, she writes steamy romances with an erotic twist. Share your thoughts about "To Have It All" at: E-mail: kwhite_writer@hotmail.com, or P.O. Box 672, Novi, MI 48376.